LAWLESS | BOOK ONE

THE DARKNESS WE HIDE

USA TODAY BESTSELLING AUTHOR

BRYNN FORD

The Darkness We Hide
Copyright © 2024 Brynn Ford

ISBN: 978-1-955349-22-2

Cover Design © 2024 Black Widow Designs

More from the Author
www.brynnford.com
brynn@brynnford.com

SERIES NOTE

Lawless is a dark romance series featuring the stories of multiple couples set in the same world. Gemma and Oz are the first *Lawless* couple! Their story is a duet, and their two books must be read in order.

The Darkness We Hide is Part 1 of the *Darkness* duet and Book 1 of the *Lawless* series. Part 1 ends on a cliffhanger, but Gemma and Oz will get their HEA in Part 2.

More couples are planned for the *Lawless* world series. Be sure to follow Brynn Ford on social media and subscribe to her author newsletter for updates!

Subscribe to Brynn's Newsletter
brynnford.com/connect

CONTENT WARNING

This dark romance series involves many triggering elements which may be upsetting for some readers. A complete list of tropes and triggers can be found on the author's website.

brynnford.com/triggers

PLAYLIST

Monster by Chandler Leighton

I Wish A Bitch Would by Delilah Bon

VILLAIN by K/DA, Madison Beer, Kim Petras, League of Legends

Pink Rover by Scene Queen

Whore by In This Moment

BEG! by Vana

Daisy by Rain Paris

PRETTY PLEASE by Dutch Melrose ft. Benny Mayne

if u think i'm pretty by Artemas

Fuck Me Like You Hate Me by Jutes

TEETH by WesGhost ft. Diggy Graves

Heavenly Bodies by Arankai

MATCH MADE IN HELL by Dutch Melrose ft. Benny Mayne

RUNRUNRUN by Dutch Melrose

Obsessed by Jutes

For Gemma.

You can run, but you can't hide.

XXX
Daddy Oz

CHAPTER ONE
Pink

Gemma

"THERE'S JUST SOMETHING about changing the color of your hair... It's so transformative." My reflection in the mirror is glossy, blurred through my tears.

I glance at my cell phone propped up on the bathroom counter and make sure the live stream on my social media continues to capture every liberating moment of my undoing. I manage a gentle smile for my viewers before looking into the mirror again.

I blink away the tears to find some clarity in my reflected image. I haven't been able to look at myself for this long in years, but now, I find a morbid beauty in the rawness of my appearance. My falling tears capture dark mascara and eyeliner, mix to form black rivers that carve canyons of dark memories down my cheeks.

There's no shortage of dark memories in my mind, but the memories I made tonight are the only ones I'll treasure.

I'll cherish this night forever.

I separate another section of my naturally blonde, unnaturally blood-stained hair, and paint on the bubblegum-pink dye.

I expected my viewer count to start dying off at this point, but instead, it's grown. I only started the account two days ago, posted a couple of rambling videos after I rounded up three of my killers—the men who took me, tortured me, and left me for dead six years ago. I told the world that I was holding them captive, that I was hurting them in all the ways they hurt me. I made it known that I wouldn't let them survive this.

The comments on my original videos told me the viewers were skeptical, but that skepticism is what skyrocketed my views and follows. It's only by luck that my videos are still up, that my account still exists, and this live stream has continued far longer than I ever expected.

I thought it would be shut down by now, but a certain type of comment has gained popularity. The consistency of its message seems to be helping me as my live streaming continues.

DO NOT REPORT THIS LIVE. It will get shut down! The longer it stays on, the more info police can gather. DO NOT REPORT!!

I shouldn't read the comments.

Nothing good ever comes from reading the comments.

But curiosity continues to beg my attention on the screen, and I can't help myself. There's a constant upward flow, then a fade of emoji reactions and clusters of text.

You go, girl!

This is fucking sick...

My hero!!! Send her all the bad men!!

OMG, where are the cops?! Is this real??

I feel sick. I can't believe this. Does anyone know where she is? What do we do?

Someone's getting Evicted...

I'm counting on getting Evicted—sentenced to life in the Territory. That's where he is: my fourth and final killer. He's the worst of them all, and I need to make him pay.

I *will* make him pay.

Through the mirror, I glance at the reflection of killer number three over my shoulder.

Colin is pale, cold, sliced to shit, and practically bathing in his own blood in the bathtub. He's silent, unmoving... Dead. He didn't deserve the relief of death—if I could have kept him alive, awake, aware, and in pain, I would have.

But he had to die.

All of them had to die.

I may be leaving this world soon, but at least I'll leave it with fewer monsters than it had before.

"They were vicious, vile, true monsters," I continue my thoughts out loud for my viewers. "I had to do this. I couldn't go another month, another week, another *day,* knowing they were still out there in the world. And after what they did to me… The things they did… You can't…" I make eye contact with the faceless viewers who continue to bombard the comments section. "I told you enough for you to understand why I did this, but you'll never know the true horror of the things they did to me. You can't even begin to imagine…" I trail off, my gaze shifting out of focus.

My mind disconnects from my body. It has to. It's the only way to shut off the memories.

A hazy fog shrouds the awful mental images, allowing me a few moments of peaceful nothingness as my fingers automatically work to separate another section of hair and trail down the strand. Halfway down the dry section of my long hair, my fingers halt on the sticky, viscous substance that shouldn't be there…

Blood.

My eyes snap to the mirror, and I see the streak of red where my fingers have stopped. It's such a vibrant shade that it almost looks fake.

The memory of blood spurting from Colin's chest when I stabbed him flashes across my mind. A misplaced smile spreads across my cheeks, yet somehow, more tears fall. Hurting him felt so good, but it didn't take away my pain. It didn't take away the years of misery I suffered in the aftermath of what they did. It didn't give me my life back or bring me a better future.

My future is Eviction. Banishment. An indisputable sentence for spending the rest of my life in the Territory once I'm charged as a violent felon. It's the future I knew I'd have when I began this. It's the future I *chose*. I decided that punishing my four killers meant more to me than anything else.

I chose revenge.

I chose to take my power back with deadly force.

Eviction is the only way for me to finish what I've started because Seb—Logan *fucking* Sebastian—is already there, already sentenced to a life in the Territory.

And I will have his blood on my hands.

I attempt to steady my twitching nerves with a deep breath. Then, I lift my brush, paint pink dye onto the section of hair, sweep right through the blood, and let it streak.

"It's transformative," I whisper. "Pink…"

Pink will soften the vivid red rage in my mind.

It's the stain of my vengeance, the remnant hue of their blood.

Pink will remind me that I'm stronger now, that their power belongs to me because I took it. I claimed it when I claimed their lives…

Pink is my reclamation.

Lyrics and melody flow into my thoughts, and I begin to sing out loud. The song has to come out. I can't think of the word pink one more time without hearing Steven Tyler's voice sing that single syllable in my head.

I sing *Pink* by Aerosmith.

There's always been a soundtrack playing in my mind. It's a constantly shuffling playlist of random songs, and each begins to play when called upon by some perfectly mundane word or thought... Like the color pink.

My viewers love the singing—at least, the ones who understand me and why I've done what I've done. But I don't sing for the viewers; I sing for me. I sing because it carries me through the moments I wish I could forget.

It carries me *through* them, though it doesn't help me *forget* them. If anything, the melody stakes its claim over the moment, gives it deep roots which tangle and burrow into the song, ensuring the memory returns whenever I hear it or sing it again.

And because the song and the memory attached to it won't fade unless I sing it through, I *always* sing them through. Too many songs are connected to these men, to my past, to the nightmare they made me endure. They tried to break my mind with the songs they forced me to connect with the worst moments of my life.

The song they played when I thought I was going to die, the one I heard every time they made me think it was really the end... I sang it for them when I killed them. I made sure it was the last thing Dominic, Peter, and Colin heard before taking their final breath.

When I find Seb in the Territory, I'll sing it for him, too. My worst memory is rooted in that melody, and I want his to be, too.

I'll make his worst memory on the day he dies...

I laugh, interrupting myself in the middle of the song. I felt such rage in that last thought, but it didn't make any sense.

"He can't hold a memory if he's dead..." I tell my reflection.

Or at least, he can only hold it as long as I keep him alive.

I don't know how long I can keep him alive.

I don't know what the world is like in the Territory; I don't know how I'll find him, how I'll overpower him, what tools or resources I'll be able to scavenge and use to hurt him. I don't know if I'll have the opportunity to do to him what I did to them. I can't plan, I can't prepare, not like I did with these three. Seb could get the upper hand. He could take me and hurt me all over again.

A sob cuts through the laughter, bringing fresh tears to drip down my cheeks, though they flow over the curves formed by the sad smile that remains. He caused me so much pain, so much sorrow and misery. But the worst feeling is knowing that he won't have to live like I did. He won't have to feel what I felt as the girl who survived and broke free. He won't have to suffer the impact of the trauma I'll cause him for years to come.

Six years of suffering...

I suffered, and they lived without consequence for what they did to me. That's what their privilege bought them. They could hurt women without consequence because Mommy's and Daddy's money could pay to clean up the messes they made— hide evidence they left, hire the best lawyers, pay off the judge. Though I guess even the Sebastian family fortune wasn't enough to buy him off when Seb killed his best friend Peter Cavanaugh's little sister a couple of years later...

"Chloe Cavanaugh." I always say her name out loud rather than think it to myself—I won't let it be lost to silence.

I would hope that if I'd been killed the way she had that people would say my name out loud. I would hope they'd say my name more than my killer's.

"Logan Sebastian was caught and convicted for murder when they found Chloe's remains." I look over at my phone screen, painting my hair blindly while I speak. "I guess you could say that I was just lucky to have survived him. Lucky to have been one of his first victims, back when he was still learning what he liked to do to women. Back when he had his little squad of obedient dickwads to corroborate on their story, and all their families' collective wealth and social resources. The justice system failed."

I huff and look away, scooping more dye onto my brush heavy-handedly.

"It fucking failed me! It failed *all* of us. Every single woman, time and time again. Men have been getting away with the most heinous acts against us since the fucking dawn of time. They keep destroying us, ruining us, breaking our hearts, our minds, our spirits, our *bones.*"

I hastily paint my hair with rough strokes.

"The broken bones... They hurt, they really fucking hurt. But it's nothing if you compare that to the pain of a shattered soul, a ruined life. They failed when they tried to kill me, but they ended my life all the same." I look at my phone. "You probably won't believe me because all you've seen of me is *this*... This violence and chaos. You've only seen the desperate, damaged parts of me. You don't know who I was before them.

"I used to be so level-headed and calm. Hard to believe, right? Before I met them, I was smart, focused, ambitious. I had dreams. There were so many things I wanted to accomplish, so much more I wanted to learn… an entire universe of discoveries I could have made."

Tears of grief warm my eyes over the life I never got to live.

"I was close… So close to having everything I ever wanted, to living my dream. I survived what they did to me, but the person I used to be is gone." I pause. "Did you know that trauma alters your brain chemistry? I won't get into the science of it, but it's true. Trauma changes you. It fucking changed *me*. I was never the same again. I never went back to finish my graduate program. I couldn't make myself—"

My voice cracks, falters, then ceases altogether.

The brush falls from my hand as the recollection of everything I've lost catches my heart in a vise. The pain seizes my lungs, and as I fight for a breath, a sob breaks free. I drop forward on my palms as they land on the countertop, letting my head hang as I cry. I let the sorrow of my stolen dreams consume me, let myself cry until my eyes dry out, until I can't cry anymore.

Slowly, I turn my lowered head to look at my phone so I can speak again, but catch a glimpse of a new comment just before it fades.

> **Excuses. Your trauma didn't kill them, YOU did.**

"I did. You're right. I killed them," I respond to the comment as if the person who made it is in the room with me. "I killed them, but they killed me first. I'm just a ghost of my former self, trying to rise from the dead and serve justice."

Another comment appears.

> I FREAKING LOVE YOU, GIRL!! YOU'RE A QUEEN! MY HERO!! I'M TOTALLY STARTING A FUNDING PAGE TO RAISE MONEY FOR YOUR LAWYERS.

I'm not a queen or a hero.

I didn't do this for anyone but myself.

Yet there's a beat of contentment that comes from the acknowledgment of another woman, in knowing that someone out there understands me, what I went through, what I'm going through, why I chose to do this.

> This chick deserved whatever they did to her. She's literally too dumb to live, recording herself murdering three men? No fucking self-control. This is why women need men. Someone needs to put this bitch in her place.

It's Seb's voice in my mind, reading the comment. It's his voice telling me that I need him. That I'm nothing without him. That I should go away with him to his summer home...

I snap, fling the back of my hand against my phone, sending it flying across the bathroom. It slams into the far wall and drops to the floor.

Self-control?

I used to have it in spades. I used to be so controlled, so disciplined, that I had myself fooled into thinking nothing bad would ever happen to me. I really used to think that a quiet, unassuming life dedicated to academic rigor would somehow keep me away from the kind of men who would take advantage of women at parties who aren't paying attention to their drinks, women who walked home alone down dark alleys, women who got too drunk at the bar or went home with a stranger hoping for a night of fun.

I did everything I was taught to keep myself safe, and it didn't matter. Nothing I did kept me safe—they found me anyway.

They always find us.

I ignore my phone, leaving it where it landed, and quickly finish painting my hair, thickly overcoating it with dye. Spatters of pink cover the wall and countertop, but I don't bother with cleaning up the mess before I leave the bathroom and enter the master bedroom attached to it. I cross the room and open the blinds so I can peek out through the window.

It's dark now, and although the suburban street is well lit, I can still see the stars—my old friends. I let the dye process on my hair as I search the night sky, silently naming the stars as I spot them.

Alhena.

Mekbuda.

Wasat.

Pollux.

Castor...

It's comforting, like counting sheep, though it doesn't put me to sleep... It just quiets my mind.

After thirty minutes or so, I return to the bathroom to rinse out my hair. I stop in front of the bathtub-shower combo and realize that I haven't exactly set myself up for success. I hadn't forgotten that Colin's body was in the bathtub, I just hadn't thought all the way through to rinsing out my hair. I could wash it in the sink or find another bathroom, but fatigue has suddenly struck me, and I just want it done.

I reach above Colin's head and turn on the faucet, letting the water run over his dead body. It pours over his paling skin, mingling with blood, tinting the water as it flows over him into the tub. I switch the flow from the faucet to the detachable showerhead and reach up to grab the handle, bring it down with me as I lower to my knees on the tile. As I bow my head, I carefully lift my hair up, bringing it over the top of my head to hang down in front of my face. I lean forward, bending over Colin's torso, which I sliced right down the middle.

I see it all.

I see exactly what I did to him.

The true horror of it is unfiltered now that the adrenaline is fading. He deserved it, but knowing that doesn't prevent the wave of nausea or the dry heave that nearly makes me vomit.

With one hand holding the showerhead, and the other digging into my scalp, I scratch and scrub as quickly as I can. Dye rinses from my hair and washes over his mangled corpse. Another heave threatens sickness, and I rush to finish.

I hold it back as long as I can, but I feel it rising the moment I've cleared the dye from my hair. I drop the handheld and somehow manage to toss my soaked hair back from my face, though I don't make it very far. I only manage to turn away from his face as I purge, spilling the contents of my stomach at his feet.

The moment I'm emptied, I spin to face away from him, drop my ass onto the hard tile, and lean my back against the outside of the bathtub. My breathing is unsteady, much like the spinning room. I try to focus, slowly drawing air in through my nose and forcing it out between my lips. When I feel like I have the strength to lift my arms, I gather my hair at the side of my head and squeeze, wringing the water out onto the floor.

As the room gradually steadies and my vision comes back into focus, I turn and reach for the toilet paper, ripping off a few squares to wipe my mouth. I move onto my hands and knees and shift my body closer to the toilet so I can drop in the used paper. I notice my phone still lying on the floor beside the wall where it landed with the screen facing up. I reach out slowly and grab it before returning to my position, sitting with my back to the tub. I unlock the screen, and I'm a little surprised to find that the live is still streaming.

The comments are flying.

Did she just puke? On the dead guy?

OMG, where are the fucking POLICE?!

I can't look away...

This whole thing has been so disgusting.

I know I shouldn't, but I do it anyway. I tap the screen to pull up the comments section and scroll through, skimming through everything that was posted from the very beginning.

She's a monster. Why hasn't anyone reported this feed? How are we still watching this?

She's not a monster. Do you even understand how they hurt her? She snapped! They totally deserved it.

Is anyone recording? This is live. Will this evidence all be gone when she ends the stream?

I've been screen recording since twenty minutes in. I will be sending it to the police!!

I'm recording.

Recording!!

Okay, but can we talk about her voice? Wow!! So talented. And the way she sang to each of them before she killed them? Damn!

Same song, too. Maybe she's a siren... Dangerous, charming, hot as fuck, great singer... LOL."

A siren? Like the mythological creatures that would sing to lure sailors to their deaths?

Aren't sirens just mermaids?

Yes, she's totally a mermaid!!

I wanna be a mermaid...

They should call her the Siren!

Pied piper of murderers and rapists.

She's such a badass. Personally, I'm proud. Maybe if this was the punishment for men who repeatedly assault women without consequence, the world would be a more peaceful place.

I'm proud of you, Siren!! Making the world a better place one asshole at a time...

> Anyone know where she is? Hit me up if you figure it out. I'd love to straighten this bitch out myself.

> This is evil. What's wrong with you people? Can't you see the Devil in her eyes?

I want to laugh at the last comment, but all that comes out of me is a sigh. I'm so tired. I'm physically exhausted, emotionally drained, and psychologically overwhelmed. I lift my phone, centering my face on the screen before I speak to the viewers, slowly and clearly.

"This is it. I've finished what I planned to do, and now I'm done. This part is over and I'm ready for what's next. My name is Gemma Hadley. I did this…" I angle my phone to capture Colin's corpse over my shoulder, making sure there's a clear view of the carnage before centering myself in the view again. "His name is Colin Kingsley, and I killed him. I also killed Dominic Brice and Peter Cavanaugh. You'll find us at 3812 Willowbrook Road in Fairfield, Connecticut."

That's it.

This part is done, and exhaustion finally defeats me.

I reach across my chest to set my phone on the edge of the tub, let the live stream continue, give the viewers a chance to confirm with each other that they heard the address right… I need the police to find me.

I slump down the side of the tub and lean my head back to rest on the edge. I stare up at the white textured ceiling until my weary eyes fall shut and the world slips into silence. Then, I drift into peaceful darkness.

When I wake again, it's to the call of sirens. Glimmering blue and red lights filter in through the bedroom window and dance across the walls. I sit up straight, lift both hands in surrender, and wait for the police to find me.

PRESENT

I PLED GUILTY from the beginning—I was never going to deny what I'd done. As expected, I was convicted of a Class A felony. It's the conviction I needed to get to Seb. I murdered them as brutally as I could manage to ensure the courts would see me as the most vicious, violent type of criminal.

The courts have been unnecessarily slow in processing my case, but I suppose they have to do their due diligence. The justice system has always run slowly, but I suppose I'd been naïve to hope my case would be quick to process given that I pled guilty right away—never mind the fact that the evidence of my crimes was so readily available. There were dozens of screen recordings from viewers who watched me murder them in real time.

As the judge told me, they have to be certain before finalizing the paperwork. Because once it's done, it's done. They can never bring me back.

The only sentence handed to a Class A felon is Eviction.

A life sentence.

Banishment to the Territory for my remaining days.

I was ready for Eviction the night I was arrested, but instead, I've spent the last four months locked up in solitary, alone with my vengeful thoughts, letting my rage simmer until I can finish what I started.

I can't let go of the rage… Not yet.

All this time, I've kept my anger just beneath the surface, saving it all for that cruel bastard.

Four long, lonely, mind-splintering months.

I survived them.

That part is over now, and today is my Eviction Day.

Today, they'll renounce my citizenship from the United States of America. I'll be stripped of all the rights, protections, privileges, and resources guaranteed by the government. I'll be transported across the country, processed, and then banished forever to the Territory. It's a lawless region occupied by the country's most violent criminals, a place they spent decades mapping out, evacuating, and walling-off so they could trap the worst offenders in the desolation of the Mojave Desert.

There's no escaping the Territory.

Eviction is final, permanent, and irrevocable.

There's no changing what I've done.

The sentence is as final as death.

But I'll take this death from the only life I've ever known because it will lead me to the end of my vengeance—the end of my hatred, my rage, my obsession.

I'll find peace at the end of this.

That's the only hope I have to hold on to.

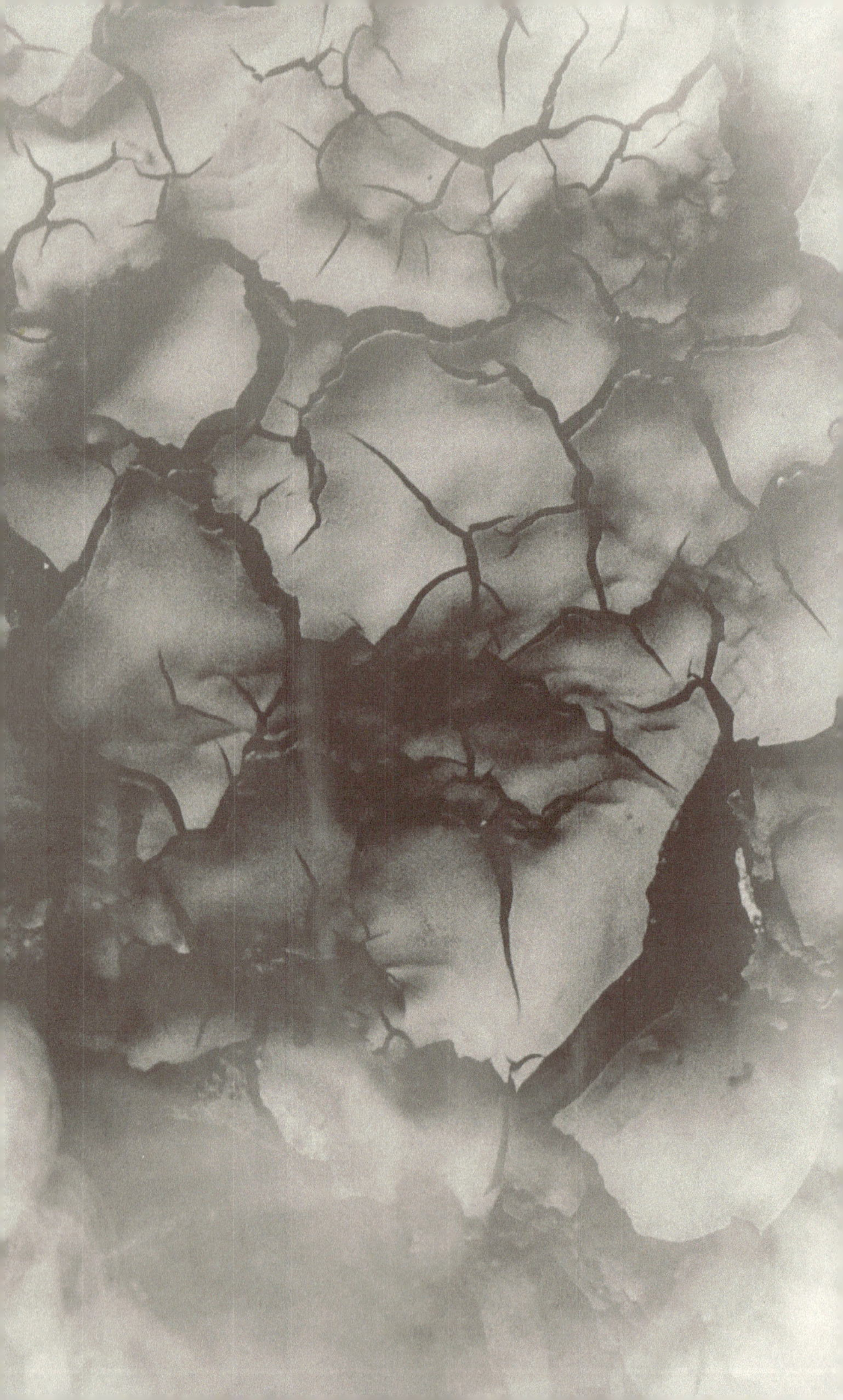

CHAPTER TWO
Rough, Wild, and Hot

Gemma

EACH AND EVERY breath requires a conscious effort—it's dry and hot, heavy tufts of thick air that have to be forcefully dragged into my lungs.

There's no air conditioning. We're packed in like sardines. My fellow convicts and I are seated shoulder-to-shoulder, trapped on an old school bus that's been repurposed for prisoner transport. My face is turned toward the open window, and I'm living for the oven-baked breeze that flows through as we travel the highways on the four-hour drive from Phoenix to the fucking inner circle of hell.

Ninety-eight degrees Fahrenheit.

"Not bad for late May." That's what the officer at the front of the bus had said.

Ninety-eight degrees, my ass.

It's got to be over a hundred.

This entire journey has been a nightmare. It began with a drive from the temporary detention center in Connecticut to the airport, which took nearly ninety minutes. Another hour passed before they put me on a non-stop flight to Phoenix. I would have savored those hours spent in air conditioning and relative silence if I'd known they were putting me on this bus next.

The fucking heat.

It's making me second guess my entire plan. I'm itching, antsy, struggling against the instinctual urge to scream and fight my way off this bus at any cost. I feel like I'd rather die than spend another second sitting still as I slowly roast from the inside out.

"I'm definitely an indoor girl."

"What?" The burly, bearded man in shackles sitting beside me looks at me as though I've offended him in some way.

I track a bead of sweat as it rolls down his cheek, drips off his chin, and lands on his lap. He looks as miserable as I feel.

I give him full, unyielding eye contact. "I'm gonna fucking miss air conditioning."

He stares at me for a minute, scrutinizing my face. "Yeah," he sighs, his expression softening, "me, too."

We share a nod in mutual understanding before we look away from one another. He stares straight ahead as I turn my face toward the Kentucky fried breeze coming in through the window.

It's mostly quiet on the journey, everyone on board silently sweating and suffering as we travel along an open desert highway. We pass through a few small, remote towns along the route, but it's mostly barren, dry land stretching out on both sides of the highway. Some sparse vegetation breaks the monotony of beige dirt, which stretches into the horizon. Rocky outcrops and mountains in the distance stand tall and overwhelming, signaling the roughness of the Earth that created these monstrous structures.

Everything surrounding me is rough and wild.

Rough, wild, and hot...

Not the kind of rough, wild, and hot a thirty-year-old woman in her prime would normally be seeking, but it's not like I ever got to have that kind of life.

I was twenty-four when those bastards broke me and left me for dead. I was too focused on achievement in the years preceding to sow any wild oats, as they say. I tried to live after what they'd done, but they froze me in time. I couldn't move forward. I couldn't be happy. I couldn't date men, and God knows, I tried.

I tried to date a woman once...

I love women—glorious, life creating, powerful creatures that we are. But I couldn't give her the physical intimacy she deserved.

I'm cursed with heterosexuality.

Fucking men.

Sweat runs down my face and soaks through my vivid orange jumpsuit. I don't even have a tie to pull back my formerly bubblegum, now faded pastel pink, hair. It wouldn't matter if

I did. These shackles around my wrists and ankles that chain me to the bolts in the floor would prevent me from lifting my hands to make a ponytail. I try not to think too hard about the sweat at the back of my neck.

At some point, we traverse a bridge over water, crossing state lines from Arizona into California. The officer at the front of the bus shouts a warning that we're twenty minutes out from the Transition Center in Needles.

It takes me a few moments to work out that Needles must be the name of some small town where the Transition Center is located. For a second, I imagined them sticking me with a hundred acupuncture needles before processing my Eviction through the Transition Center.

The Transition Center *in Needles.*

They'd have to stick me with all the needles they can find to distract me from this heat. I'd kill for a fan. I laugh because I *did* kill, and that's what put me on this bus to suffer the heat in the first place.

I look out at the river beneath us as we cross the bridge, imagining how refreshing it would be to hurl myself over the edge and plunge into the cool stream.

Is it the Colorado River?

Whatever it is, it feels so contrary to the land around it. A winding flow of water cutting through such a dry, barren world feels misplaced.

I find myself thinking about the river long after we've crossed the bridge. Sometimes I feel like a river finding its way through an unforgiving world...

We turn off the highway, transitioning from pavement to navigate desert back roads, bumping along dirt paths. The wheels kick up dust, which floats in through the open windows. The cloud of dust dries out my eyes, mingling with the air to make each oppressive breath more stifling than the last.

I'm approaching a breaking point, where the intense need to escape the heat consumes me, threatens to send me into a panic. The last few minutes of this trip feel like the longest. Anxiety claws at my chest, makes me itch with the urge to scream.

Then, finally, the bus slows.

We come to a stop.

I peer out the window, watch the cloud of dust slowly settle to reveal a gray, unassuming building in the middle of the desert. A wide concrete canopy stretches out from the roof of the building to shade the entrance.

"Attention upfront." I look toward the voice to find one of the officers at the front of the bus, stepping out from his seat, turning in the aisleway to face us. "Listen carefully. We've arrived at the Transition Center, and yes, this is your final destination. In just a few moments, we will direct you off the bus in a quick and orderly fashion. You will form a single line, standing shoulder to shoulder, and parallel to the bus. You will stand quietly and await further instructions.

"We are bus number three arriving today, and five more are coming in behind us. The Center will be processing just under three hundred and fifty of you outlaws for Eviction over the next three hours. While that may sound like a large number to you, I assure you, it's not. We've averaged processing just over five hundred outlaws on each monthly Eviction Day over the last six months.

"Why do I tell you this? Because I want to make it crystal fucking clear that we are well-equipped to control each and every one of you. You may think that stepping off this bus is your opportunity to run, but let me assure you, it is not. There is only one Center that processes outlaws for Evictions, and that, right there," he stretches his arm, pointing toward the building, "that's it. This is a well-funded federal operation. Do not delude yourself into thinking you can run. Our officers are granted permission under federal law to use any means necessary against fleeing or combative outlaws, including the use of deadly force.

"Make no mistake, ladies and gentlemen, you *will* be processed and Evicted today, despite any futile plans you've made to try to escape your fate. There will be plenty of opportunity for you to run out into the desert and do whatever the fuck you want once you've entered the Territory, so please, hold your half-baked, stupid plans until that time. Thank you."

He quickly turns and steps off the bus as two other officers in the front and three more in the back stand, moving into the aisle and barking orders. I wait impatiently as they visit each seat to work one person at a time, carefully unlocking a portion of the chains. The cuffs remain tethered between wrists, but they're detached from the ankle chains, which are bolted to the floor. Then, the ankle cuffs are removed, and those chains are left behind. One outlaw at a time, the officers unshackle us from the floor and lead us off the bus.

At least fifteen outlaws are ahead of me, forming a shoulder-to-shoulder line when it's finally my turn to escape the oven on wheels. I step into the line and turn my back to the bus like the others, facing the entrance of the building. We're feet away from the shade provided by the awning, but shadows from my left and right block me from direct sunlight all the same—it appears I'm sandwiched between two tall men.

I look up at one, then the other, then look all the way down each side of the line before I come to the realization…

"Am I the only woman in this group?"

Someone down the line says, "Sure are, princess."

Someone else whistles as a few others chuckle.

"Quiet!" an officer, who's probably younger than me, barks the command.

He closes in on the line, heading in my direction, and I notice then that there's at least a half dozen new officers who came out from the facility when we arrived. He makes a beeline for me, swings his rifle back over his shoulder so it hangs strapped to his back, wielding his unearned power in the same way he probably flings his dick around with vulnerable women.

The fucker moves right in front of me, stops and stands with no more than a foot of distance between us, invading my personal space. I can already feel my lip snarling, the rumble of a warning growl looming in the pit of my stomach. I can sense right away that he's not well-intentioned, but I still raise my eyes to meet his without fear.

He plasters a wide, shit-eating grin across his face. "Are you feeling a sense of pride for being the only one with a cunt on that bus full of degenerate losers?"

I hear a couple of snickers from a few who must think that's a gut-punching insult to a girl like me. It isn't, and their response doesn't surprise me. But I *am* surprised to hear a few of those so-called "degenerate losers" speak up in protest on my behalf. I even see one of them take a step forward, out of line, before being ordered back by another handsy officer.

That was... nice.

I don't ever recall a man standing up for me. I'm not really sure how to process that.

The officer glances sideways, then tilts his head. "Did you suck that guy's cock on the bus or something?" He smiles again, and it makes me want to vomit on his bullet-proof vest. "Come on now. Give us a smile. I'll bet you're pretty when you smile."

Though my hands are still cuffed together, I'm able to lift them between us to show him both of my raised middle fingers. I use the tip of each one to push up the corners of my lips, forcing my mouth to curve up into a sarcastic smile.

His hand floats up, then lands too gently on the chain attaching my handcuffs. Slowly, he pushes my hands down, then takes a step forward, leaning in so close that I can smell the mix of aftershave and sweat on his cheeks.

He lowers his voice. "I know who you are."

"You have no *idea* who I am."

"I watched your live stream."

His nose touches mine and I jerk my head back, my face scrunching in disgust, but my movement only encourages him to inch closer, to further invade my space without permission or invitation.

"I saw what you did to those men."

Glancing through my peripheral vision, I see that other outlaws from both ends of the line are being dismissed. The other officers move quickly to identify, check in, and filter each person into the building. Yet a lone guard stands in front of me, far too close and threatening.

"You're a filthy little cunt, and you deserve everything that's coming to you out there. Pretty little bitch like you won't last twenty minutes."

Anger claws in my chest, scratching to get out of its cage, but I fight it. I keep it caged, keep it as fuel to add to the fireball of rage I'll unleash when I find Seb.

Instead, I keep the sarcastic grin plastered on my cheeks, hold his stare, despite all the ugliness I see behind his eyes, and remain silent. I won't give him another word because that's what he wants. He gets off on a reaction, and I won't give him that satisfaction.

"Do you have something to say to me? You had a lot to say on social media, but you're awfully quiet now, aren't you? Do you wish you could sing me a little song and cut me open, too?"

I remain silent.

I give him nothing.

And then, he collides with me, pushing me backward until my spine hits the metal side of the bus.

"Come on, Siren. That's what they call you, right? You sing your little songs and men come crawling just so you can hurt them?"

I turn my head just enough to keep his face from touching mine, but I keep my eyes locked on his, holding him to his quiet commitment to threaten me. "Seems like it worked on you. Crawled right on up out of the sewers to find me, yeah?" He slams his hand so hard against the bus beside my face that I can't help but flinch. I recover quickly, though, managing a small laugh. "Go ahead, officer, put your hands on me. Hurt me. I *dare* you."

His eyes show the exact moment when he decides that accepting that dare is worth the risk—though maybe it's not a risk at all for him. Who's to say whether anyone would care if an officer hurt an outlaw on their way to Eviction?

"Hey!" Another officer suddenly appears at my side, latching onto his arm. "Step back, Officer Smith."

"Officer Cruz." Smith backs up with haste, taking two quick steps backward in compliance. He gives me a contemptuous look before dragging his hateful stare from mine and addresses Officer Cruz directly. "Sir, I'd like to request permission to do a cavity search on this outlaw. I have a reasonable suspicion that she's attempting to smuggle drugs into the Territory."

"Gemma Rose Hadley?" I turn my head to look at Officer Cruz when he calls my name.

He's an older gentleman—probably in his fifties—with a hardened expression and kind eyes. He looks down, and I follow his gaze to the electronic tablet in his hands. "Gemma Rose Hadley, correct?"

"Yes."

"Please hold still." He lifts the tablet, holding it in front of my face as though he's going to take a picture. "Both eyes open wide for a retinal scan."

I hold still and wait.

"I apologize for the delay you seem to be having here with Officer Smith." He lowers his tablet when it beeps, then taps the screen. "We'll get things straightened out for you right away."

Pinned to the bus and caught in a power struggle, I wouldn't have noticed that I'm the only remaining outlaw left standing outside.

"Your identity has been confirmed, Ms. Hadley." Officer Cruz tucks the tablet between his arm and waist, pinning it there with his elbow as he turns to Smith. "Okay, Officer Smith. I'm listening. Please tell me about your reasonable suspicion that she's… what did you say, smuggling drugs into the Territory?"

"Well, she's a violent felon, Officer Cruz." He puts on that nasty smile I know he thinks is charming. "Isn't that reason enough?"

"No." Officer Cruz is sharp and serious with his response. "Anything else?"

"I don't trust her."

"Has she given you a reason not to trust her?"

"She murdered—"

"Has she given you a reason *today*? Since she's stepped off that bus, what has she said or done that's given you a reasonable suspicion that she's somehow managed, not only to access drugs, but to place them in a body cavity since being searched at the last security checkpoint?"

"Female outlaws are—"

"I'll stop you right there. Request denied, Officer Smith. You can move along now. Another bus comes in twenty, and you have tasks to complete before then."

Smith looks me up and down with a clenched jaw. "Yes, sir." He takes his time turning away, then finally heads inside the building.

A relieved breath rushes out of me.

"Apologies, Ms. Hadley. I'll ensure you make it safely through processing to the Red Zone, but I'm afraid that's the best I can do for you." He looks at me squarely. "I'm afraid you're going to find yourself staring down a lot of angry men for the rest of your life."

"I'll be fine."

"I'd suggest you make fast friends with the right people."

I feel like I'm dying from the heat, sweating buckets, especially after Smith's invasion of my personal space. "Can we go inside now?" All I can think about is taking two steps forward into the shade.

But Cruz steps in front of me, blocking any escape. "There are places in Lawless Land that you don't want to find yourself." His voice is quieter than it was before, like he's telling me something he doesn't want anyone else to hear.

"Lawless Land?"

"Stay away from the Reborn. Don't let them convince you that they'll take care of you. They won't. Avoid major roads and highways. If you hear an engine, hide—"

"An engine? Like a car or—"

"Sometimes. Cars, motorcycles, dune buggies... There aren't a lot of them out there anymore since usable gasoline is scarce, but there are some pickers with access to resources, some who look for women coming through on Eviction days, and they usually have vehicles."

"Why are you telling me this?"

"Just listen. The Reborn will target you. Pickers will target you. There are going to be a lot of pissed off men who will target you, and that's going to start as soon as you enter the Red Zone. Find women who know you as the Siren, who appreciate what you did. Seek them out the moment you go through those doors and make friends with them. Connection is how you survive."

I don't need to tell him that I'm not interested in survival beyond the time it takes me to find and kill Logan Sebastian. Instead, I ask, "How do you know all this?"

"Officer Cruz?" We both look at an officer standing at the entrance. "Do you need back-up?"

Cruz waves a hand to signal he's okay. "I don't know anything." He says it in a way that suggests he knows more than he should. "Let's just call it wild speculation and leave it at that. Now, go on." He jerks his head over his shoulder toward the main entrance. "Head on in. Might be the last time you experience air conditioning… Unless you can make it to the city."

Maybe he really is spouting wild speculation about the Territory, but I'm not going to stick around to ask. The moment he confirmed the building was air-conditioned, my feet started moving me toward it. I take a step to move past him, but he gently taps my arm.

I stop beside him as he leans sideways, close enough to speak in a soft voice. "I know it's a long shot, but I have to try. If you ever meet a girl named Nova Cruz, would you… Could you maybe just tell her that her dad said hello?"

Ah, that's it, then…

His daughter was Evicted.

His child was banished to the Territory.

She may be dead.

For obvious reasons, I'm curious. Naturally, I wonder what crime this cop's daughter committed to wind up with a life sentence in the Territory.

"She's a quiet girl. A good kid," he tells me. "She got mixed up with a bad crowd and made some mistakes—one life-altering mistake. For what it's worth, I wouldn't call what you did a mistake. You're a strong woman, Ms. Hadley. If my girl's still alive out there, I'd hope she could find a friend with some backbone. Someone like you."

"I'm not planning to be friends with anyone out there." I soften my expression and tell him a lie, a promise I can't keep. "But if I happen to come across her, I'll tell her."

He gives me a tight smile and nods his gratitude. "Okay. That's it then. Meet Officer Johnson at the door."

I finally step into the shade created by the awning, and it's glorious. It encourages a quick stride toward the air-conditioned building. I pause before going through the door Officer Johnson holds open for me, stealing one last look at Officer Cruz. He's lost in thought, gazing off down the dirt road we traveled in from.

I scan him, waiting for a stab of instinct, a knowing feeling of his deception, but it never comes.

Maybe his kindness was genuine.

Maybe he does know things about the Territory.

Maybe his guidance is worth following.

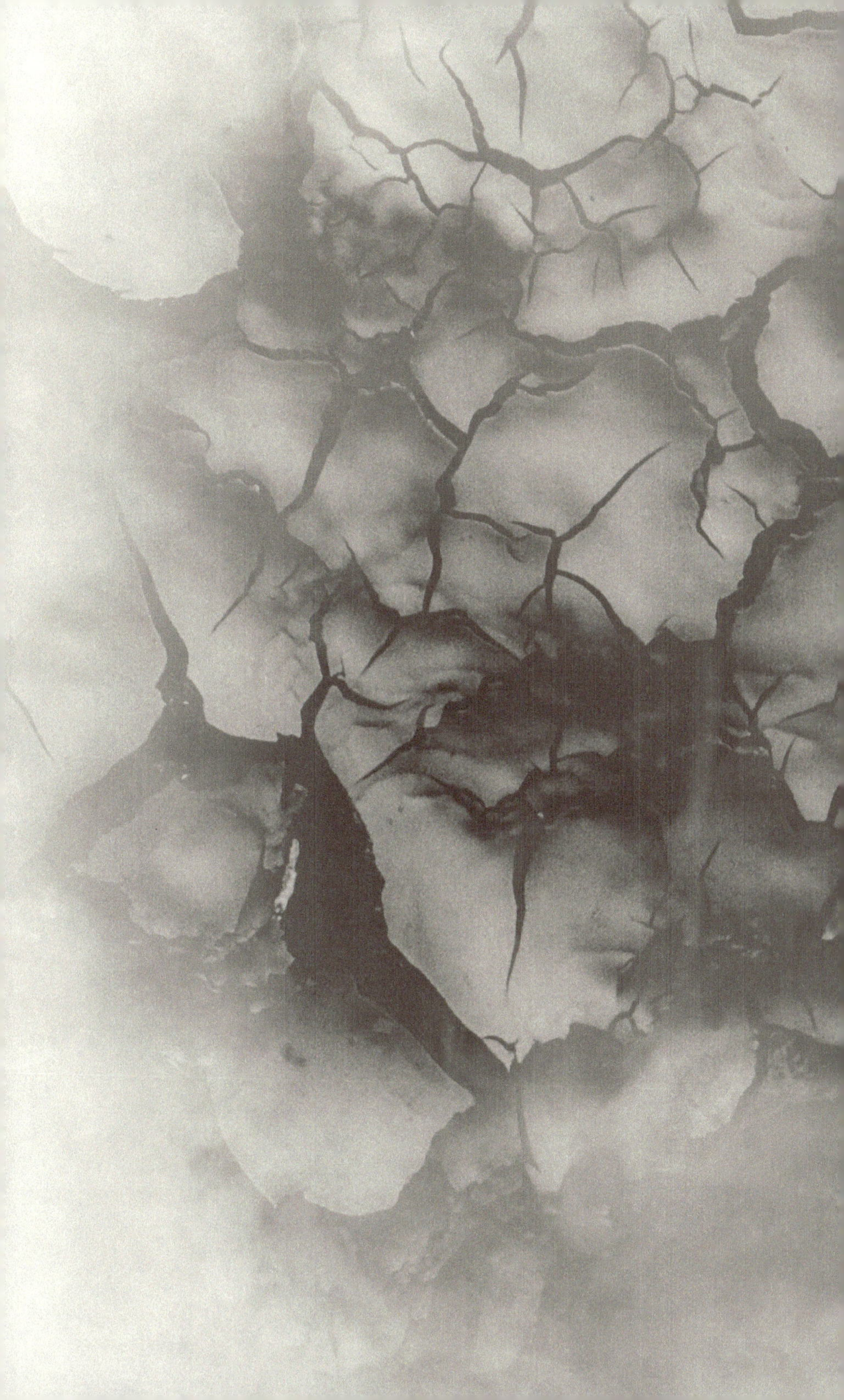

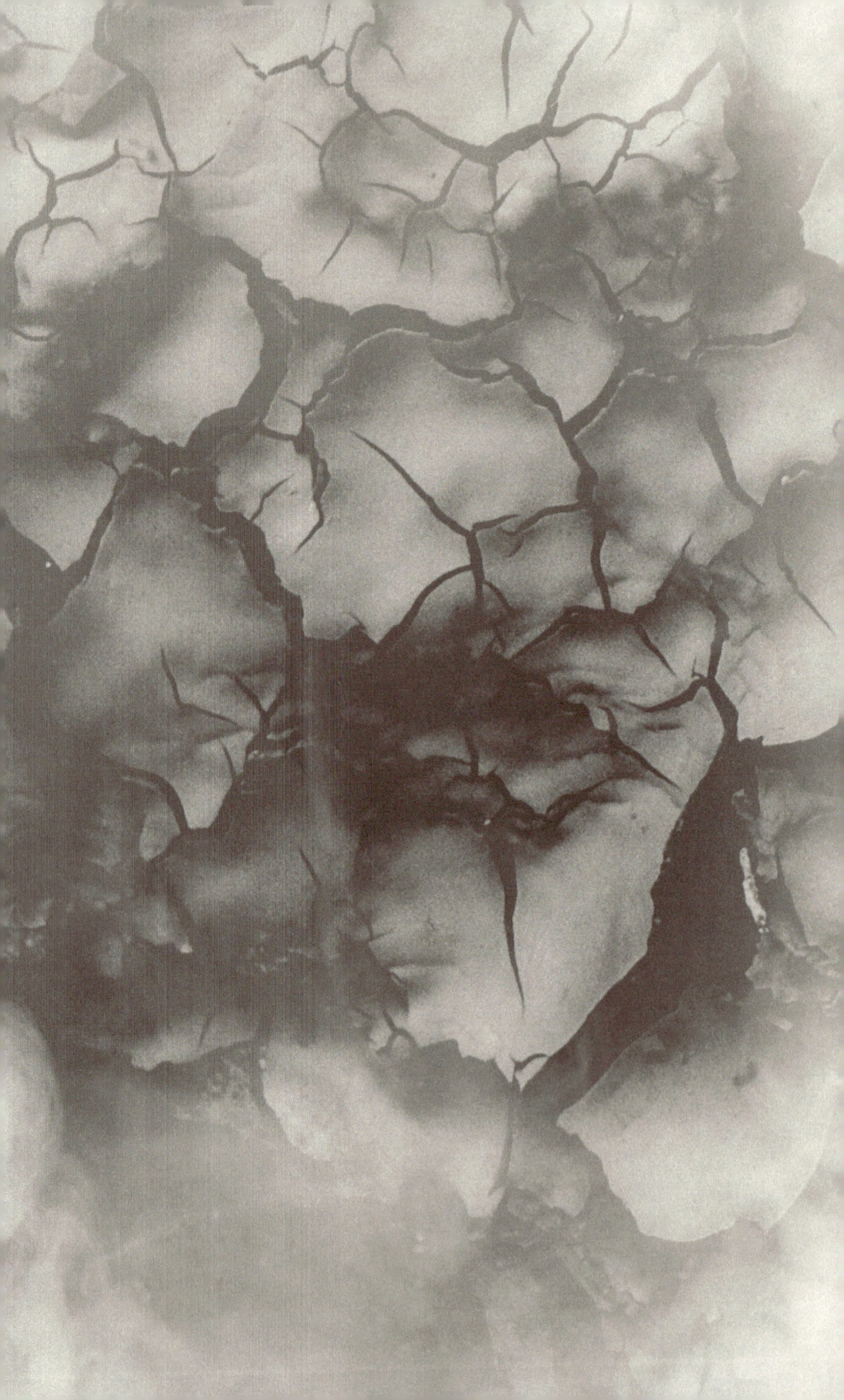

CHAPTER THREE
Lawless Land

02

SMOOTH AND STEADY, I roll on the throttle, and she rumbles between my thighs. After months of searching for and salvaging parts, I finally finished her last night, crafted her with care, piece by precious piece.

My bike dips and bumps along this long stretch of rough highway, testing her agility as I steer to dodge potholes. These old highway roads in Lawless Land are unmaintained—decades' worth of wear and tear without repair or restoration. Some stretches, like this one, are harder to navigate than the open desert terrain.

There's a wide-open flat patch of desert between the road and the mountains in the west, so I pull off to my right and take my bike off-road. I carefully navigate over a strip of uneven terrain that's dense with creosote and brittlebush, plant life that draws a line along the highway, separating road from desert.

I pass through the thicket, then drive out a few hundred feet away from the road before aiming south. I pause to survey the land before me, noting flat, smooth land stretching out ahead. There are no obstacles in my path as far as I can see.

I rev the engine and take off.

Goddamn, the way she purrs.

I pick up speed and stretch her legs, slicing through the wall of dry heat and splitting it apart as I rumble through.

She's doing so well...

So fucking good.

Her engine purrs sweetly, riding so smoothly.

I roll the throttle and give her some real speed.

Sun.

Sweat.

Speed.

Adrenaline spikes as I push her to the limit, open her up to an unreasonable pace beneath unending clear, blue skies. I blaze a trail through the desert, dragging dust into a cloudy line that traces the path of my wake.

My reputation buys me certain precious resources, including the gasoline fueling my new motorcycle for today's Eviction sweep. New lawless are arriving, and as vultures do, we fly across the desert to find them, circle them, and take our picks of the fresh meat.

I manage a quick mile before I hear the approaching roar of our salvaged crew cab pickup finally catching up, following off-road behind me. I'd left the Gates fifteen minutes ahead of them to scout out the first few miles.

The wandering lawless want our compound's resources—resources I fought for the privilege of having, that I worked hard for and grind every day to maintain.

I'd kill to protect what's ours.

I *have* killed to protect what's ours.

And I *will* kill again.

Ahead, I can see the end of the flat, open terrain in the distance. I'll have to ease off soon and get back to the road, but there's still some distance before I need to draw back.

I kick up my pace and race ahead.

The crew cab's rumbling engine gets louder as they close in behind me. I easily stay ahead of them where the land remains clear and barren, but I'm forced to ease off the throttle ahead of the uneven, upward slope closing in.

Dotting the rocky incline are clusters of beavertail cacti in full bloom. Bright pink flowers blossom above the flat cactus spires which, as the name suggests, resemble the wide, flattened tails of beavers. The vibrant shade of pink brings color to our drab, beige world.

I ease my speed to a crawl, but the pickup doesn't slow. As they plow past me, I catch a glimpse of Santi in the driver's seat, laughing with Hayes, who sits beside him. The old Toyota Tacoma is built for off-roading, so they easily climb the rocky slope as I'm left shrouded in a cloud of sand. At least my aviator shades and the black handkerchief tied around my head keep my nose and mouth protected from eating their dust.

I know my motorcycle won't be able to traverse the uneven, rocky passages between the approaching batch of small mountains and mesas, so I make my way back to the empty interstate. I take the next exit onto a narrowed backroad that cuts through the rocky hillside.

The winding, rolling road around the mesas and plateaus is absolute shit for speed. It's cracked and bumpy, but it's the only path my bike can navigate. It's a few miles before my path meets the end of the pickup's offroad shortcut.

As I come around a bend, I see them parked sideways in the middle of the road, nestled between the slant of a rocky hillside on my left and a jutting mesa on my right.

Santi leans against the side of the truck, a metal baseball bat held down at his side. He looks over at the mesa and his lips move inaudibly as he says something to Hayes—who's gleefully painting a swirl of piss on the rock face—which makes them both laugh manically.

Tucker's head only rises at the sound of their laughter, pausing in the middle of the line he's silently pacing behind the truck. The pacing stops when he looks up, but he keeps twisting and twirling the tire iron in his hand like a fucking baton—I don't think he ever stops moving.

Santi sees me first, pushing off the truck and taking a few steps in my direction as I close in. I stop a few yards back from the truck and, with some hesitancy, cut the engine. I scan the road along the mesa to watch for wandering lawless while Hayes zips up, then bends to pick up the heavy-duty length of chain piled beside his feet.

I'm wary, on edge, as I climb off the bike and slide the handkerchief off my nose and mouth. "Why the fuck are you stopped here? Get back in the truck and keep moving."

Santi halts as I take furious steps toward him. "Hayes had to take a piss."

"I saw." I grab Santi's shoulder and forcefully spin him toward the truck, shove between his shoulder blades until he walks to the driver's side door. "But you don't stop beneath a vantage point where you've only got two exits."

This is why I built the damn bike.

They have to take the truck for Eviction Day sweeps. It has enough room for these three dumb fucks and their picks, but they don't need me taking up the valuable cargo space, and it would be wasteful to fill the tank on a second truck for these long trips.

But my guys need to do their work, and I need to make sure they can do it with minimal risk, despite the unseen dangers hiding around every turn—especially when they do dumb shit like park between two towering vantage points and limit their exits.

They should know better, but they don't.

They're lucky I give a shit enough to go with them now as added security.

Tucker gives me a quick glance and a tight-lipped, humble grin as he moves to the back door of the crew cab, spinning his tire iron one more time before opening the door.

"My fault." Hayes approaches me, one palm lifted in surrender, the other holding his looped chain. "I swear we're not usually this stupid. I honestly couldn't hold it anymore. It's okay, though..." He turns his palm into a fist, then jerks his thumb over his shoulder to indicate the mesa at his back. "I marked our territory. That mountain's our turf now." He flashes a cheeky grin.

I wanna break his fucking teeth.

I give him a look that says as much without words, and his face falls. Sometimes I find humor in his banter, but not now, not here. I don't fuck around outside the Gates.

I grip his shirt at the center of his chest, gather the fabric in my fist and jerk him close. "Rule number two, dumbass. We don't fuck around in Lawless Land."

Rule number one... you don't fuck around with *me.*

I push him back as I release him. He stumbles a bit but recovers easily. "Sorry, right, I'll—"

He rattles off a string of apologetic words, but I don't hear a single one of them. My attention is stolen by shadows creeping along the flat, vertical rockface behind him. Two dark, morphing figures—the shadows of two people approaching.

My one-word warning is sharp and clear. "Lawless."

We all act at once.

Tucker and Santi leap out of the truck.

Hayes turns, drops one end of the chain looped tightly around his fist to let it dangle, ready to use it as a weapon.

I bend and pull the folded butterfly knife from its sheath in my black boot, then rush past Hayes around the back of the pickup. As I move, I flick my wrist with a perfected twist to open the balisong with skill. The two handles swing apart around the pivots, turn a full one-eighty to collide with each other on opposite ends as the blade rotates outward between them. The handles and blade lock perfectly into place with a satisfying *snick.*

"Uh uh." I hear Santi's voice, and he quickly comes into view as I circle around the truck. "You can stop right there."

He's got his bat up, his arm outstretched and raised, the end of it pressed to the center of an unknown man's chest.

There's two of them.

Two men who have the fucking nerve to step right up to me and my crew. Except it's not just the two of them. The tall, brawny man on my left, who resembles Sasquatch—months overdue for a good shave—has a limp, unconscious woman draped over his shoulder. The slightly shorter man on the right has the longest nose I've ever seen... Looks like the goddamn witch of the fucking west when he shows us a crooked grin.

Long Nose raises his palms in surrender, held back at the end of Santi's bat. "We don't want any trouble. We thought you might be interested in a trade."

I don't buy it.

His jovial tone is unconvincing.

His hands are steady.

His expression is smug.

His arrogance is so thick, I can practically smell it.

Santi takes a step toward Long Nose, pushing him back with the end of his bat. "We don't do trades. Turn around, walk away, pretend you didn't see us."

"We'll give you the girl," says Sasquatch, boldly stepping up beside his friend. "We're done with her."

Santi doubles down. "I said, we don't do trades. One more chance to walk away before we fuck you up."

Santi's doing what I taught him to do...

Impose an immediate threat.

Give two chances, never any more than that.

Be prepared to throw down without compliance.

And never, *ever* barter or trade.

What's ours is fucking ours.

Except...

I see an opportunity to kill two birds with one stone here, to kill two wandering, lawless men, and take...

"She alive?" I ask, twirling the handle of my balisong, making a show of my agility and skill with a few unnecessary tricks. I want them to know that I'm well acquainted with my weapon and won't hesitate to use it.

Long Nose shrugs. "I think so. If she's dead, she's still fresh."

Tucker, Hayes, and I all move closer at the same time—we share the same collective priorities.

"You think so..." I repeat as I close in. "How do you not know?"

Both men chuckle, the vicious rattle of pure evil. I've been here long enough to recognize the sound of it.

"She was breathing when I picked her up, but then she passed the fuck out. We haven't exactly gone easy on her." Sasquatch lifts his hand from her bare thigh to smack her ass.

She doesn't react.

"Is she injured?" I snarl.

"Yeah, but her cunt's still warm." Big Foot looks over at his buddy Long Nose, and they share a good laugh.

At the same time, I throw Hayes a meaningful look, and he subtly lifts his chin with acknowledgment.

I close the space between me and the Yeti. "We'll take the girl."

"What'll you give us for her?" he asks.

"I don't think you heard me right." I glance at Tucker, who moves past us, circling around behind them. "Tuck, did you hear me agree to a trade?"

"Nope, didn't hear you say anything about a trade." Tucker twirls the tire iron. "All I heard you say was, '*We'll take the girl.*'"

I nod, meeting Sasquatch eye-to-eye. "That's right. All I said was that we'll take the girl."

Like vultures, we circle them.

Long Nose scoffs. "You're out of your fucking mind if you think we're handing her over to you alive without getting anything in return."

"But you don't know if she's alive," I taunt.

"Right, but if she is, I'm keep—"

"You said you were done with her."

"We are, and I'll trade her for something you've got."

"I've got a lot of things." I narrow my eyes, lean in close, cock my head to the side. "Tell me what I have that you think you deserve in exchange for that girl."

"You got smokes?"

A smile of disbelief stretches the corners of my lips. "Cigarettes?"

I glance over at Santi when he fails to stifle a laugh. Our eyes meet, and I give him the same look I gave Hayes before, silently affirming my intent to bring violence.

"Yeah..." Long Nose gives an apathetic shrug. "Or weed. "

I purse my lips and spin, pacing away. With a few feet between us, I turn to face them both. "I want to make sure I'm understanding the deal. You want us to give you smokes, and you'll give us a girl who may or may not be dead?"

The two men look at each other, then back at me. "Yeah, man. We're easy."

They're not easy.

They wanna see if we'll cave.

They wanna know our dynamic, how we react together.

They're gonna stalk us until they figure out how to kill us with minimal risk. They're gonna dump the girl on us to get their hands free, follow us in secret, try to kill us at our next vulnerable moment, and take our vehicles.

I know this game.

I've been through this before.

I won't allow it to happen.

I soften my expression and pretend to concede. "Okay. Deal. Tucker, get that last pack of cigarettes out of the glove box and hand it over to them."

"But the pack is—"

"*Yours.*" He was going to say it's nearly empty, but I cut him off before he could. "The pack is yours, I know, Tuck."

We haven't been able to get cigarettes in almost a year, and Tucker's been saving those last few for a rainy day. He looks confused, which isn't exactly an unfamiliar look for him, but the stress that shows in his furrowed brow gives me a sharp pang of unease. I wanna tell him I'm not giving these men what they want, but I have to be cautious, I have to be cryptic, I have to time things just right.

"I'll get you more later, Tuck." I try to help him understand with my eyes, without saying the words out loud. "I wanna take that girl with us, and it seems a trade is our only option."

That statement alone should be enough for him to understand. He *knows* I don't do trades with wandering lawless. I only deal in debts owed and negotiated contracts with people I trust, which are few and far between.

But Tucker's young, relatively new, as he's only been a Vulture for half a year, and he's a little dense sometimes. I don't know if he gets it or not, but he gives me a small nod and complies anyway, moving to the truck to get the nearly empty pack.

"Santi, Hayes..." I wait for each of them to look at me. "Sounds like a fair trade, right? They get our last box of cigarettes, and we get the girl?"

"Yeah. Sounds fair." Santi hardens his expression as he cracks his neck to prepare for a fight.

Hayes widens his stance. "Fair is fair."

I look at Sasquatch and Long Nose and give them a phony grin. "Pack of cigs is about all she's worth, am I right?" I rib, putting on a fake laugh to put them at ease until the girl is in our possession.

I watch each man carefully, give them each a chance to show me just a flicker of hesitation.

But there is no hesitation.

Each of them snickers independently of the other.

They just made that their last fucking laugh.

"Here," Tucker says at my side, handing me the nearly empty pack of cigarettes.

I take it from him and hold it in my palm, wave it at the walking dead men. "This is yours as soon as you put her in the truck bed. Lower the tailgate, Tuck."

Tucker moves without question and does what I told him to. I don't know whether he's aware of my inclination to always pull him back from the front lines—I don't really know why I do it. He's no stranger to violence. Violence is why we're all here. I guess I just want him to keep his hands clean as much as possible.

He does better at keeping the women calm, anyway.

Long Nose gives his buddy a nod of permission, and he carries the woman to the back of the truck. Tucker climbs up on the tailgate and moves back to stand in the center of the bed as Sasquatch approaches.

"Lay her down easy," Tucker tells him, holding out his palms like he's going to catch her if she's dropped too fast.

The Yeti huffs with annoyance but brings her off his shoulder with relative ease, laying her down with a surprising amount of gentleness for how bruised, battered, and bloodied she appears.

"Take a step back," I demand the moment she's down.

Sas moves away as he's told, stepping back to stand beside his friend.

"Now hand it over." Long Nose stretches out his arm and opens his palm expectantly.

I hold out the pack, but then I jerk my arm back before he can take it. "I'm gonna give it to you, but before I do, I just have to say one thing…" I pause for two reasons—dramatic effect and asserting my authority. "You get what you deserve in Lawless Land, and you both really fucking deserve this."

I toss the box at his long fucking nose, and as it flies, I swing my arm, thrust my blade with force, and sink it to the hilt into Yeti's gut. Santi swings, hitting a skull-crushing home run at the back of Long Nose's head. Hayes whips a length of heavy chain around Sasquatch's neck and pulls.

His hands shoot up, attempting to loosen the chain as Hayes grunts with the exertion of dragging the giant backward. I'm pulled along with them, my knife catching on a rib as I try to pull it out. I have to twist before I can yank it free. Then I stab him again, again, then one final time that finally has him slumping to his knees.

I step back as Santi delivers a second hit to Long Nose, who's facedown on the road, making sure he's good and dead. Hayes chokes the last bits of life out of Sasquatch as he bleeds profusely from the middle. Then I look at my hands, my tattoos hidden beneath a thick layer of blood.

I study it to the sound of a dying man—the man whose blood coats my skin. It's a slightly different shade than my own blood, which is exactly what I expected. I've scrutinized the blood of every kill and found that no two people share the same exact hue. Maybe it's just me who can see the subtle differences...

Maybe I'm wrong.

Maybe I'm crazy.

Maybe I'm lying to myself.

It's impossible to prove or disprove when I can't compare samples side-by-side, but I know what my eyes tell me, and every shade has been unique.

It fascinates me more than it should.

The blood on my hands now is less vibrant than my own. His has a brownish tint, similar to the shade of dried blood, though it's still fresh, warm, and wet. I get lost in the flow of it, watch a single drop as it glides down the back of my hand, slips along the side of my arm, and drips to the concrete beneath my feet.

"Heads up," Tucker's voice interrupts my obsessive observation.

I look up and he tosses me a towel.

"She's waking up," he says, still standing on the truck bed and crouched behind her head.

The tan woman with long black hair mutters quiet protests as she stirs, gradually creeping back into consciousness.

"Good." I start to wipe the blood from my hands. "You and Santi put her in the cab with the A/C. And Hayes?" I look back at him just in time to watch as he releases the chain from Sasquatch's neck, letting his dead body fall sideways to the ground. "Help me load these two fuckers into the bed. We'll take them back to store in the freezer."

We make quick work of it, clean the blood from our hands as best we can, and get back on the road. It'll be another ninety minutes before we arrive at the Crevice—a spot where a mesa sits beside a miles-long plateau, creating a long, narrow path in between. It's the first major landmark that new lawless will encounter on their journey into the Territory. It's where the Reborn lie in wait to entice them with false promises.

We don't make any promises.

We just take what we need.

And what we need are four new girls for Eden.

We hadn't expected to pick up a new girl so quickly, but it's one less that we'll have to find and fight to take at the Crevice.

They always put up a fight.

Conscious women tend to do that when they see us coming.

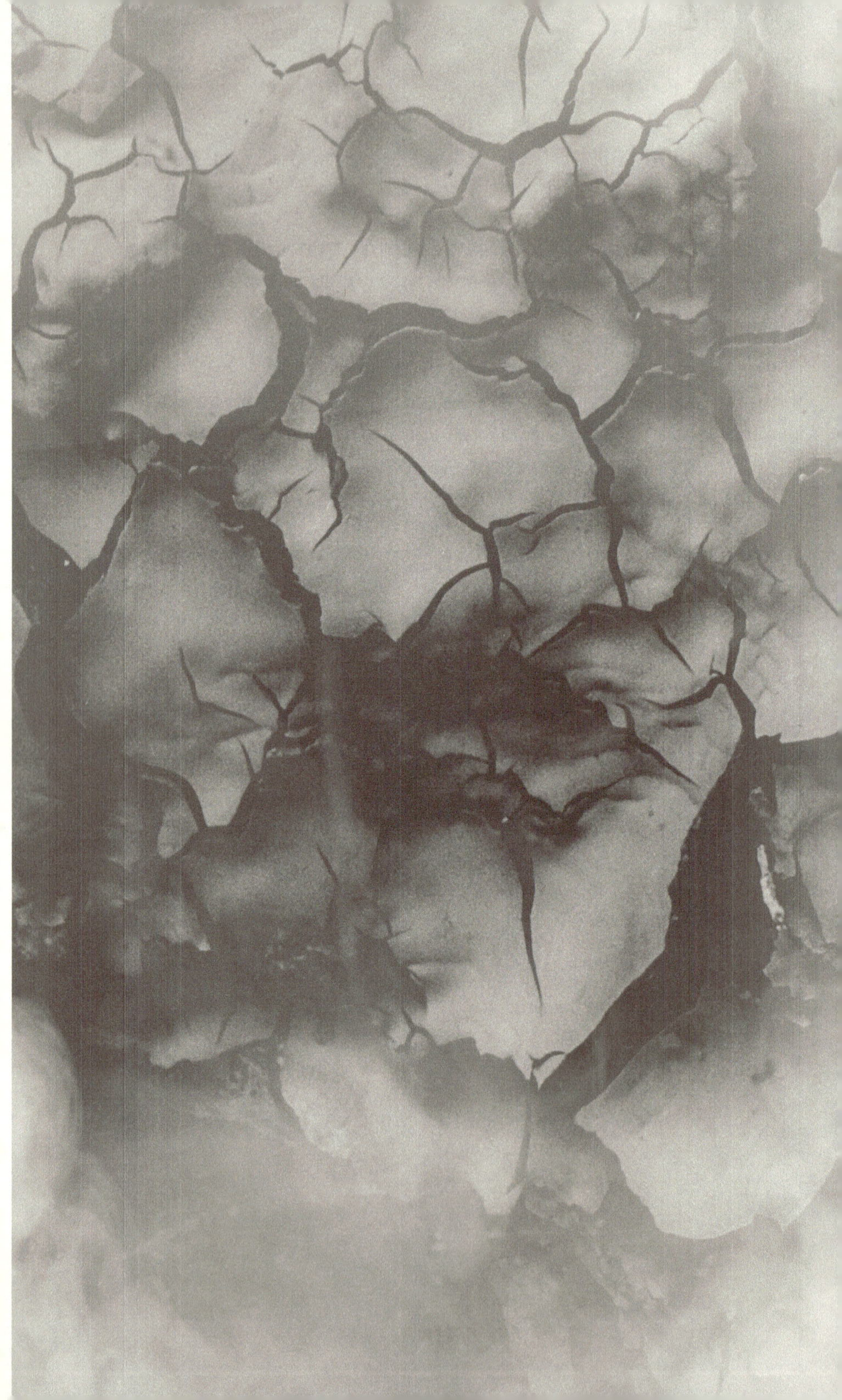

CHAPTER FOUR
Kill Pill

Gemma

"THIS IS YOUR kill pill."

"My *what?*" My eyes snap to the woman with unassuming features and plain, brown hair behind what I presume is bulletproof glass.

She sits behind a counter on her side of the divide, packing a tan backpack with basic survival items—standard issue for each outlaw on the brink of Eviction. She waves the item she's holding to get my attention, waiting until my eyes land on the small, translucent packet pinched between her finger and thumb. Inside the packet is a single, unnaturally bright neon green pill.

"You only get one," she continues. "Standard issue for female outlaws. Women like you are often targeted upon entry."

I jerk my chin back. "Women like *me?*"

She sighs, but not with annoyance. If the dark circles under her weary eyes are any indication, her sigh is a breeze of deep exhaustion spilling out.

"If you find yourself in a position where death is preferable, just rip the packet open." She taps her finger at the side of the packet to indicate a small perforation. "It's notched for an easy tear. The pill can be chewed or swallowed. Once it's ingested, you'll be dead in three minutes or less."

"Great, that's my plan B. Thanks for that. I didn't expect you all to make it so easy."

She ignores my comment and finishes her well-rehearsed statement like a damn professional. "Swallowing it whole is more efficient if your situation warrants a quick conclusion."

A quick conclusion.

I'll admit, it's tempting.

The thought of falling asleep forever and being done with all the pain has a certain appeal… Though the thought of hurting Seb in all the ways he hurt me is *far* more appealing.

"Eviction begins in ten minutes."

Ten minutes?

It feels as though an entire lifetime has passed since the journey from my jail cell in Connecticut began. Yet only an hour has passed since our bus arrived at the Transition Center.

Herded and filtered.

Stripped and showered.

Implanted with a microchip just behind my ear.

It's been a mad rush—an unexpectedly quick and efficient process—and I haven't taken a moment to reflect on how drastically my life is about to change.

The woman on the other side of the glass unzips the front pocket of the tan backpack and slips in one easy-open kill pill before zipping it closed. She presses a button on the countertop and a hinged door rises to reveal an opening that's conveniently backpack-sized.

"This is yours." She drops the backpack into the hole and slaps the door shut with her palm.

Her finger descends on a second button, triggering a brief but irritating buzz. Something shifts and clangs within, then another hinged door springs open against my thighs. Inside is the backpack.

"These items are granted to you as a goodwill courtesy by the federal government of the United States of America."

I grab the bag and slip it on over my shoulders. The weight of it settles, and though there isn't much inside, it feels heavier than I expected—heavy enough to drag me down with the weight of reality.

I'm afraid.

Everything is about to change—permanently and irreversibly.

I no longer have a choice.

I have no control.

"The backpack and items contained within it are the only possessions you will be allowed to take into the Territory." She pauses. "Please raise your right hand."

Shit, this is happening.

"Please state your full name and date of birth for the record."

I swallow hard. "Gemma Rose Hadley. January thirtieth, twenty-thirty-four."

"Gemma Rose Hadley, you have been processed for Eviction from the United States of America. On this day, May twenty-fourth, twenty-sixty-four, your citizenship is hereby renounced, effective immediately. Please acknowledge your understanding by stating, 'I understand.'"

My sight is unfocused, blurring as I struggle with the truth of this moment, but my eyes are fixed on hers, watching her speak through the haze. "I understand."

"You no longer retain the rights and privileges of a citizen. You are here and forevermore an outlaw, and all outlaws of the United States must be Evicted. Your Eviction is a life sentence. You are effectively banished to live your remaining days—however many that may be—in the Territory. Please acknowledge your understanding by stating, 'I understand.'"

"I understand."

"The Territory has no unifying governing body or system of law, and therefore, no law enforcement or public safety services. All outlaws assume their own risk for injury, bodily harm, or death from the moment they enter the Territory. Please acknowledge your understanding by stating, 'I under—'"

"I understand," I spit out the words before she finishes.

Fear crawls beneath my skin, and it scratches me, rubbing me raw with impatience.

I'd thought the four months of waiting in solitary were the worst part of all this, but I was wrong... It's *this*. The pomp and circumstance, the formality behind my Eviction, the ritual of this transition.

Get on with it.

Just send me away already.

There's a slight pause before she begins again. "Immediately upon receiving directions, you must exit this Transition Center. All outlaws will enter the Red Zone, pass through the tunnel, and enter the Territory for outlaws. At no point will you be allowed to re-enter the Transition Center, nor any part of the United States beyond the border walls of the Territory."

She takes a deep breath, then blows it out, and the hopeless sound somehow draws me back and focuses my vision—it has me sweeping my gaze across her face, noting the exhaustion in her features. This job must be draining, sending people off to their potential demise.

How many of the people in this room will survive a week in the Mojave? A month? Will one of us die today?

"Gemma Rose Hadley, do you acknowledge your renouncement of citizenship and imminent Eviction from the United States as the sentence for your crimes as judged in a court of law?"

Do I acknowledge...?

Why ask a yes or no question when they'll only allow you to answer one way?

I let my head fall to the side a little. "What would you do if I just said, 'No?'"

"You would be removed from the facility by force."

"Where would they take me?"

"Same place. You would be forced to enter the Red Zone all the same."

"A man would put his hands on me to do that?"

Her brow furrows at the line of questioning. "Yes, as I said, you would be removed by force. As many of our officers are male—"

"Got it. Not worth the argument for argument's sake. I've had enough men put their hands on me and take me by force to last me a lifetime, you know?"

Her eyes scrutinize, but I see a hint of softness there. Still, she's all business, just trying to get this done to move her day forward. "Gemma Rose Hadley, do you acknowledge—"

"Yes, I acknowledge. I understand, and I acknowledge."

She gives me a short nod. "You can lower your hand. Please join one of the lines on your left. Outlaws must stay behind the black-and-white line until they are called forward to enter the Red Zone."

I glance left to see the lines of outlaws forming and growing, the head of each line stopped behind a black-and-white line painted across the cement floor. A row of five fire-engine-red doors stand ominously about ten feet beyond the black-and-white line. Armed guards stand between the lines and the doors, watching the outlaws with careful scrutiny and skepticism.

And on each door, the same sign is affixed, bold and clear with thick black letters on a stark white background.

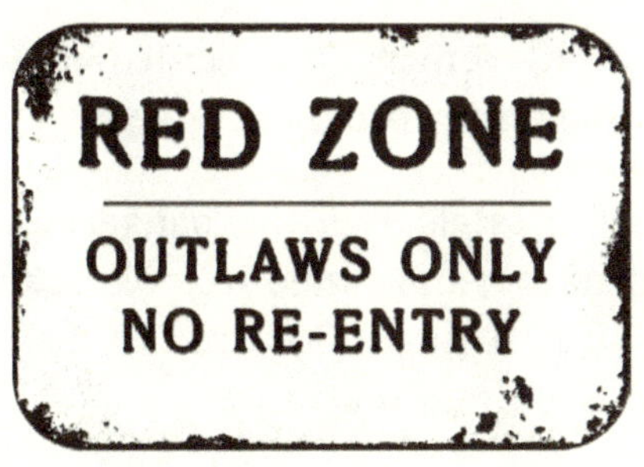

No re-entry...

None.

Once I pass through those doors, it will be final. I'll never return home again; I'll never see my family or my friends again. Any chance I could've had at a normal life will be gone forever.

"So, that's it, then?" My voice is soft. "Through the red doors and no turning back..."

It's not as if I have a choice anymore. I made my choice the night I killed those three bastards.

"Please join one of the lines."

I blink at the sound of her voice, realize that fear and weakness must show in my expression, and I quickly fix my face—this isn't the time or place to show fear.

I mutter a quick and quiet, "thank you," adjust the weight of the backpack, and naturally gravitate toward the line that's second from the right—one of only two lines, as far as I can see, with women.

I join the line behind two young women, chatting vibrantly. The energy and intonation in their speech reminds me of the roommate I had during my sophomore year of college and how she interacted with her sorority sisters. They had the social connection I secretly envied but denied myself—I was too obsessively focused on my program.

I'd thought their lifestyle was the dangerous one—with all the partying, drinking, and random hook-ups with strangers. When I was young, it never occurred to me that I was prey simply because I had tits and a pussy.

My mistake.

Maybe if I'd developed more friendships and let myself have a little more fun, I wouldn't have been so lonely and vulnerable when Seb and his friends found me.

The woman directly in front of me faces the red doors, fussing with her shoulder-length brown, wavy locks, freshly washed from the showers we were required to take and air-drying in soft waves. She speaks to her friend in a hushed voice, but at a rushed pace.

The other woman—shorter than her friend by at least three inches—was matching her energy until I stepped into the line. Every time I glance, I find her looking at me before she quickly diverts her eyes back to the brunette. She pulls her long dirty-blonde hair over one shoulder, absent-mindedly twisting the strands into a braid in front of her.

I don't know why she keeps looking at me, but it puts me on edge. I don't know her. She's here because she's a violent criminal. I know my motivations for violence were justifiable, but I don't know what *she* did or *why*. She might recognize me from the media, and if she does, she could be one of those women I don't quite understand—the ones who hate me so passionately that they wish me dead.

I don't judge those women.

I imagine them as the unfortunate wives of men like Dom, Peter, Colin, and Seb. If I were one of them, I would probably misdirect my suppressed rage, too.

Regardless, I have to remain vigilant. I'm about to enter one of the most dangerous places in the world, and I can't let a moment's hesitation, fear, or weakness—however fleeting that moment may be—stand in my way of surviving long enough to get my final revenge.

My brow furrows as I harden my expression. I start to ask her what she's looking at, but before I can get a word out, she decides to give up on the sneaky glancing and go all in on full eye contact instead. She leans to the side a little so she can look at me squarely over her friend's shoulder.

"You're that girl, right?"

I draw in a subtle but deep breath as my fingers curl around the straps of my backpack. With feigned innocence, I ask, "What girl?"

She smiles softly, almost sweetly, and lets go of her unsecured braid as her friend whirls around to look at me, too. "You're *that* girl... The one who single-handedly murdered three men in revenge before dyeing her hair pink on social media..."

I shrug. "Am I?"

The brunette's eyes widen as she gives me a once over. "Oh, my *God*!" Her gaze darts wildly to the shorter blonde. "That's her... It's *her*!" Her expression morphs instantly from excitement to annoyance, and she taps the back of her hand against the blonde's shoulder. "How long was she standing there, and you didn't say a fucking word?"

The blonde is staring at me, paying no mind to the brunette. She nods slowly as a grin lifts her cheeks and scrunches her nose. "Oh, my fucking God. It's the *Siren*." She enthusiastically throws her hands out in front of her with her palms angled toward the ceiling. "You're the *fucking* Siren! I fucking *knew* it!"

She's not angry.

Her tone is… *joyful?*

Like she's meeting a celebrity.

They're practically bouncing, gleeful in front of me, staring like I'm the second coming of Christ or something.

I don't love it, but I definitely don't hate it, either…

Okay, maybe I like it a little.

"The motherfucking Siren." The brunette sinks her fingers into her hair, overcome with disbelief. "Girl, you're my *idol*. I fucking *love* you! I've been following your story from the beginning. You inspired me. For real, though, you're the reason I'm here."

She hesitates, then launches herself forward and throws her arms around me, giving me a hug. I'm stiff as she squeezes me tight, stunned and frozen in the way she embraces me.

"Thank you. Seriously, thank you for doing what you did." Her words are soft and sincere. "Watching you gave me the strength I needed to survive."

Oh… Wow.

I didn't expect that.

I'm not exactly sure what she's thanking me for, and I'm still shocked as hell when she releases me and steps back.

She flashes a wide, star-struck grin. "I'm Quinn." She puts her hand on her chest as she introduces herself, then places it on the shorter blonde's shoulder. "This is Katie. It's so funny we both have the same Eviction date. We were friends in high school, but we lost touch for a bit. Graduation was three years ago, and we haven't seen each other since…"

They glance at each other, then Katie says, "Yeah, but we both ended up on the same prisoner transport flight out from Tallahassee and rode the same bus here."

"Who fucking knew we were in solitary in the same damn detention center this whole time?" Quinn laughs.

"We were actually just talking about you on the bus ride," Katie tells me. "Found out we were both in for basically the same crime…" she pauses, "which was inspired by *you*. The Siren. Oh, my *God*, I can't believe you're literally standing in front of me right now!"

The hairs on the back of my neck rise as they speak, though not because of them… It's because I feel eyes on me.

They've said the name I'm known by several times now—the Siren—and they aren't exactly using their indoor voices. I'm relieved that these two women don't hate me, but there are a lot of men in this room. Men who know what I did, but don't believe the reason why I did it. Men who think of me as nothing more than a lying, man-hating bitch who would try to kill them simply for having the wrong tone of voice.

Maybe I would…

Becoming the Siren changed me.

"Shit," Quinn whines. "I wish I had my cell phone so I could take a pic."

Katie puts her fists on her hips and turns her body to Quinn, looking up at her. "Girl, you're never gonna have a cell phone again. Accept it."

"I know, and I hate it! At least I could text on that cheap phone one of the officers snuck into solitary for me…"

As they chatter on about cell phones, I recall something Officer Cruz had said to me outside…

> "There are going to be a lot of pissed off men who will target you, and that's going to start as soon as you enter the Red Zone. Find women who know you as the Siren, who appreciate what you did. Seek them out the moment you go through those doors and make friends with them. Connection is how you survive."

Make friends?

I'm not sure I even know how.

Yet, I feel my shoulders shrugging against the tension in my neck—a physical manifestation of the unease I'm feeling as attention is drawn in my direction. Maybe I do need connections to survive this. And these women are standing in front of me offering exactly that.

When I find a natural spot to join in the conversation, I take advantage of it. "I'm pretty bummed I can't do any live streaming in the Territory. I'm willing to bet I'll find more than a few men who deserve to hear me sing…"

There's a brief pause as they both look at me, and I wonder if they understood what I meant. I know they did when they both break out into laughter.

"Girl, yes!" Quinn cheers.

"Pretty much every man in this room, right?" Katie leans in. "We should start a fucking uprising out there. Find all the women, work together to wipe out all the men, and then take over the Territory for ourselves."

"Sounds like a dream." I nod, giving them a small smile.

That really does sound like a dream.

A head-in-the-clouds, get-real-it's-never-going-to-happen dream, but a nice dream, nonetheless.

Quinn looks me up and down. "You're such a fucking goddess. Honestly, you're so pretty. I thought you were pretty in the clips from your live stream they showed on that network special, but you even look fucking cute in these hideous orange jumpsuits."

Katie looks at her and grins. "I know, right? She's a queen!"

I think maybe this is where I should return the compliment, but before I have a chance, something heavy bumps into me from behind, shoving me forward. I nearly collide with Quinn and Katie, but they both put out their hands to halt me, to keep me upright as their eyes rise over my shoulder, their expressions twisting from excitement to rage.

Speaking over each other, Quinn punches out the words, "Back up, asshole."

Katie gives attitude with hers. "Ever heard of personal space, dickwad?"

"Shut the fuck up." It's a deep male voice at my back, booming down from somewhere above my head. "No one asked any of you dumb bitches to speak."

Excuse the fuck out of me?

Slowly, I turn and come face-to-chest with a wide, tall, mountain of a man. His predatory energy is overwhelming, consuming, palpable. I'm immediately disgusted by this man, unease crawling beneath my skin from his disturbing energy.

I lift my chin, slowly dragging my eyes up to the nasty motherfucker's face. He towers at least six inches above my head and probably thinks that makes him intimidating. I ball my hands into furious fists held down at my sides.

White-knuckled.

Jaw tense.

Pulse racing as chaos thickens my blood.

"Say it again." My voice is quiet, but insistent in my growing rage.

His head tilts down as he meets my eyes, his bushy eyebrows angling down toward his nose. "What did you say to me?"

I quickly scan his face, hyper-vigilant as I take in every twitch, every subtle twist in his expression, every wrinkle, every freckle, every bead of sweat. There's a nasty-looking scar across his left cheek, and I can't help but think it looks like some of mine, which were made by the wild slashes of a knife.

I hold his stare as I emphasize every word. "Say. It. Again. Tell us one more time to shut the fuck up. Call me a dumb bitch again. Say it."

He's already too close to me, but then he leans forward, his protruding belly pressing into me.

I'm disgusted that his body touches mine, and my heart races from the adrenaline of fear, from memories of my most traumatic moments rushing around somewhere in the back of my mind, warning that there's something wrong… Warning me that *he's* like *them.*

Despite my fear, I won't step back.

I refuse to step back from men like him ever again.

"Shut the fuck up, you dumb bitch."

Quinn and Katie are hyped that he dared to say it again. I can feel their anger as they make utterances of disbelief at the man's audacity and give me encouragement to fight him.

I don't want to fight this man.

I don't *need* to fight this man.

The last man I'm going to hurt is somewhere out there in the Territory, and I'm not giving an ounce of my building vitriol to any other. Logan Sebastian gets all my remaining fury.

Ease off, Gem.

Save it for Seb.

"That's what I thought you said. I guess I'm just such a dumb bitch that I didn't understand you the first time."

So much for easing off.

I force an exaggerated smile, one that uses every muscle in my cheeks so I can ensure my dimples pucker.

He counters my sweet smile with a dark grin.

"You'd better look out for me and my boys out there, *dumb bitch.*" He really doubles down on the dumb-bitch shtick. He lifts a massive finger and jabs the scar on his cheek with a filthy fingernail. "This is your fault. You're the reason my girl tried to take me out. But I don't fuck around with bitches like you and her, you understand? When I knew what it was coming to, I put her down for good. And I'm gonna put you down, too."

My breath catches momentarily, but my sweet smile never falters. "I don't know what you looked like before she cut you, honey, but I'm willing to bet she did you a favor."

He lunges, bumping me backward into Quinn and Katie again. They catch me before I topple backward, grab hold of me and pull me behind them. They willingly step up to the giant to defend me, shouting obscenities and gesturing wildly. I almost have to laugh at the extreme height difference between the man and Katie, the way her neck cranes backward to look up at him so she can make eye contact without fear.

The urge to laugh rushes out of me in a wave when the man's hand snaps forward and latches around Quinn's throat. My fury begins to unsheathe, but a familiar voice leaps from the crowd somewhere behind me.

"Outlaw!" Officer Cruz appears on my right, walking down the line of outlaws in my row. His hand lands on the giant man's and yanks it down, forcing him to release Quinn. "You keep your goddamn hands to yourself. You are still standing on US soil."

The man's face is contorted with rage, but he lifts his palms in surrender at Officer Cruz.

"You three," Officer Cruz indicates me, Quinn, and Katie with his hand, "move to the front of line one."

As we move to pass, Officer Cruz gently grips my elbow. He walks me along behind Quinn and Katie toward the front of the line, nearer to the red doors.

Leaning in, he keeps his voice quiet but speaks to me quickly. "That man is going to try to kill you. Line one enters the Red Zone first, so you girls will have a head start. As soon as you enter, *move*. Get as far ahead of the crowd as you can and move quickly through the tunnel. When you step out into the Territory, move faster. Don't stop until sunset."

He walks us along the black-and-white strip on the floor to the first line, and places us at the front. "You can survive this. Good luck to you."

And just like that, he's gone.

"What the hell was that?" Katie looks at me, bewildered.

"He's… I think he's trying to help me survive Eviction."

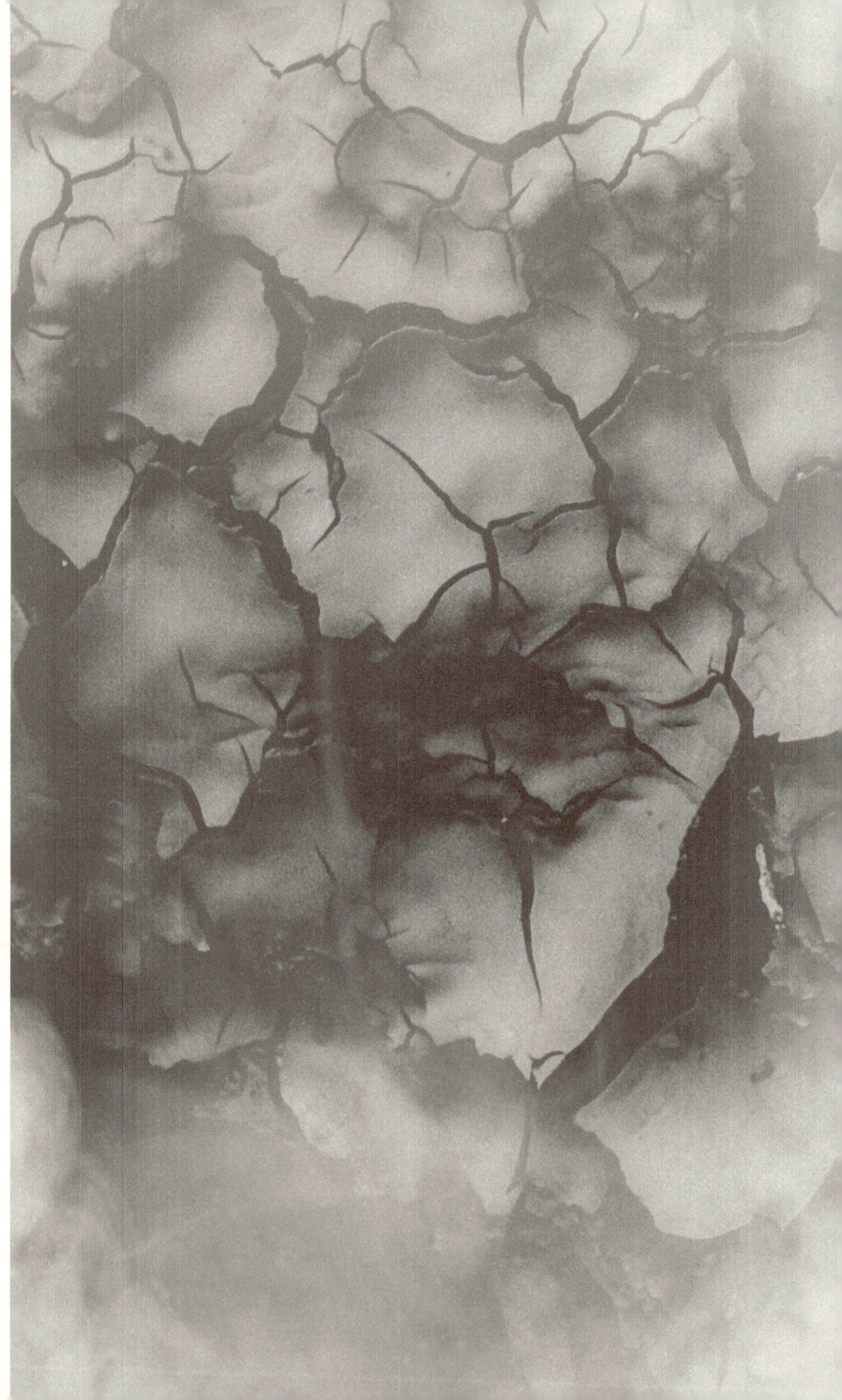

CHAPTER FIVE
Eviction

Gemma

THE RED DOOR opens, and the world I knew is gone forever.

From that moment, it's a mad dash from one reality into the next, and everything happens too quickly for me to process.

All I can do is move.

I have to move to survive.

I have to survive to serve justice.

I have to serve justice to satisfy this insatiable need for revenge.

Maybe then I'll find some peace.

Four of the five red doors remain closed—it's only the one in front of us they've opened, and we're immediately ordered through.

We cross the threshold and enter the Red Zone.

There's no turning back, no time to think about the world we just left behind forever.

No re-entry...

Just keep moving.

The Red Zone is dark, a dimly lit cave.

A flat slab of concrete beneath our feet stretches as long as the five red doors, ending with stone walls on either side.

The only direction is forward, toward the edge of the concrete, which descends into a wide staircase, dropping into the darkness beneath a concrete header that has the words *Red Zone* painted across it in vibrant red paint.

Ten long strides to cross from the door to the staircase.

I urge Katie and Quinn to keep up with me as I step down, but I don't look back to see whether they do—I have to focus on myself, on my mission.

Less than ten steps to the bottom.

In this bizarre underworld, we find the tunnel.

It stretches out before us, wide enough for ten people to pass side-by-side, carved out through natural stone. There are lights on either side of the passage, but they're small and dim with darkness lying beyond them.

Keep moving.

"Whoa." Katie grabs my elbow, jerking me to a stop. My head whips sideways, my brow furrowed with frustration as I meet her eyes. "Maybe we should hang back a sec. I don't wanna be first going in there..."

I briefly glance away from her, look over my shoulder to watch the other outlaws from our line moving in through the only open red door, slowing their pace as soon as they enter. Their eyes sweep the dim space with both wonder and worry.

I can't let myself slow down.

I can't let myself think about what's happening.

I could drop too easily into the fear of what lies ahead... That fear creeps beneath the surface, begging for indulgence.

Threatening.

Cracking.

Crumbling.

It's a flood of panic behind a dam wall that's moments from falling apart. It's *going* to fall apart, but I might be able to outrun the surge for a little while if I just keep going.

"We have to move," I tell them. "We can't stop."

The red door slams shut behind us with a vibrating *clang*, startling everyone. There's a beat of silence before the second red door opens and the next line enters.

"Let's *go*." I shake my arm from her grip, turn away, and move.

"HOW FUCKING LONG is this fucking tunnel?" Quinn huffs.

I feel nauseous from fighting adrenaline.

There are lights throughout the tunnel like the ones at the entrance, but they're placed few and far between, shifting us between periods of light and stretches of darkness.

"God, we've been walking for like fifteen minutes." Katie's voice is tinged with annoyance. "Is this some sick joke? Do we all just walk the tunnel forever until we die?"

As if in response to her question, we edge around a curve, and a brilliant light floods the passage.

It's the end… It's the beginning.

"Thank fuck." Quinn sighs. "Never thought I'd be so damn happy to walk my ass into the desert."

She and Katie laugh, but levity evades me.

The onrushing reality of entering this lawless world, coupled with that outlaw's threat to *put me down for good* like he did to his girl, weigh heavily on my shoulders. If he catches up to me and I die here today, all of this will have been in vain—Seb will never suffer the way he deserves to.

I quicken my pace toward the sunlight that reveals the end of the tunnel. My eyes burn as we approach. I squint and blink rapidly as we pass through a haze of blinding light.

We enter a new world.

We've arrived in the Territory.

I have to stop as my eyes adjust to the sunlight, but I start moving again as soon as I'm able to make out my surroundings.

Massive walls—taller than anything I could've imagined—stretch out forever into the Mojave. Walls that keep outlaws trapped within their bounds. In front of me is barren land—an expanse of dry, cracked earth in drab beige, coated with a thin layer of shifting sand—and in the distance are mountains.

Hot, bright, empty.

Desolate.

Home.

This is home now.

The fear I fought so hard finally breaks the dam and it surges through my veins. Adrenaline streams through me and my head feels light. I double over, dropping my hands to my knees, letting my head hang as I force myself to take a slow, deep breath.

"You okay?" I'm not sure exactly who asks, but a gentle hand lands on my back.

I take in another breath, blow it out slowly. "Just give me a second. We have to keep moving."

Another in, another out.

I force myself to stand, though I still feel dizzy.

There are so many voices behind us, the volume ever-growing.

It's dangerous for us to stop here.

I make myself move.

Ten steps, twenty, thirty… Katie and Quinn walk beside me, matching my stride. We move forward together until a force knocks me off my feet.

The weight of a rolling boulder slams into my back and I fall forward. I manage to fling my arms in front of me before I land, slam my palms to the hard ground, and slow my descent enough to avoid breaking my face as someone heavy falls onto my back.

I know immediately it's the man with the scar, the one who threatened me in the line. I hear Katie and Quinn descend into rage, shouting with madness, their voices rising in volume as they come to my aid.

But there are other voices, too.

The voices of men.

Furious, violent men.

The shouting turns to screaming.

Scar Face twists me beneath him, violently whipping me onto my back before straddling my waist, crushing me with his full weight bearing down. "No one to save you now, *dumb bitch.*"

Those two words strike me like lightning, sending a jolt of electricity through my veins. It vaporizes fear but leaves adrenaline for the fight.

I grit my teeth. "No one ever saved me."

His hands clamp around my throat.

There's chaos around me, and I can't focus…

I can't breathe.

My hands latch around his wrists, pulling uselessly against his strength as he squeezes and presses down.

Fuck.

If he presses down much harder, he'll snap my neck.

My legs thrash.

I scratch at his arms, dig in my nails.

He feels nothing.

I reach for his face, grappling at his chin, arching into his grip as I fight with the urge to hurt him, rip him, tear his skin with my nails, gouge out his fucking eyes.

I blink as Katie appears above me, slams her fist into the side of his face, knuckles punching right into his scar. It's enough to stun him. Though he doesn't release me, his grip loosens enough for me to draw in a decent breath. If she hits him again, I might be able to get away.

Her fist is clenched, ready to strike as she pulls back her arm, but then her head jerks back, and she disappears from my sight with a scream—dragged away by some man trying to hurt her, too.

Fury consumes me.

I claw at his arms, digging my nails so deep that I can feel his flesh tear. He cusses, and his arms twitch as I cause him pain.

Maybe he'll kill me, but I'll give him the scars to remember me.

Maybe he'll kill me...

The truth is a trigger for the song inside my mind. The one they tortured me with every time I thought I was going to die. The one I sang to them when I killed them. The one I want to sing to Logan Sebastian as I watch the light leave his eyes.

I have to watch him die.

All I can do is fight, so that's what I do.

I fight.

Even as I creep toward unconsciousness, still, *I fight.*

"That's right," I hear Quinn's triumphant voice. "*Die,* motherfucker."

I hear the sound of a man coughing, choking, dying.

What did she do?

"Hang on, girl." I think she's talking to me, but her voice isn't coming from the same place. I hear her on the opposite side of me now, where I saw Katie before.

Grunting. Smacking. Slapping. Breaking.

They're fighting someone together.

"Gimme your pill," Quinn says, both of them panting. "Let's make that motherfucker choke on it."

I'm fading.

I'm still fighting, but I'm fading.

My vision blackens around the edges. I blink and see flashes of red. There's blood on my fingers, blood that coats Scar Face's arms where I rip his skin.

Katie appears behind him, wraps her arms around his thick neck, and squeezes him with the force of her entire body. His right hand lifts from my neck, and though his left remains on my throat, I can sneak in shallow breaths.

I can fight him harder.

As I squirm and thrash, Quinn appears.

"I'll kill you bitches, too," he says, but while his mouth is open, Quinn slaps her palm against it and presses hard.

He lets go of me all together so he can reach for her, but he merely claws at her side, unable to get a grip at this angle. I wiggle my body out from beneath him as he tries to fight both women.

His eyes go wide.

He coughs behind her palm.

"That's right," Quinn soothes, grunting as she struggles to keep her palm clamped over his lips. "Just take it. Swallow it down. It'll all be over soon."

I don't even know why, but I feel the corners of my lips twist into a grin.

Within seconds, his body goes limp.

His eyelids droop.

He slumps in their grip.

They release him at the same time, and he falls sideways, crashing to the ground.

Panting, I blink up at them.

Quinn looks at me with concern wrinkling her bloody brow. There's a cut that stretches from the middle of her eyebrow halfway to her hairline. "Are you okay?"

"Shit." Katie takes a step toward me. "You're gonna have bruises."

I lift my hand and brush my fingers across my neck.

I blink away droplets from my watering eyes.

Inhale a deep breath through my nose.

Blow it out in a rush through rounded lips.

It takes me that long to find my voice. "I can deal with a few bruises. But how's my hair?"

Quinn chuckles. "Fucking fabulous."

"Flawless." Katie smiles as she reaches down.

I take her hand, let her help me to my feet. I brush my hips and butt, skimming away the dirt on my ugly jumpsuit as I glance around, noting three dead men on the ground.

The one to my right is bloodied and broken, his face smashed, caved in on one side. A heavy rock rests beside his skull—the obvious murder weapon. The man on my left is scratched up a bit, but just like Scar Face—who lies dead on the ground in front of me—I can't immediately tell what killed him.

"How did you do that?" I ask.

Quinn lifts her hand and shows me a familiar translucent packet, the plastic torn across the top perforation, hanging on by the corner.

She twists her wrist to show me both sides of the packet.

Empty.

"Kill pill," she says with a grin, then tosses the plastic onto the asshole's dead body. "They were right. It did come in handy."

I guess these women came in handy, too.

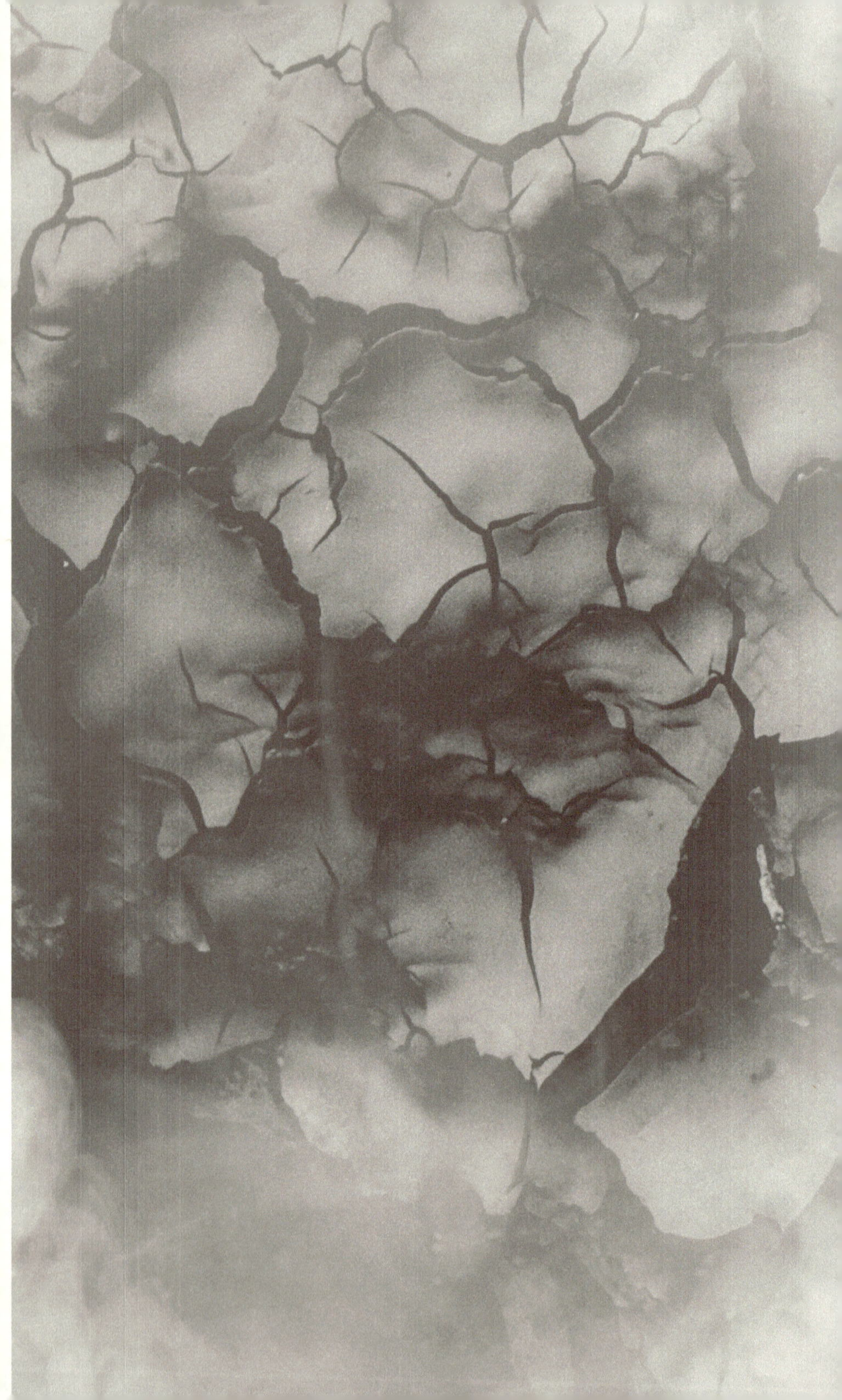

CHAPTER SIX
Motorcycle Man

Gemma

THE TIME AND distance we've traveled into the unforgiving desert is indiscernible. The only thing on my mind is moving forward, finding something resembling shelter, anything that will shade us from the overwhelming light and heat.

My skin bakes under the glaring sun. I'd be burned from head to toe if they hadn't provided a single travel size bottle of sunscreen in my backpack.

Would it have killed them to throw in a hat and sunglasses?

My eyes are so dry they beg to be shut, so I close them every once in a while and walk blindly for as many steps as I can manage before feeling the overwhelming urge to lay down, fall asleep, and wait for death to take me.

We haven't encountered another attack in the amount of time that's passed. The unexpected connection with Quinn and Katie, and the way they worked together to defeat our attackers, naturally fostered some kind of unspoken alliance that's granted us strength in numbers.

Of the hundreds Evicted today, I'd estimate that maybe fifty of them were female. At least half of those women move with us in a loose cluster, like stars orbiting an unseen body in the night sky—gravity from a black hole dragging us all toward an infinite, unknowable fate.

We move in silence.

We keep moving forward through the miles of misery.

Miles of barren land, no trees to grant us shade.

Just when I begin to feel as though I may give into exhaustion, right here and now, I see something in the distance.

There's a rock formation up ahead.

The end of a long plateau curving toward us.

The wide expanse of it stretching infinitely into the horizon.

Just beyond the edge of the plateau, I spot another formation that's just as tall, but not nearly as long—a mesa. I think the formations must have been connected once before, separated from erosion, which carved a space between them.

A crevice.

A passage.

A small canyon.

Quite possibly some shade.

A reprieve from the sun.

At the head of the pack, unintentionally leading this group, I turn toward the landform and pick up my pace. The hope of shade is worth every ounce of energy I have left.

It feels like another decade has passed by the time I'm close enough to confirm it with my own eyes—there are pockets of shade within the passage between the plateau and the mesa. I hear sighs of relief from the women all around me, utterances of approval for a respite from the sunlight.

Each step brings us closer to comfort, but it also brings us closer to something else…

Shit.

To my right, there's a gray line stretching out along the horizon, drawing parallel to the passage. It's an old, paved highway, one of many routes through the desert that were cut off from civilization when the wall was built around the Territory.

> "Avoid major roads and highways. If you hear an engine, hide—"

Cruz warned me to stay away from the roads.

Though what did he mean, exactly?

Stay far enough away that you can't see them?

Don't cross them?

Don't walk along the paths they carve through the desert?

Are we too close to this road or far enough away to be safe?

The questions exhaust my dried-up, shriveling brain cells. There's only one decision I can make in this hell on earth, and that decision is comfort at all costs—I keep moving toward the passage. I have never been so desperate to crawl into the shadows.

But then I hear a low rumble in the distance.

A rumble that gradually stretches into a roar.

Two vehicles appear from the end of the road where it fades into the sky, racing down the highway, heading in our direction. The road is farther from us than the passage that promises shade and concealment, but we're not close enough to hide before we're spotted.

Voices rise, expressing confusion, making plans, trying to make sense of how there are vehicles on this road and who the fuck would be driving them. A few women break off and make a run for it toward the passage, while some stand still in silence. I can sense others backing away.

I feel like I'm internally screaming at myself to *run*. To get to that passage between vertical mountains, find a place to hide, and hope that whoever is driving those vehicles just keeps going.

But I don't run.

I don't even stand still.

Inexplicably, I move toward the road, one small step at a time until they're close enough for me to make out the shape of them.

A white pickup truck leads.

A man on a motorcycle follows.

I stop and watch this stupid man without a helmet race down the highway, weaving around vegetation that has worked its way through the cracks in the pavement.

"Hey," Katie calls for my attention. "Let's go."

"Yeah," I mutter, but take another step in the direction of the road.

"What are you doing?" Quinn's tone is tinged with frustration. "Come on. Let's get away from the road, try to hide."

The man on the motorcycle turns his head, and appears to be looking right at me. He slows, turns his machine to face me, and eases to a stop at the very edge of the road where pavement meets dry, cracked earth.

My breath catches.

My eyes are wide—I can't seem to drag them away.

Heat causes the air to ripple, like a curtain of invisible waves that distorts the sight of him. You could almost convince me this is a fever dream, that he's not really there.

Someone's hand is on my arm, gently pulling, and a voice is frenzied in telling me that we have to go, that we need to run.

She's right.

I should run.

But I can't seem to connect my legs with good sense.

It's the heat... I'm delirious.

Motorcycle Man subtly inclines his head, and I swear, he's watching me the way I'm watching him—with some mix of curiosity and fear. I can almost feel the air vibrating between us from the rumble of his engine.

I think he's wearing sunglasses… His eyes look like giant black pits from this distance, and I can't quite make out his face. His mouth and nose are covered by a small piece of black fabric, a bandana that he must have tied around the back of his head. It has some white image printed on the front of it that I can't quite make out.

His hair is charcoal brown, cut closer on the sides, gradually thickening into a tuft at the top of his head. It's windblown, a few longer strands falling toward his face. His arms are covered, but not by sleeves. Tattoos blanket every visible inch of skin from the backs of his hands all the way up his arms, disappearing beneath the short sleeves of his black T-shirt. They appear again at the collar, creeping up the sides of his neck, finally stopping beneath his jaw.

What kind of maniac wears black in this heat?

That maniac right there.

And I must be a maniac for standing here, watching him stare at me when I should be running for cover. I attempt to refocus, draw in a deep breath, but only choke on the dry heat. I'm trapped with curiosity for his next move until suddenly, he turns his head, his chin rising as he looks in the direction of the mesa.

I take a step backward.

"What the fuck?" Katie's tone is wary. "Look…" She grabs my arm and tugs.

"Who are they?" Quinn wonders.

They're both looking up at the top of the mesa, the same place that drew Motorcycle Man's attention away from me.

I lift my chin skyward and look up.

Atop the mesa, standing at the edge and looking out at all of us, are three women, all dressed in black.

The sight of them is consuming...

They form a triangle, one woman standing at the precipice, the other two a step back on either side of her. Their flowing black skirts catch the arid breeze, fluttering in light waves. The two women behind wear dark sunglasses, hiding their faces beneath the rims of black sunhats. They each hold a black umbrella, reaching forward to shade the woman in the center.

She smiles, holding out her arms with her palms toward the sky. "There's nothing to fear," she calls out, her long black hair flowing in time with her skirt.

Everyone on the ground stops moving.

Everyone falls silent.

The only sounds are the empty breeze and the woman's echoing voice as she speaks. "Come with us, Daughters of Darkness. All are welcome here. We have shelter from the wretched sunlight. Food and water. Friendship and camaraderie. Join us, and we'll take care of you."

There's a long pause, a shared hesitation, and the silence stretches through it.

She waves her hand toward the canyon. "Come through the passage. You'll be safe with us."

A dash of bright orange moves in my peripheral as one of the female outlaws who walked with us rushes toward the passage.

Another outlaw moves, then another…

More and more women make their way toward the promise of shelter and care.

"More maniacs wearing black in this heat," I mutter.

Quinn looks at me. "What?"

"Let's go," Katie demands. "I'll trust those maniacs up there any day before those men out on the road."

The women in black look like fallen angels atop the mesa, ethereal in their darkness, bewitching, beguiling…

"This isn't right…" I take a step back.

I turn my head toward the highway.

Motorcycle Man is still there, staring right at me, half-risen from the seat of his bike and leaning forward as though he's compelled to leap off the thing and run after me.

"Siren?" a voice calls out to me from the top of the mesa.

"Is that her?" Another from above.

"It is!" They speak as though they've spotted their favorite celebrity. "Our Siren! She's *here*. He told us she would be here, and she is!"

"How do they know who you are?" Quinn asks, exactly what I wondered.

How could they know about things happening outside the Territory?

Motorcycle Man glances up at them, then fixes his stare on me once again. He seems to make the connection that I'm the one they're talking about—that I'm the Siren.

He drops onto the seat again as three men appear at his side, presumably from the pickup truck I saw with him before. He must be saying something to them from beneath his bandana because they nod and turn away, step off the highway and into the desert, and begin to walk toward us.

Motorcycle Man revs the engine.

"Fuck!" I step back, reaching out to my side without taking my eyes off the man. My fingers brush Quinn's shoulder, and I start to push her toward the passage. "Go. *Move.*"

Though my instincts warn me against the women in black, they also warn me against these men. I have to choose between two dangers, and the passage feels like the best option.

With Katie and Quinn, I make a run for it.

"Yes, come join us, Siren!" They continue to call for me from above. "We'll keep you safe."

"Be reborn with us, Siren!"

I slam to a stop.

Reborn?

There was a warning from Cruz...

> "Stay away from the Reborn. Don't let them convince you that they'll take care of you. They won't..."

Suddenly, I'm captured by indecision.

I'm stuck in place as Quinn and Katie continue running.

And then I hear the engine roar to life.

My head whips toward the highway. He's racing toward me, kicking up a cloud of dust in his wake. Adrenaline punches through my veins and instinct takes over. I turn and sprint away without direction.

I push so hard, it hurts.

I'm overcome with a rush of fear I haven't felt since... *Fuck.* Since the night Seb chased me to the lake. I blink, and I travel through time, back to that dark night, to the terror I felt. Air catches in my lungs, but I keep moving.

He's close...

He's too close.

The roar of his engine resembles the triumphant growl of a lion about to pounce on his prey.

Is he going to crash into me?

He could be some nasty sicko who gets off on mangling women with his machine. He could run me over. I nearly scream when I feel the heat from the engine at my back, closing in, skimming my side so close it nearly knocks me off my feet. He speeds ahead, turns just before he would slam into the edge of the plateau, and skids to a stop.

He's off the bike in a flash.

I'll collide with him if I don't stop. My shoes slip over sand, and I almost stumble as I twist to change direction, nearly turning all the way around to backtrack toward the passage, which I somehow blew right past in my hurry to get away.

I hear his boots plodding behind me as he chases me on foot, following me into the passage. Ignoring exhaustion, I dig deep, tap into my reserves, and run faster.

Sunlight dims as we chase deeper into the canyon. It's still bright, but less abrasive between the vertical walls of rock. There are pockets of shade found beneath ridges at various heights.

I touch darkness as I pass beneath a ridge, find a moment of relief within its shadow. But the relief is gone a second later when I feel him grab my backpack and pull. I shrug it off my shoulders in a rush, but he slowed me enough with the pull to catch up, and his large hand encircles my arm.

"No…" The word whispers out with a sigh of disbelief.

He grabs me with both hands.

My momentum is lost. I can't get away from him.

I've been caught.

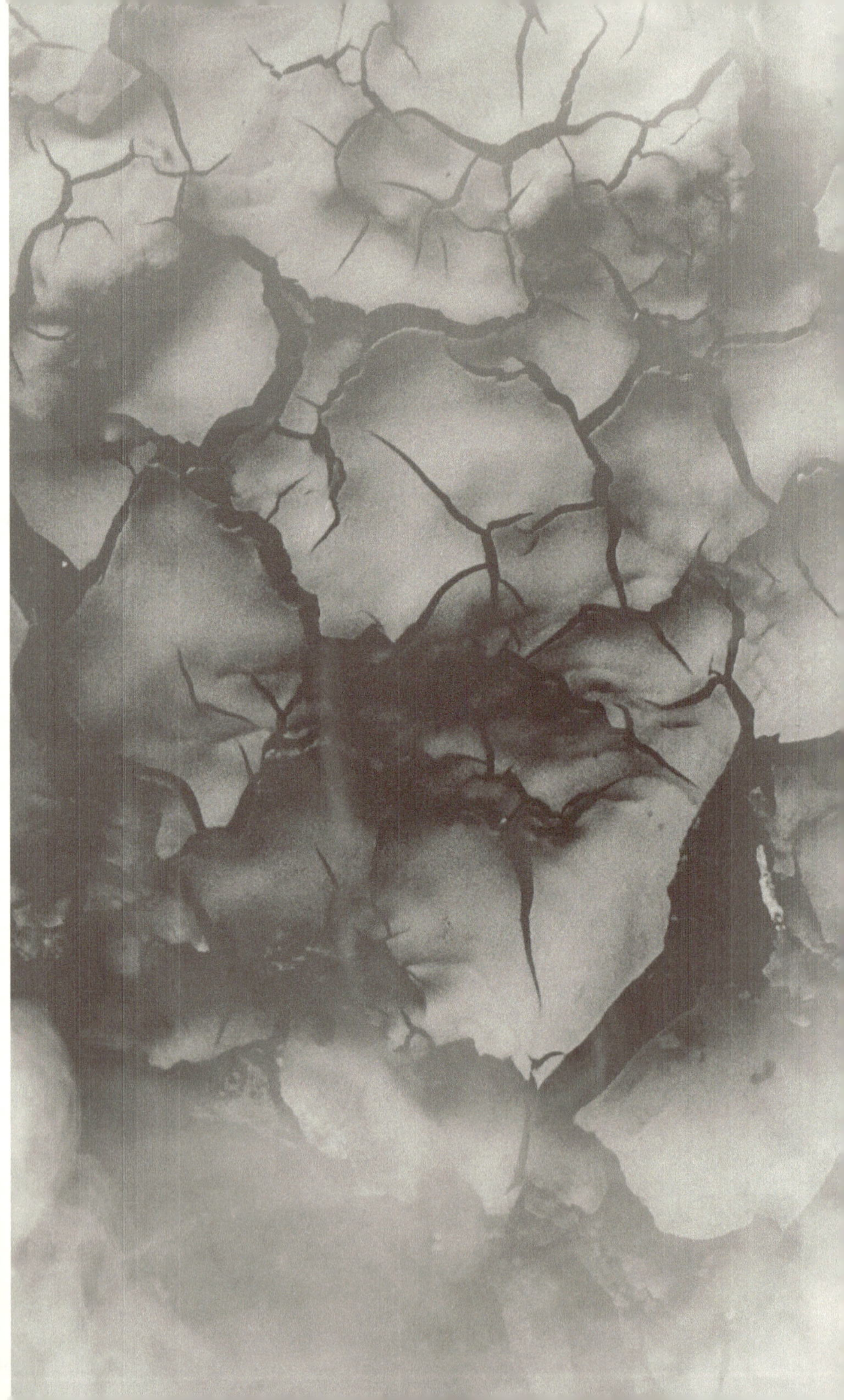

CHAPTER SEVEN
That Monster Right There

Gemma

I WOULD ABSOLUTELY fall on my ass if Motorcycle Man didn't have such a firm grip on me, but his hold is steadfast. He drags me back until I slam into his chest. His large hands wrap around my upper arms, fingertips digging into my flesh as he whirls me around to face him. He walks me backward and shoves me against the rock wall. The air is knocked from my lungs as my spine crashes into hard stone, as his hard, stone body crushes me against the mountain.

I tilt my chin to stare up at him.

Eyes concealed behind aviator sunglasses.

Mouth and nose hidden behind the black fabric.

I can make out the white design printed on the front of it now—the nose and mouth of a skeleton.

He hides his face behind an image of death.

I snarl, my lips curling with rage. "Show me your eyes, coward. Let me see your violence."

Something resembling a warning growl vibrates through his gut. I feel it rumble where his body presses to mine, and a strange heat washes over me—something internal, a feverish discomfort more consuming than the desert sun could produce.

He lifts one of his hands to clutch my throat and leans in close, his fabric-covered cheek touching mine. His other hand slips up my arm, over my shoulder, and he twirls his finger around a strand of my faded bubblegum-pink hair.

His lips brush my ear. "You've made yourself an easy target, little cherry blossom."

I make a fist and land a punch to his gut. There isn't enough momentum in my swing, and it lands with little impact. He groans at the strike, but hardly flinches. He releases my hair to grip my wrist between our bodies, widens his stance, and presses closer.

Literally stuck between a rock and a hard place...

He's so close that I can't move, can't fight. His grip on my wrist is painfully tight, knuckles digging into my stomach where he holds it still.

"The women in black aren't trying to help you." His voice rumbles, and I feel it vibrate through my skin, striking just beneath my ear and shuddering down the side of my neck. "If you go with them, you'll regret it."

"I'm not going anywhere with anyone," I hiss. "Get the fuck off me!"

"I like the way you fight me, bubblegum." I feel his face press into the crook of my neck, and it stuns me, freezes me like ice. "Keep trying."

His false familiarity shocks me.

I'm enraged but stunned by how confidently he speaks to me.

I'm petrified by the boldness of his touch.

It's rough, aggressive, possessive—everything I've ever known a man's touch to be. But somehow, it's also restrained. My mind can't make sense of the restraint in this dangerous moment. The contradiction of it is so heavy that the feeling sinks in my gut, flips and twists around, then sinks deeper. It's like an anchor that drags an unexpected thrill down with it to my very core.

My stomach contracts with the sensation, trying to fight it, wanting to *feel* it.

I hate the way my body responds to it.

I shouldn't feel... *that.*

It makes me feel weak and vulnerable. It reminds me of all the ways Seb fooled me before luring me away from the life I had planned. This man is the worst kind of dangerous for me, and I need to get away from him as fast as I can.

I use every muscle in my body to push, throw my weight against him, struggle and fight as hard as I can. Yet he remains an unyielding statue that pins me with ease—he's lean, but he's all fucking muscle.

"Siren!" a female voice calls out to me.

Not Katie or Quinn...

Where are they?

Are they safe?

Motorcycle Man turns his head to look toward the voice, and I do, too. Rushing in our direction from somewhere deeper within the passage are three women in black—I'm almost certain it's the same three women I saw atop the mesa, but they're on the ground with us now.

How did they get down so quickly?

It's the woman at the center who speaks, just like before. "Help her!" she shouts, turning her head back over her shoulder. "She's the Siren... We need her!"

What the fuck do they need me for?

My fear shifts, drawn toward the women in black, and then to the handful of men emerging from behind them.

Fuck.

Motorcycle Man's head swivels, bringing us nose to nose. "I guess they want you like I do. You'll have to choose between us, won't you?" His hand clutches my throat again, but his grip is light, just a touch. "You already know the right choice, pinky. *Make it.*"

He lets go and steps back. It feels like an invisible rope was attached to his hand, and when it lowers, he pulls all the danger and fear through my body, twisting and mixing them with the thrill in the pit of my stomach.

I always knew this day would come...

The day my trauma turns into kinks.

My mind is so fucked up that it confuses danger with desire.

I laugh out loud as the word "desire" crosses my mind, one hand reflexively going to my throat. I bend, placing the other on my knee as shallow breaths stutter through my laugh. My pink hair falls in front of my face as I laugh at the absurdity of this life. I fight unexpected tears from spilling down my cheeks.

I jerk my head, tossing my hair aside, and slowly lift my chin to look up at him. Just as my gaze lands on the black bandana, he raises his right hand to his face, revealing the nose and mouth of a partial skull tattooed on the hand that gripped my throat. My eyes narrow with curiosity as he quickly pulls down his bandana, then removes his sunglasses.

I draw in a sharp breath when I finally meet his eyes. They're lighter than I expected… light where I anticipated darkness. They seem blue, though the shade is faint and the light now spilling over him makes them look almost foggy gray. Like wispy clouds across a bright blue sky or a rare blue star beyond a nebula's haze… I get lost in them for a moment.

He glances right, then holds out his hand, as if he expects me to take it and…

Do what?

Ride off into the sunset together?

I blow the heady air from my lungs and straighten to my full height—all five feet six inches—and take a step toward him, looking directly into his breathtaking eyes. "I'm not going anywhere with anyone." I take another brave step closer, my chin rising to maintain eye contact, as he's at least six or seven inches taller than me. "I suggest you fuck off now before you really piss me off. You have no idea what I'm capable of."

His expression remains serious, though his cheek twitches just above a dimple—a dimple with a line that cuts as hard as the rest of him. "That's not what I wanted to hear, baby. Try again."

"*Baby?* Are you fucking—"

The song...

Before I snap, I hear the song.

The melody's strong and clear, and I'm not just hearing it in my mind. The whistled tune grows louder, bouncing off the two towering walls.

I turn and step toward the sound as the women in black stop. I stop, watching them warily as they stand side-by-side about twenty or thirty feet away. It's not any of the women whistling the song that I reclaimed for my vengeance; it's someone else approaching.

A man I've never seen before comes around from behind the women, dressed in black, lips still. It's not that man whose appearance strikes me in the chest, reaches inside me and rips the tainted melody from the place where it's imprinted on the shadow of my soul.

It's the man who follows behind him.

At the sight of him, I stumble backward.

Motorcycle Man's hand clamps around my elbow, keeping me upright and holding me steady. But I'm unconcerned with him at the moment. Because the man whistling the song that he played to torture me time and time again stands before me.

Logan fucking Sebastian is dressed in black, standing in front of the women who called to me. His eyes find mine, and he stops whistling mid-chorus to grin at me, showing his straight teeth and deceptively charming smile.

What kind of fucking monster stops a song before resolving the goddamn melody?

"That fucking monster…" The words grit from between my teeth. "*That* monster right there…"

"Professor Hadley…" The monster tilts his head and twists his expression toward condescension. "No, I'm sorry, that's not right, is it? I heard you never did go back to finish your PhD. It's a shame. Should I just call you Gemma, then?"

He takes a single step closer, and I feel as though I could spit fire. I'm leaning in, itching to wrap my hands around his throat, but some vice-like grip on my elbow keeps me from pouncing.

"Gemma Hadley. The fucking Siren herself. That's what they're calling you now, right?"

Seb takes another step, and I bend my knees, something primitive within me preparing to lunge.

"I have to admit, when the news reached me that you were convicted of killing my three best friends, I felt a little something…" He thumps his fist over his heart. "Pride. Just look how far you've fallen, Gem."

"Don't call me Gem—"

"I remember you were one of the most promising young academics at Yale," he says with an air of feigned nostalgia. "Top of your doctoral program, right? You were still years from finishing your degree, but already entertaining offers from Ivy Leagues. You were so fucking uptight, so focused and driven, so goddamn *boring*."

I'm fuming.

The grip on my arm is the only thing keeping me in place.

"You were so fucking fun to ruin. And you know what? I'm actually glad you survived what I did to you. Just look at us now." He waves his hand between us. "I made you what you are today—a violent, vicious villain. And now we can be family."

He spreads his arms wide, glancing over his shoulder at the women who stand behind him. "You can become a Daughter of Darkness." He grins sadistically. "I fucking love my daughters."

I jerk hard against the grip on my arm. Disgust and the need to claw out his goddamn eyeballs turn me into a feral creature.

 Seb lets his arms drop against his sides. "I'm afraid I'll have to insist that you find a new Siren song, though. I have to say, it hurt my heart to find out what you sang to my best friends when you killed them. Seemed a little unfair that you didn't give me credit for the choice of your signature song. It is *our* song, after all, isn't it?"

He just hammered the final nail in his coffin.

Pure carnal rage explodes within me.

I'm gonna kill him.

I'm gonna tear him to pieces with my bare fucking hands.

Violent fury grants me a moment of supreme strength, and I use it to rip my arm from Motorcycle Man's powerful grip.

I run after Seb, intent on clawing the grin off his face.

I dig my nails into his cheek as soon as I reach him, draw flesh beneath my fingernails, and triumph in the moment I hear him cry out in surprise.

But then I'm captured.

Strong arms close around my waist from behind, dragging me back. I scream at Motorcycle Man to let me go, my arms and legs wildly flailing in my desperation for violence against Seb. My movements knock him off-balance and we twist; he falls back on his ass with me writhing and clawing the air in his hold.

"Down girl," he mutters before he rolls, dropping me on my side.

Oh, he has a death wish.

Before I scratch him, too, he slams me onto my stomach. His weight shifts above me as I thrash, kick, and scream like the undead, possessed, and singularly focused on the attack.

Motorcycle Man fists a thick chunk of hair at the base of my skull. Rising to his feet, he hoists me straight up from the ground with a single, inhuman tug. My hands shoot back, grappling at his wrist, but his grip is firm. He walks backward and drags me with him.

"I'll fucking *kill* you, Seb!" My feral voice is demonic, and I barely recognize the sound of it. "I'll cut out your goddamn Devil's forked tongue and make you choke on it, motherfucker!"

Not as eloquent or sophisticated as I'd hoped to be, but it gets the point across.

Motorcycle Man chuckles. "That's it, strawberry shortcake, you let him have it." His voice is low and quiet as he flattens his palm over my belly, drawing my body back against him.

If I could twist against his hold, I would backhand him so damn hard… But then a cold, sharp line of metal touches my neck, and fear comes back to quell my fight.

Motorcycle Man holds a knife to my throat.

"I told you to make the right choice, *professor.*" The way he whispers *professor* is taunting.

I'm gonna kill him, too.

"I don't know your history with her," he bellows, speaking to them rather than whispering to me, "but she's mine now, and she's coming with me. Try to stop me, and I'll slit her throat. She'll be no good to you then."

I nearly laugh. Seb would *love* to watch me bleed out and die here in front of him. But his face doesn't show that he would… He touches his palm to his bloody cheek, looks at Motorcycle Man with a tense jaw and slightly widened eyes.

Oh, I get it…

Seb wants to kill me himself.

He'd be pissed if he were denied the opportunity to do it himself.

But then the woman at the center of the three who stand behind him steps forward, worry etched in her expression. She lightly places her palm on Seb's arm.

"You can't let him take her. We need her. She's perfect. You promised she would be ours."

What?

Seb doesn't look at her—his eyes are fixed on the knife at my throat. "I know. I'll take care of it." He shoos her away with a flick of his hand, and she steps back in line far too easily. "We're willing to make a trade for her." Seb motions behind him at the women in black. "Take one of ours."

The women exchange confused looks.

"Any of them will go willingly at my command. Take your pick."

"I don't make deals with the Devil." Motorcycle Man steps back, and I move with him.

"What do you want, then?" Seb steps forward.

We take another step back.

"Name it," Seb offers. "Tell me what you want, and it will be yours. All we want is the Siren."

Motorcycle Man moves backward so slowly, one creeping step at a time, almost like he's stalling.

What is he waiting for?

Why doesn't he just fucking kill me?

He must be a monster like Seb. They both threaten my life, but it's only to control me. They want to control me so they can use me, abuse me, get off on my suffering. I'd rather be dead than suffer either of these men.

I could just turn my head... Slash my own throat against his knife.

The intrusive thought consumes me.

Do it.

Take back control of your life.

End it now.

Look Seb in the eyes while you bleed out.

Enjoy the look of disappointment on his face while you die.

I tempt fate. I lift my chin before slowly turning my face, and the razor thin edge of the blade lightly slices across my skin. I feel the dragging sting of it, the hot burning pain and wet, sticky heat as blood trickles down my throat.

The people in black jump in response, calling out, "No!" and "Stop!" as they lunge, fighting the urge to run after me or reach out a hand as though they could stop this from a distance.

What did I just do?

I draw in a sharp breath of panic.

I pull back, press the back of my skull against Motorcycle Man's shoulder, retreating from the blade. I know I didn't cut myself deep—no more than the depth of a hair's width—but throats are tender, and I *will* die here today if I'm cut any deeper than the short line I just drew beneath my own chin.

The people in black are anxious over my spilled blood, but Seb remains calm, wearing an arrogant smirk that reminds me of how fooled he had me in the beginning with his lies and manipulations. He probably has all these people fooled, too.

He creeps forward slowly, both palms raised. "Take it easy with her. Her blood is precious… it needs to be preserved. Spill another drop, and you'll give us cause for retaliation."

Motorcycle Man turns his head, cranes his neck to look at my profile. I lift my eyes to meet his—those nebulous blue star eyes—and watch them skate down my cheek until they land at the knife he still holds beneath my chin.

"Look at that…" The corners of his lips twist into an oddly pleasant grin, and his eyes lift, connecting with mine. "So eager to bleed for me, aren't you?"

My mouth drops open in shock, but I'm at a loss for words.

It's the way his celestial eyes light up the shadows of my soul.

But then he blinks away, fixating on my throat. His hand rises from my stomach, my entire body flinching against his touch as the side of his hand grazes my breast on the way up.

"Don't worry," he tells them as his index and middle fingers trace a delicate line up my throat. He turns them just beneath the blade to trace the cut, gathering blood on his fingertips. He lifts them away and holds his two blood-soaked fingers out to show them. "I can put it back."

His fingers press hard to my lips without warning. He rubs them forcefully along the seam until I'm forced to let them part. He shoves both fingers inside my mouth, slips them across my tongue, feeding me the metallic taste of my own blood. He pushes deep and doesn't stop until I gag. I finally recover from the initial shock just as he draws them back.

I bite—not nearly as hard as I intended, but hard enough to leave marks on his fingers before he yanks them out. I know it had to hurt, but he barely reacts other than shaking out his hand. He stretches his arm across my chest, curves his palm around my arm to hold me tightly against him.

His lips brush the shell of my ear as he whispers, "I wouldn't dare waste a drop of you."

He drags me back three quick steps, and now I see that he and I are no longer on our own. Three men step up from behind Motorcycle Man. One holds a metal baseball bat across the back of his shoulders, another flexes a heavy chain, and the third spins a tire iron. I think they must be the men from the pickup truck I saw speaking to Motorcycle Man on the highway. They move together, forming a human wall between us and the people in black.

That's what he was waiting for... backup.

Motorcycle Man spins me around to face him.

The world turns beneath my feet.

He shoves me backward until my spine hits the vertical wall of the plateau, taking us back into the shadow where he caught me the first time. He pulls the blade from my neck and replaces it with his palm, fastening his hand around my throat with a firm grip. He gives a quick flick of his wrist with the other hand, the blade neatly folding into the handle, and he slips it into his back pocket.

My backpack—which I'd thrown off during our chase—skids across the ground after he kicks it backward with his black combat boot.

"Hayes," he calls out.

 The man with the chain glances back, spots the backpack, and gives Motorcycle Man a quick nod.

He dips in front of me and wraps both arms around my waist. I yelp as he lifts me from the ground, easily tossing me over his shoulder. He walks back toward the opening of the passage, carries me, kicking and screaming, to the sounds of protests and fighting behind him. Moving quickly, we're back through the passage in no time.

Fighting him every step, I don't even realize we've reached his motorcycle until he lifts me off his shoulder and plops me backward on the seat. He grabs my right leg and forces it over to the other side, making me straddle the machine. I try to lift it over again to join the left, but he has me beat in size and strength. He wrestles my thighs apart with both tattooed hands, pressing down so hard it hurts.

He leans in close, touching the tip of his nose to mine. "I promise, you're safer with me, pink."

I snap my teeth at him, threatening without words to bite him again—any part of him that he dares to put in my face.

But then he smiles, and it knocks me back.

His provocative grin shows me his own straight white teeth that could chomp me right back. His thumbs dig deep into my thighs.

"You're cute, like a nipping puppy. But if you're gonna nip at a pit bull," he climbs onto the motorcycle, tightens his grip on my thighs, and pulls me close, "don't be surprised if he bites back."

He holds me to his chest, my legs draped over his thick, muscled thighs. I can feel his cock right there between my legs, and I fully expect blind rage to strike as my hands shoot up to his chest.

But it doesn't strike... and I don't push him away.

His sculpted arms reach around me to grip the handlebars, caging me in. The engine revs, and the machine eases into motion. He turns the rumbling beast between my legs— between *our* legs—circling back to face the highway.

At least the man and the machine face the highway, while I only face the man who now holds my life in his hands.

Fuck, I hope he knows how to ride this thing.

My fingers bunch the fabric of his black shirt as he straightens out. He rolls the throttle. I drop my face, pressing it into his chest to shield my eyes from the sand. He gears up, punches the invisible wall of heat with a burst of speed, and the forces of nature thrust my body into his.

I throw my arms around his waist and hold on for dear life.

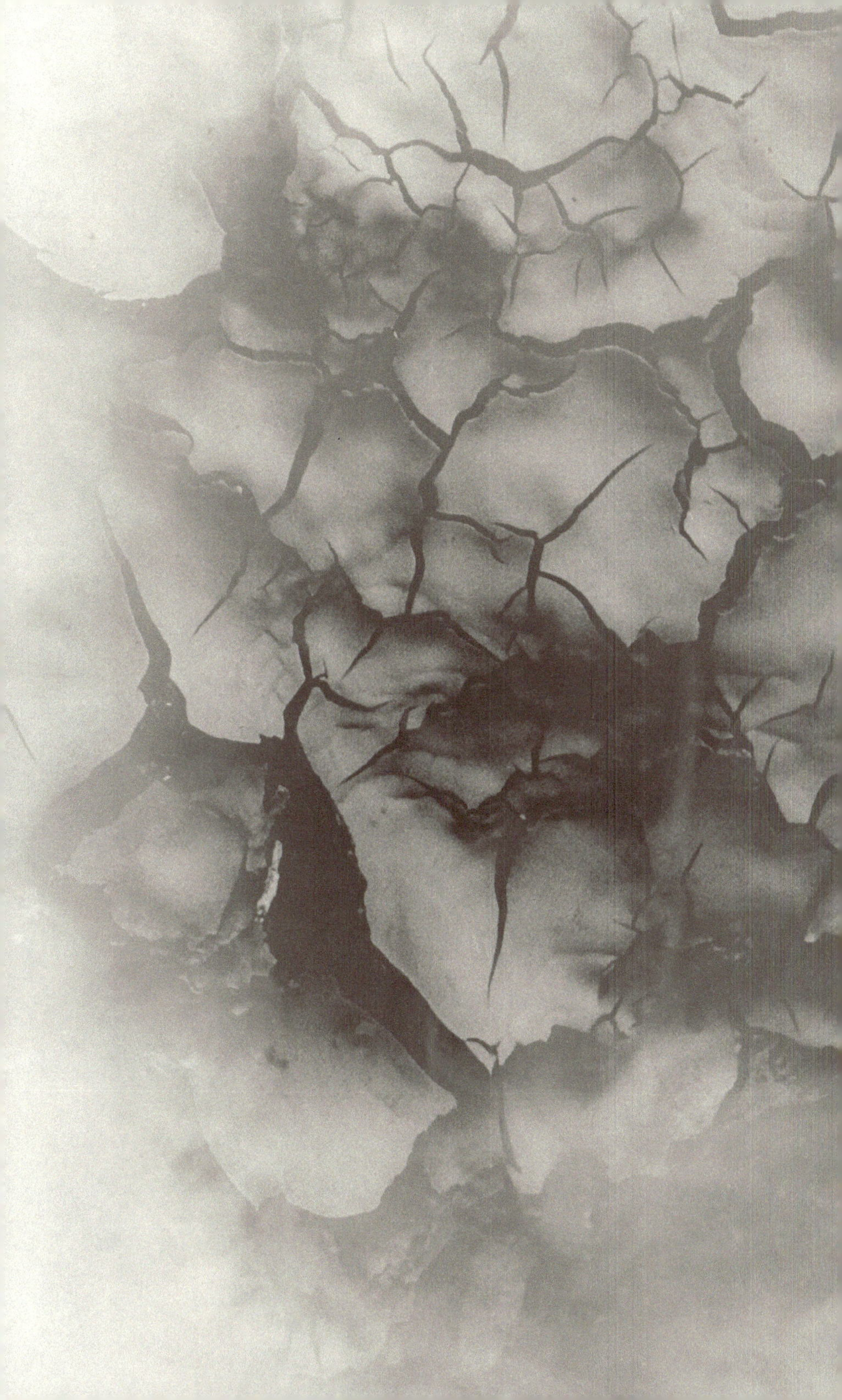

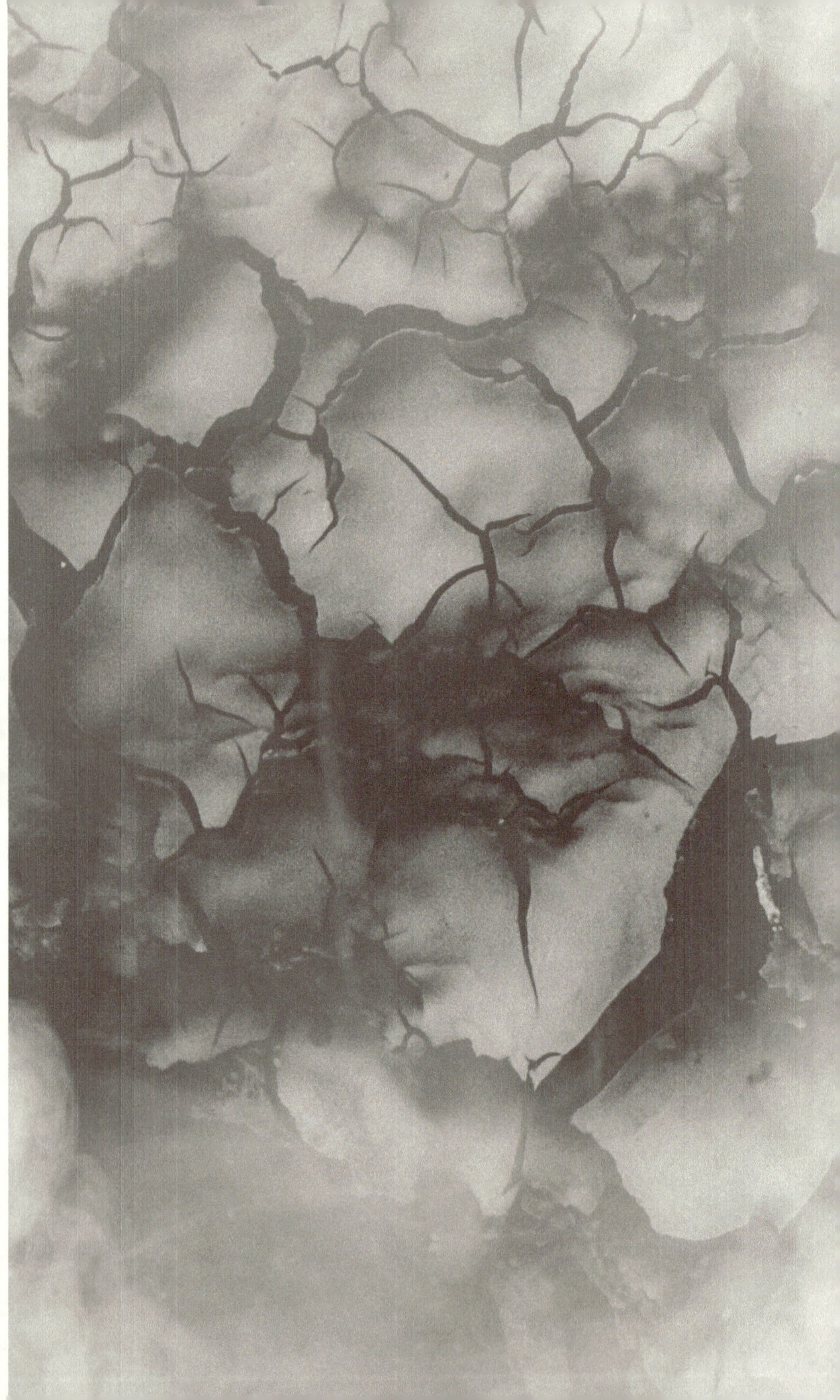

CHAPTER EIGHT
Break Her

Oz

SHE WAS A bright pink bloom in the beige desert. Amidst a sea of women all dressed in the same orange jumpsuit, she stood out like the fuchsia flowers that grow atop beavertail cacti in the most barren parts of Lawless Land.

They all saw us coming down the highway, but this one—this adorable little pink-haired praline—was the only one who stopped to watch me.

She saw me.

I saw her.

And she easily became my target.

She clings to me as I turn onto the freeway and hit the throttle. It's too damn hot for bodies to be this close, but I can't say that I mind the feel of her wrapped around me. There's a natural vibration to her chaotic energy, an electric buzz I felt the moment I laid eyes on her.

I want to claim her for myself, the darkness within already throbbing with the pulse of a quickly forming obsession. This adorable creature could become a dangerous compulsion that, perhaps, I should've left behind.

But I couldn't leave her behind.

I couldn't let the Reborn have her.

I wouldn't let that man break her.

If any man is gonna break her, it'll be me.

Though the pleasure of her company will be shared among the Vultures.

Salem made space for four more in Eden, and requested we provide the women to fill those spaces. So, as part of our agreement, that's what we'll provide. It's what we promised, and I'm nothing if not a man of my word.

They get what they need.

We get what we need.

That's how it all works.

And as long as I keep my word and hand this one over, along with the other three with my boys in the truck, it doesn't matter that I cherry-picked the *professor* to suit my own interest.

She stood out like a sore thumb with her delicious cotton candy hair. At first, I thought that's why the Reborn singled her out, simply because there was something visibly unique to call her out on. The Reborn prey on lawless women in that way all the time, but it seemed they knew exactly who she was the moment they spotted her.

They'd called her *Siren*, and that has me fucking curious.

I'm just as curious to know *how* they knew her. I occasionally receive updates about the world beyond the walls, but that's a privilege I've earned from the connections I made while building my community. It's beyond me how the Reborn would know her, though clearly it had something to do with that man she hated so viciously.

Brutality is their favorite trait.

They only want the most vicious and violent criminals as intensely as they wanted her. And she displayed it so boldly. She was absolutely feral trying to get to that man in black.

Vicious, violent, soft, and pretty.

Feral little princess.

Sweet, bleeding baby girl.

Goddamn...

I felt something for her. I felt the way she fights, the way she takes what she wants and refuses to answer to anyone but herself. But if she wants to survive in this barren wasteland, she'll learn to answer to me. I'm the only man with the resources to keep her safe.

Though I may not be able to keep her safe from *me*.

CHAPTER NINE
Hazy Blue

Gemma

THE AIR IS on fire, but racing down the highway keeps it moving, providing some relief as it breezes across my face. Motorcycle Man's body is a furnace, but the steady thumping of his heart is strangely calming.

It's infuriating.

This is the first time I've felt anything resembling a moment's peace in weeks, months... maybe years.

Has it been years since I felt peace?

It's a false sense of peace, though. In reality, it's a moment of deception. It's my own desperation for a second of relief from the rage and fear that always threaten to consume me.

Peace is a good feeling... And good feelings are dangerous when they come from someone else because they always demand something in return. I can only imagine what this man will demand from me.

I won't let this moment fool me.

He's just like all the rest—a dangerous man who thinks I owe him something.

I owe him *nothing.*

If anything, he owes me a free ride back to that rock formation and the courtesy of a weapon I can use to carve out Seb's heart while it's still beating. For good measure, I might just carve out Motorcycle Man's heart and shove it up his ass because the way it calms me is so damn irritating.

I have to stop listening to the way it *thump, thump, thumps* inside his ribcage. Once we've reached a steady speed on a straight lane of highway, I ease my grip on him, and slowly, carefully pull away. Then we hit a small bump, and my fingers curl, clinging to the sides of his shirt as I stifle a yelp.

"Hold on tight, little flamingo."

I lift my eyes to meet his with annoyance, but the stunning blue in his hazy-gray gaze stops me.

Goddammit.

He's staring out at the highway, and I can't help but stare at *him.* I thought he looked less like my teenage wet dream before.

Cue the old Katy Perry song...

I'm pissed off that he was blessed with handsome features, but that's how nature works. My scientific area of expertise is astrophysics, but I'm not ignorant of the biological principles that make the strongest and most virile of the species the most attractive. But the most powerful, most handsome men aren't always the best men. Some of the worst of mankind are the most beautiful creatures.

Looking up at my kidnapper, I try to make his features ugly. I try to hate how plump and soft his lips look; I try to find disgust in the hard, chiseled lines of his jaw. I try to convince myself that the snide smirk reminds me of Seb and his haughty grin, though it doesn't.

I should be screaming at him to stop, trying to hit him, trying to *hurt* him, trying to do anything that would make him slow down so I can jump off and get away.

I have to get away.

I have to go back.

Seb was right there... It was as though all the stars in the universe had aligned in some strange cosmic intervention so I could commit my final act of violent revenge.

And then this asshole showed up and ruined everything.

He's a violent criminal.

He's going to hurt you, Gem.

My inner voice speaks with reason, though it's treasonously faint. The swirling blue nebulas in his eyes are so bewitching, they could hypnotize me against good sense.

He glances down at me, just long enough for his eyes to meet mine through a maddening beat of false alliance. I quickly blink away to sever the connection. But then I feel his open palm curve around the back of my head to pull me in, to press my face toward his chest again, but I immediately resist his demanding hand. We struggle back and forth, fighting each other until the bike swerves, making a quick jog to my right.

His hand finally falls away—I assume to grab the long handlebar as he quickly gains control of the motorcycle. Then he decelerates, slowing the bike to a steady crawl. The engine rumbles with a pulsing rhythm, like it has its own heartbeat.

He raises his voice so I can hear him over the roar. "Are you trying to get us both killed?"

"Are *you*? Don't touch me like that again."

"Kinda hard not to."

He's not exactly wrong, given the way my arms and legs are wrapped around him, but it's not as though I'm sitting here by choice. It'd be easier for both of us if I were sitting behind him, facing forward, but that's not what I want. What I want is to get the fuck off this bike and get away from him.

"Stop for a minute, let me move behind you." I have no intention of moving behind him if he stops.

He's rolling along at a slow but steady speed, steady enough to give me a look with the tilt of his head. "Do you think I'm stupid?"

"As far as I can tell, you're a man. Same thing, right?"

I deliver the insult and reflexively draw back. My mind is hypervigilant, preparing my body for a violent retaliation in this powerless moment.

Powerless?

He doesn't retaliate.

Instead, he grins.

His smile is wide and handsome, showing genuine amusement. His smile could have me fooled into thinking there's no malice lurking behind it. My four killers would grin at me just as wide, but I think I could always see the violence hiding behind the false charm—even in the beginning. And if I can't even see it in this man, then he must be more dangerous than they ever were.

He's dangerous...

But I'm not powerless.

The bike is moving slow enough that I could jump, and if I land just right, I'd be able to run away with nothing more than a few scrapes and bruises. I decide to test my balance. Slowly, I pull back, unwrapping my arms from his waist. I watch his face as I unwrap, see his eyes flicker back and forth between me and the highway as his smile fades.

"I know what you're doing." He rolls the throttle to increase our speed, and the lurch of acceleration throws me against his chest again. I can't jump at this speed, but with me between him and the handlebars, he can't easily control the machine at this speed, either.

I'm not powerless...

I know how to take back control.

Instead of wrapping my arms around his waist to hold on, I bring them between us, sliding my palms up his chest. I bunch the fabric of his black shirt, gripping it over his pecs, and hold myself against him. I gaze up at him, lock my stare on his ridiculously beautiful eyes, and set my intention on distraction.

If he's distracted enough, he'll naturally slow his speed.

I stare until he glances away from the road and meets my eyes. I keep staring while they dance back and forth between me and the highway, as he holds each look longer and longer. I pull down on his shirt as I lift my face closer to his, lengthening my spine. And when his eyes hold mine as long as two heartbeats, I plant the ultimate distraction on his lips with mine.

A soft, deceitful kiss for a lonely, dangerous outlaw.

A means of distraction and nothing more.

It's "nothing more" that buzzes electric in the pit of my stomach.

His guttural groan vibrates through my lips, and that's… good. It's good because it tells me the distraction is working. That, and the fact that his speed reduces drastically for the few seconds I hold my lips to his.

He slows nearly enough for me to jump, but I need a gut-punch moment first—something that will distract him long enough for me to unwrap my legs. I drag my lips from his and lean back, noticing the way he naturally leans with me.

Stuck his whole damn face in that sticky honey trap, didn't he?

I lay it on thick, smother him with it, give him bedroom eyes, parted lips, and a breathy whisper that has him slowing to a crawl. "I wanted to do this from the moment I saw you…" I slowly draw back my right knee.

He lowers over me as I lean away. "Don't tell me lies, baby."

Baby…

The way he says it grinds my teeth.

I tighten my grip on his shirt as I inch my right leg back a little more. I'm nearly lying back on the fuel tank, and he's right there with me, practically on top of me. "I'm not lying, blue eyes."

He comes to a sudden stop, dropping his black boots to the concrete to balance the machine. I can't tell if calling him *blue eyes* made him horny or angry… but neither really swings in my favor. Regardless, my leg is where I need it now, so this is my moment.

"Honestly," I whisper, tugging at his shirt to pull him closer, to tilt him off-balanced from his center of mass. "From the second I saw you watching me, I wanted to do this more than anything."

With a single, forceful motion, I push, throwing him backward as I pull my right knee to my chest. Then, I thrust my leg out in front of me, slam my foot into the center of his chest, striking him hard in the sternum. I hear the air rush out of him on impact.

He falls backward, and I twist, rolling toward my left leg and off the bike. I try to catch myself on my feet, but the bike falls in the opposite direction, the unexpected motion knocking me off balance. I land on my hip, but I'm ready for the impact, letting my body roll through it. Then I scramble to my feet and whip around, expecting to see him lunge for me. Instead, I see him flat on his back with one leg sandwiched between the fallen motorcycle and the pavement.

But he's not completely pinned.

He's already fighting to free his leg.

And his face is twisted in rage.

Fuck.

I turn away from him and run, ditching the highway to sprint into the open desert… The vast, open, barren terrain.

There's nothing to run to.

There's no place to hide.

What do I do? Where do I go?

Just run, Gem.

I keep running, even when I hear his footfalls in the dirt behind me, the sound of his boots plodding after me. I'm panting, fighting for a replenishing breath against the consuming heat.

The heat, the hunger, the adrenaline fatigue of this fucking exhausting day—it all weighs me down and eases me back.

I feel like he has a lasso around my waist, and he holds it taut; he doesn't pull me to a stop, but he doesn't allow me to move, either. It feels like running in place as his steps grow louder and he closes the distance between us.

It's not long before I feel his hands graze my arms.

He throws his arms around me from behind and tugs me to a stop. The abrupt movement unbalances us both, and though he tries to keep us upright, the way I struggle against his hold knocks us sideways. We land together on our hips, both of us groaning at the painful impact.

Then, he's on top of me in a flash, twisting me onto my belly, straddling my hips to pin me down against the dry, cracked earth. I can't move, can't crawl out from beneath him. Being trapped under his weight unsettles me, but it's the way he slaps his palm to my cheek and presses my face into the dirt that disturbs me.

There's a growling vibration in his tone that intimidates me. "Feisty little scrapper, aren't you?"

Panting, he removes his hand from my cheek to grip my wrists. I struggle beneath him, but he easily wrestles my arms behind me as he sits on my ass, holding them together at the small of my back.

"No…" I grind the word between my teeth.

I fought.

I ran.

I tried.

I lost.

I'm not powerless…

I am powerless.

Every time I think I have it, a man takes it from me.

I liberate the primal roar that's been building in my gut, scream it out with a blast of heat from my lungs.

I hate this world.

I hate this place as much as I hated my life before.

I hate men and the way they hurt me.

I hate the way they steal from me, break me, make me bleed.

This hatred doesn't fuel me the way it used to. Instead, it fills me with shame, exhausts me with guilt for the fact that I've once again found myself powerless to a man.

I'm here because I chose to be. I'm here because I was so desperate for revenge that I lost myself in violence. It's my fault. I chose to kill them—

No.

It's their fault, not mine.

It's what they did to me that brought me here.

Their fault or mine, I've failed all the same.

Unexpected tears fill my eyes. "Take me back..." My voice cracks. "Take me back and let me kill him."

"I'm not taking you back." He doesn't move; he just sits there, straddling my hips, holding me down.

I stifle the sobs, but I can't hold back the tears as they flow from my eyes, dripping from my cheek, falling to the ground, and are drunk by the thirsty earth.

He shifts my wrists, holds them both in one large hand, and I flinch as the other touches my forehead. A fingertip drags my hair back from my sweat-soaked skin, and then he strokes my hair... With a gentle hand, he fucking *strokes my hair.*

"That's good, baby. Just be still. Everything will be okay."

It's silent beyond his voice until the faint rumble of an engine fades in from a distance, the volume gradually increasing.

"You hear that? Vultures are on the way. We'll get back on the road soon."

"Take me back." My voice is quiet, and it shakes. "Take me back or—"

"Or what?"

"Or kill me." I spit the words with forced fury that tries to mask my pain.

"I already told you I'm not taking you back." His knuckles stroke down the side of my cheek. "And you're no good to me dead."

I'm no good to him dead?

I don't know if it's the words or the hopelessness of my situation that completely undoes me, but I can no longer hold back the pathetic sobs that ache for me to unleash them—so I let them out. I let myself cry, embarrassingly loud and long. I let despair have me.

"That's it," he soothes. "Let it all out, *professor.*"

With the speed of a lightning strike, despair retreats.

Professor.

That's the word that brings me back, that snaps me out of sorrow and drenches me in rage.

I'm not a *professor.*

I never got to *be* a professor because of *them.*

They broke me so tragically, so effectively, that no amount of therapy or rehabilitation could ever fix me. Seb said it to hurt me, and this no-name Motorcycle Man is doing the same.

My jaw tenses as I force a warning out from between my grinding teeth. "Don't call me that again."

He bends over me and his lips graze my cheek as he whispers, "I'll call you whatever I want, *professor.*"

My head jerks up from the ground as I try to bash his fucking nose with the side of my face. He rises quickly, and I miss him by a mile. With my eyes turned, I can see him smiling down at me from where he sits, perched on my ass.

Before long, three dark shadows block the sun, slowly moving over me. It's the men from the truck—the three who stood between me and Seb, holding their weapons as Motorcycle Man dragged me away.

I quickly take stock of my situation.

One man is holding me down.

Three men are watching me.

Four men are about to take everything from me all over again.

A flood of traumatic memories wash over me, forcing fear to take hold of me. In a sudden panic, I use every muscle to thrash beneath him, fighting like hell to get out from under him as I scream, "No!"

He flips me over beneath his spread legs and brings my hands in front of me. I swing my arms, try to punch him, hit him, slap him, scratch him, but he's so much stronger than me. He brings my hands between his legs, presses down on my wrists to hold them steady against my waist. Then a new deluge of fearful tears fill my eyes, and everything becomes blurry. The four men become faceless, nameless… Dark shadows of the men from my past who still haunt me.

Is it all happening again?

Am I dead? Is this hell?

Am I doomed to suffer this nightmare forever?

Motorcycle Man lifts his head to look at one of the men. "Did you find two more girls at the Crevice?"

That same man—whose face is blurred behind a sheen of tears—moves in close and takes a knee beside me. He touches one of my wrists and I flinch, jerking away. But then another man on the opposite side of me bends, too, helping them hold my hands together. They wrap something plastic around my wrists—a cable tie—and pull it tight.

"No, no, no..." My head shakes slowly from side to side.

It's all happening again...

"Yep," one of them says as he rises to his feet. "Got two girls at the Crevice, plus the one we took from the lawless men on the highway before... And your runner here makes four."

I know they mean me. I'm the runner.

Four hands grip my wrists, my arms, and hoist me to my feet. I blink my eyes as much as I can, trying to clear away the tears, but no matter how much I dry them, reality remains a hellish blur.

A waking nightmare.

These men may as well be my killers—my delirious mind can't seem to tell the difference.

It's Seb standing in front of me.

No... That's not right.

It's Motorcycle Man.

"Did you get her bag?" He tucks my hair behind my ears, runs his hands down my shoulders.

"It's in the cab," someone says.

"Did any of the Reborn follow you?"

"Nah. Santi slammed the back of that blond dickwad's knee pretty good, and they were more concerned about him than us."

Blond dickwad...

Seb?

"Did you break his leg?" Motorcycle Man asks.

"I don't think so."

"Swing harder next time." He grabs my bound hands and lifts them up high, setting my wrists on his shoulders as he steps into me. Then he dips, lifts, and hoists me up over his shoulder. "Let's get back on the road. Pick up my bike and help me put her on behind me."

"She can go in the cab. Tucker can ride in the truck bed with the dead guys."

"Why do I always have to ride with the dead guys?"

"No," Motorcycle Man snaps. His hand lands on my ass, and he squeezes. "She rides with me."

I'm so out of it, so lost in this frightening daydream, that I can't even muster a reaction—no anger, no great expression of sorrow, not even a smart-ass, sarcastic quip in response.

I fucking hate it.

I feel like a ghost reliving my haunted past.

Maybe this fate is inevitable.

Maybe I cheated death when I survived my killers.

Maybe I'm doomed to relive the hell they made until they finally succeed in ending my life.

What's the point of fighting destiny?

I retreat into my mind, find a dark corner to hide in, and focus on the shifting shadows. It's always black here in the darkness where I hide, but now the purity of darkness is tainted with swirls of hazy blue, dancing to an old song by Katy Perry about a *Teenage Dream* that speaks of a life I never got to live.

It speaks of an intense passion I could never hope to feel, and a love that could never endure in a world ruled by men.

I start to cry again, pathetic as I've ever been.

I'm breaking my own heart. That voice inside my head is destroying whatever's left of my soul. It tells me to give up, to give in, to accept my weakness and the inevitability of my death. It tells me to let them inflict their irreversible damage because fighting back didn't save me the first time—not really.

It didn't matter that I killed the men who hurt me.

It didn't make me stronger.

It didn't give me back my power.

It only brought me to this world, where all the worst men are gathered and needy, aching and desperate to defile me without consequence.

And that's exactly what these men will do.

CHAPTER TEN
What All Men Want

Oz

THE REMAINDER OF the journey is uneventful. She's been still and quiet since we got back on the road.

Her arms are wrapped all the way around my waist, wrists bound with the zip tie, and held at my navel. My Vultures helped to get us situated on the bike so she's sitting behind me, and I feel every inch of her along my spine.

I'm not one who cares much for gentle touch, but I'll admit that I feel something about the way she holds me. She's forced to embrace me, but she's accepted it, and her body is soft against mine, her cheek resting between my shoulder blades.

She surrenders to the inevitable.

I might've mistaken that for a weakness if I hadn't already witnessed her violent, fighting spirit firsthand.

She's fucking fascinating.

I haven't been this intrigued by a woman since Emaline—

She's gone.

Don't think about her.

I force haunted memories to the back of my mind and focus on the visceral, the feel of a wild woman against my back. She's tumultuous, unpredictable, overflowing with raw, unfiltered emotions. There's no guessing what she's feeling when she's feeling it—she presents emotion without reservation, and I like it.

I like it a little too much.

It might be the reason I fixated on her so quickly. Obsessive thoughts itch for the next opportunity to poke and prod her until I've discovered every point of passion, toed every delicate boundary line, and witnessed every private feeling etch itself across her adorable fucking face.

And then I wanna do it all again.

We approach the suburbs of the city from the south, gradually creeping out of the open desert landscape, crawling toward the ruins of civilization. A concrete barrier separates one side of the freeway from the other, though it's cracked and broken in spots along the way.

Old billboards still stand, proudly advertising businesses and attractions that once made the city one of the most popular tourist destinations in the world. We pass one for a limousine rental service, another advertising real estate—new construction homes that never got the chance to be sold. Then, a promotion of a topless revue on the old Las Vegas Strip.

That's the city—we call it Prosperity.

It exists within the border walls that separate Lawless Land from society, but it's inaccessible to most lawless. It has walls of its own, and a certain birthright is required to live there. Most lawless reap no benefits from their existence, but I do. I may not have their birthright, but I have connections with the right people.

Rows of cookie-cutter homes begin to appear as we approach the outlying suburbs. From far away, they look normal, like any other house on any other street. It's not until you get closer that you see the chipped and fading paint, the broken windows, and the disappearing roof tiles. You could almost fool yourself into believing this place exists beyond the border walls, but it doesn't.

Life beyond the walls is over for us.

It took me three years to accept that as the absolute truth, another three years of devolution and deconstruction to learn this new way of life, and three more to build what I have now. Nine years in Lawless Land is a lifetime beyond the walls—our reality is brutal and unforgiving.

Pinky here ought to be grateful she's coming home with me.

I exit the highway and dash beneath the overpass. I blow past the dangling, long-dead traffic light, and speed past meaningless stop signs. My turns are sharper, and my speed is faster than it would normally be on these streets, but that's only because of the girl straddling my bike.

She's the literal target on my back.

I need to get her to the Gates before we're attacked by a starving criminal intent on consuming her—the delicious little strawberry shortcake she's bound to be.

We occupy the largest community in the suburbs—a cluster of several gated neighborhoods surrounding a central structure—that sits about twelve or thirteen miles south of the city's center. Our community, and the other neighborhoods surrounding our gates, would have been limited to occupancy by only the most affluent of society in the time before the Territory existed.

Our community is as safe as it could possibly be in Lawless Land. I've vetted my men carefully, recruited purposefully, and with their help, secured and fortified our gated borders, leaving only a single point of entry. As I turn onto our road, I ease off the throttle, slowing to a crawl as I approach the gated entry.

The guardhouse-style structure spans the entire width of the two-lane road. Concrete pillars, positioned in the center and on both sides, support an angular roof that juts from the top, providing some shade for the Vultures assigned to guard duty for their shift. The gate's dark metal bars stretch from pillar to pillar, blocking entry and exit. It's a fortress-like access point, both beautifully architected and severe, a silent warning to anyone approaching.

Malik steps out from the shadows beneath the gatehouse roof, holding a large, scoped sniper rifle—mostly for show, as we hardly have any ammunition for it.

I come to a stop as he steps down from the curb, greeting me with a quick lift of his chin. Malik raises his voice to be heard over the idle rumble of the engine. "How'd it go?"

I glance over my shoulder to see our truck turning into the drive behind me, gradually approaching. "Can't complain. We all made it back."

Callahan appears from the gatehouse and begins the process of unlocking the chains that hold the black metal gates closed.

"How many new girls are we tracking?" Malik asks.

"Four. One needs medical right away. A couple of lawless had her, and she was unconscious when we took her."

Malik gives me a nod. "I'll send Zuri over to the holding house for her. And the men you took her from?"

"Dead. In the truck bed."

"Callahan's shift ends soon. I'll send him over to pick up the truck and put 'em in the freezer." I track his eyes as they move to the beautiful woman at my back, and I feel a sudden tension in my neck. "What's her deal?"

He's wondering why she's strapped to me on the back of my bike instead of sitting in the truck where he'd expect her to be.

"Attitude problem."

"Fuck off," she mutters, though she doesn't move an inch.

One corner of Malik's lips curls in amusement as he nods. "I see."

As Callahan unloops the chains and begins to pull open the wide, black gate manually, a bad idea comes to mind… A thought that sinks its claws into my better judgment and rips it to shreds.

"This one won't be at the holding house; she'll be with me."

Malik's eyebrows knit together. "At *your* house?"

I nod. "She'll need medical, too. Send them to my place when they're done with the other girl."

"Okay, you've got it." He still has that look of apprehension, but he knows better than to question me further.

My word is law here.

I give Malik and Callahan a nod as I pull through, and the truck follows. Slowly, I navigate the twists and turns of our suburban community roads, crawling along past what used to be the homes of the wealthy.

The homes selected by each vulture are well kept, a stark contrast to the rows of vacant houses which melt into ruin. Some are uninhabitable, neglected for decades and unoccupied since Lawless Land came into existence. Others could be livable with a little work, but mostly, those homes will remain vacant. We don't welcome just anyone into our piece of this world.

These girls have no idea how lucky they are to be here.

We roll past rows of houses, making several turns before heading toward the road that leads to the cul-de-sac. The holding house is the first on the left, and that's where I should stop. I should follow protocol and leave Gemma there with the others.

That would be best for everyone.

That would certainly be best for *me.*

Yet I wind up at the far end of the cul-de-sac, pulling into my own goddamn driveway.

I place my feet on the cobblestone—half of which I replaced myself—and hesitate, thinking about turning back and returning her to the holding house where she belongs. The hesitation becomes a pause, and the pause stretches into a full stop. I convince myself that this is fine, that I won't have any issues holding her in my home until it's time to send her to Eden.

I'm equipped to manage this.

It'll be fine.

I cut the engine and let out a heavy sigh, resigning myself to this potentially dangerous decision.

Then *she* sighs.

It's an overly dramatic imitation of mine.

"Rough day, huh?" She's mocking me.

I grin, though she can't see it.

Bending sideways, I reach toward the ground to pull my butterfly knife from the sheath in my boot. Then, I grip her left wrist and hold it steady while I flip the knife open with a flourish of my right hand. Her arms jerk back instinctively, tightening around my waist at the sight of the blade.

"What are you—"

I slice through the cable tie binding her wrists. Her arms remain around my waist as it takes her a few beats to realize I've cut her free. When she starts to pull them back, I clamp my hand around her wrist and hold it firm to my stomach.

"I hope the scenic drive was eye-opening, *professor.*"

Her freed right palm presses flat against the middle of my back, just to the right of my spine, and she attempts to push me away while simultaneously pulling back on the arm I still have trapped. It's a pointless waste of her waning energy.

I lean back and she gasps, her body forced to tilt with mine. Her fingers curl at my back to grip my shirt, and her hand around my waist stretches wide, fingers splaying to catch herself from falling backward—instinctive reactions to the sudden feeling of falling.

My hand glides along her wrist, turns it as I slide my palm over the back of her hand, and then I quickly thread my fingers between hers.

She tugs her arm. "What the fu—"

I tighten my grip between her fingers, holding her in place.

"You can try to run away from me, but you won't get over the gates before you're caught. Even if you did, you'd never survive Lawless Land on your own." I twist my neck to look at her over my shoulder. "I advise you give up the fight now and come inside with me, desert rose."

I give her hand another quick squeeze, then release her and climb off the bike before she can respond. I turn to face her and find some twisted pleasure watching the assortment of raw emotions that tangle into an expression I don't know how to describe… It's a blend of shock, anger, and disbelief mixed with a hint of amusement and a dash of shrewd calculation.

I close the knife and slip it into the back pocket of my jeans. Then I hold out my palm, silently offering to help her off the bike, but she doesn't take it. She doesn't move. She doesn't even spare a quick glance at my hand.

Her eyes are locked on mine, and for a moment, they hold me in place. The setting sun casts a glow that highlights the warmth in her hazel eyes, sharpening the green around the edges. Her pink hair complements the color with unnatural perfection, the soft rose petal shade drawing out the gold halo circling the center of her irises.

Stunning...

My gaze lowers to the dried blood beneath her chin. Flaky pieces cling to her skin where it ran down her neck and crimson stains the collar of her shirt. The bleeding seems to have stopped, and thank fuck for that... The last thing I need is an excuse to obsess over the features of her fresh blood and spiral down a dangerous path.

She still doesn't move to take my hand, so I let it drop, lift my eyes to look beyond her toward the holding house at the end of the road, spotting the white Tacoma now parked at the curb. Santi, Hayes, and Tucker climb out, shooting me confused glances before carrying on with their work.

"I know what you want from me." Her voice is venomous, and I meet her eyes in a hurry.

"Do you?"

"You want what all men want."

"Hmm..." I know exactly what she's thinking, but I play dumb for the hell of it, cock my head to the side, and let my eyebrows furrow. "What do *all* men want? I know we're all simple-minded, sex-crazed fiends, but it's got to be something special if we *all* want it... Something like happiness, peace, maybe love?"

"You're fucking obnoxious."

"No, you're thinking of something simpler, something basic, fundamental…" I reach forward and run my finger down a strand of her long hair. "Something like *pleasure*."

"Something like *violence*." She flings her arm, swatting my hand away like a fly. "Don't fucking *touch* me."

In a single motion, I close the space between us, rushing forward to sink my fingers into her hair. I reach over the bike with my other hand, place my palm on her hip, and quickly slide it down her thigh. I grip the flesh just beneath her knee, and before she can react, I lift her leg, dragging it over to meet the other, forcing her body to turn and face me.

Her eyes go wide at the forceful motion, and she gasps as I press in between her legs, my fingers slipping through her hair to cup the back of her head. Tugging the tangled strands, I force her to crane her neck, tilting her chin skyward as I grip her waist with one hand.

Her nostrils flare and her cheeks pinken with rage. She turns her gaze skyward, intentionally playing keep-away with her eyes.

"Oh, no, princess. We're not playing that game. I'm gonna need your eyes on me. Be good…Show me I have your full attention."

All she gives me is defiance.

Not so much as a glance.

"Eyes on me, baby."

I curl my fingers, fist a chunk of her hair, and tug back so hard it makes her yelp. Her gaze drops with a snap of seething rage. She glares, unable to stop herself from showing me the pure hatred that burns through the halo of gold in her hazel eyes.

Her rage stuns me.

It's this beautiful, tangible thing that lives just beneath the surface—so raw, so strong, so accessible. She may as well have handed me the stick I use to prod her.

"There you are." I give her a full-toothed, condescending grin. "That's perfect, baby. I knew you could be such a good girl."

That snaps her into the feral little creature who was out for blood at the Crevice. She thrashes, snarls, bares her teeth, and screams profanities at me.

It gives me a rush, makes me instantly fucking high in a way I've never felt before. The threat of addiction is what makes her dangerous... I'm not exactly skilled at suppressing my compulsive urges, and I'm quickly developing the compulsion to make her react.

I pull her hair harder, bring my other hand from her waist to her throat, and grip it tight enough to scare her, forcing her attention back on me.

"You're not exactly in a position of power here, pink."

For some reason, that reminder makes her go still. Her fury hasn't left—it's still visible in her eyes, etched in her expression, rippling from her in unseen waves.

"I suggest you watch your words with me. You're in no position to tell me not to fucking touch you. You have no *idea* what I've done for you by bringing you here. You wanna safe place to sleep tonight? You wanna eat? Take a fucking shower? Show a little goddamn respect for me, baby."

"I'm not your fucking—"

In a smooth rush, I step backward, dragging her off the bike and jerking her against my body. I wrap an arm around her waist to pull her close, though my fingers stay tangled in her hair. I bring my lips to her ear and whisper, "With all due respect, *professor,* shut the fuck up and get in the house."

I release her, turn away, and move toward the front door.

I rise two steps onto the landing, which is shaded beneath an arched, Mediterranean-style portico. I stop at the front door—made from sturdy, black painted wood, and the view through its window is obscured by frosted glass, hidden behind black metal bars I added for security.

I begin the process of unlocking it with keys attached to the same ring as the one for my motorcycle. First, I turn the key for the deadbolt near the top of the door, next, the one just above the handle, then finally, the lock near the base.

But I don't open the door right away.

I turn sideways and lean my back against the inner wall of the portico, kick my boot up on the wall behind me, and twirl my keys around one finger. "It would be easier for both of us if you just walked your pretty little ass on in here yourself."

I don't have a good view of her from where I'm standing, but I don't need a better view to know she hasn't moved. "Or you could just sit out here and roast. That's a choice I guess you could make."

It's not really.

She's coming inside either way—willfully or by force.

But the goal is compliance, and it's easier to get someone to comply with another's demands when they think *they're* the one who made the choice.

After a few moments of silence without any movement, I give her a more compelling reason to come inside. "Power comes on soon. I'll probably turn on the A/C and make something to eat. If you're not hot and hungry, you could stay out here and pout all night—"

Suddenly, she appears, framed by the arched portico entry, standing at the bottom of the porch steps. "You have power?"

I stop my keys mid-twirl and pocket them. "Four nights a week from eight to four."

Her head tilts. "How? *Why?*"

"Come inside, and I'll tell you."

She crosses her arms and juts her hip to one side. "Do you think I'm stupid?"

"No." I push off the wall and turn to face her, match the angle of her slightly inclined head. "Why? Do *you* think you're stupid?"

She scoffs. "What kind of question is that?"

"I don't know." I briefly glance behind her when I see Tucker come up the street in our direction, breaking into a light jog. "You're the one who asked."

"Have you ever heard of a rhetorical question?"

"Oh, that's clever." I grin, taking a single step down from the landing.

"Excuse me?"

"Asking me rhetorically if I've ever heard of a rhetorical question."

Tucker reaches the driveway, slowing to a brisk walk.

"What the fuck is *wrong* with you?" she says at the same time Tucker asks, "Want me to bring her in?"

I give him a nod as I tell her, "I could make you a list, but you'll have to come inside first."

"I'm not—" Her words morph into a surprised shriek as Tucker hoists her off the ground.

I turn and open the door, step inside my home, and wait as he carries her inside. He plops her down on her feet in the entryway, and she steps back to catch her balance after the quick drop. Tucker steps back, blocking the open doorway with his body. He pushes at the tan straps on his shoulders and removes the backpack Gemma received at Eviction. He holds it out to me, and I take it, slipping one strap over my shoulder—I'm not giving it back to her just yet.

"You really keeping her here?" Tucker rubs the back of his neck in an anxious sort of way that implies concern. I wonder if it's for me or for her.

"Yes, I am. And you don't need to worry about it. You need to get back to the holding house. You know the rule: one-to-one ratio for vetting. I'll manage her here. You can tell Brady he's off the hook for this round."

Tucker hesitates—looks at her, then looks at me.

I turn to face him, blocking his view of her, and my teeth grind from the tension in my jaw. "What the fuck are you worried about, Tucker?"

If he knows what's best, he won't answer that question. If he knows what's best, he'll turn around and walk away.

"It's just that…"

My head falls to the side as I send him a warning glare.

It's subtle, but I notice the way he leans back in recognition of my authority. "She's *bleeding*."

"She *was* bleeding, but it's dried now. Medical's coming here after the holding house." My expression hardens. "Any other concerns about my ability to manage one little pink-haired princess in my own fucking home?"

I take a step forward, and he takes a step back. He lifts his palms in surrender with another backward step, and a look of contrition filters the features of his face. "Sorry, you're right. It was just that Santi told me…"

I know exactly what Santi told him.

He shakes his head, looking down at his feet. "Forget it."

I unfold my arms, grip the outer edge of the door in one hand. "I never forget anything, Tuck."

His eyes snap wide, and he looks genuinely bothered, nodding furiously as he moves backward down the first porch step, nearly tripping over his feet. "Okay. Yeah, okay. Sorry."

Fuck.

He's young, he's dumb, and he's a fucking handful most of the time. But I guess I have a bit of a soft spot for the way he tries. He begins to turn away, but I call out to him, "Hey. You guys did good today."

There's a slight pause before he lets the hint of a grin tug at his lips. "Yeah, thanks. Uh… Thanks."

Just as he turns to jog back to the holding house, Gemma gasps.

"Is there…" she stammers. "Are you holding someone *hostage?*"

Hostage?

I'm taken aback. The sound of horror in her voice instantly begs my curiosity. I shut the door and turn to face her. Her eyes lift from the small, white piece of paper in her hand to meet mine.

"You have a girl collared and chained up?" She stomps toward me, shaking the paper in my face. "You have a woman locked up in a room here?"

What in the actual fuck is she talking about?

I pluck the paper from her hand, and she starts to back away from me, shaking her head with rage. "You sick son of a bitch—"

"No need to bring my mother into this—"

Her eyebrows shoot to her hairline. "I'm not letting you do this to her."

Do what?

To whom?

She turns and sprints off into the house, and though I instantly have the urge to chase her, I pause to read the scribbled message on the piece of paper.

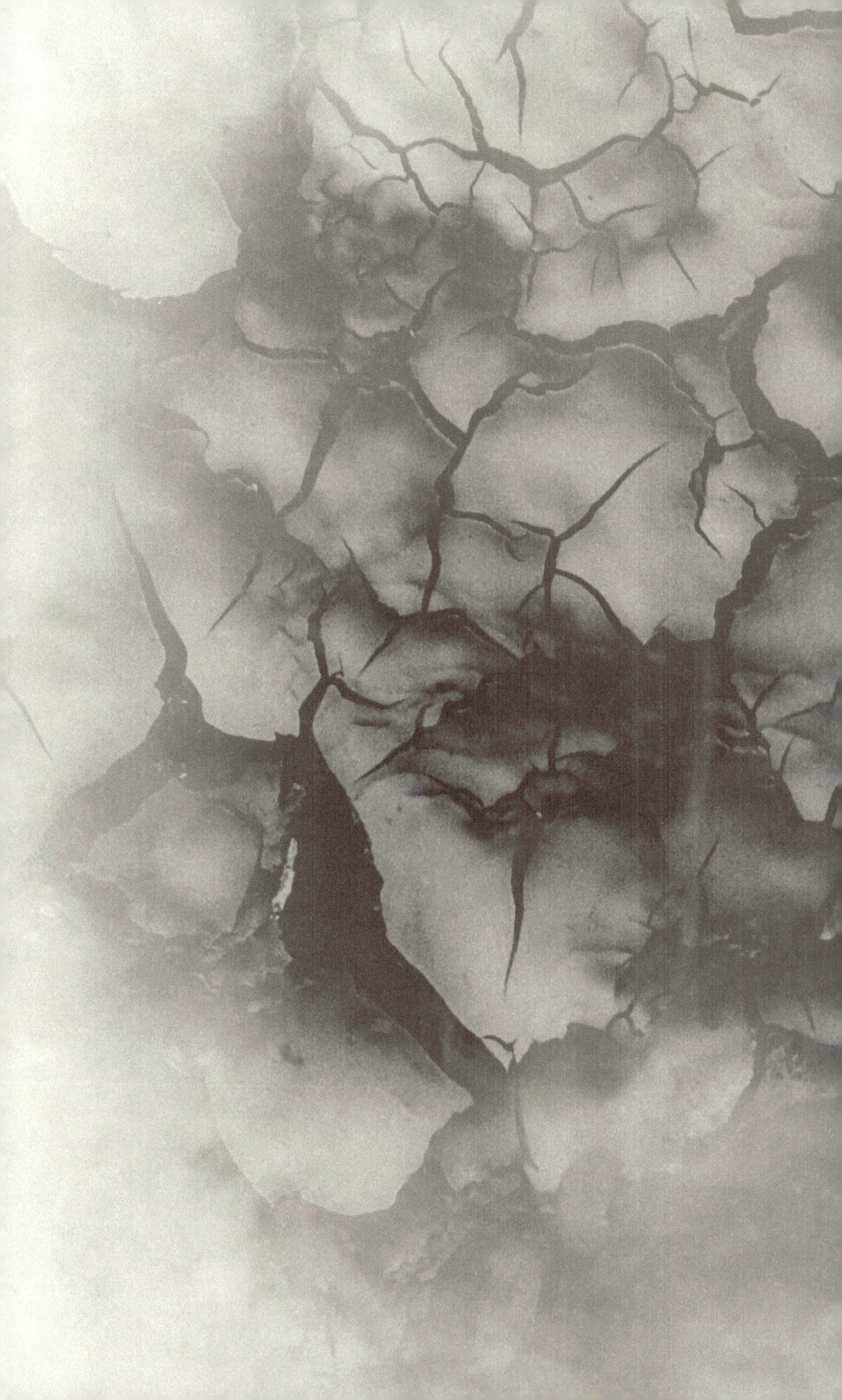

CHAPTER ELEVEN
Violent Intimacy

Oz

I TURN TO lock the front door—all three bolts, plus a security chain—as Gemma dashes through my house on some unknown morality mission. I quickly read the handwritten note I assume she found on the small entryway table standing beside me.

. . .

Oz,

She was such a good girl today! Brought her back, fed and exhausted, at 7:00pm.

We really have to find her a different collar. She hates the one she's got, and it's driving me crazy watching her pull at it all the time. Took it off for a while to give her a break. It's back on her now, and she's chained up in her room. You know that feisty little bitch is leashed and locked because she kept trying to follow me out when I left? She might actually love me more than she loves you. . .

(Obviously, I'm kidding. Unclench your jaw, Daddy Oz. You know she only has eyes for you.)

Hope everything went well. See you soon with the new girls . . .

XOXO.

Salem

So, from that, the bubblegum beauty has gathered that I'm keeping a female chained up and locked inside a bedroom. She's not exactly wrong, but she also isn't right.

I toss the note from Salem onto the entry table, drop Gemma's backpack onto the floor, and slowly move toward the sunken living room. I stop before stepping down, though. I stand quietly, waiting and listening.

I listen for her footsteps, for the chain, for the sound of Angel's low, rumbling growl as she waits for my command to attack or heal.

But it's surprisingly quiet.

I scan the living room as I wait for a sound to tell me where she is, my gaze sweeping across the furniture filling the space.

My living room is the most recent renovation in my home, though in hindsight, the black leather sectional and matching armchairs were probably a poor choice—they already feature scratches from Angel's claws.

A decent couch is a luxury in Lawless Land. Here, we can only have what we can salvage and repair. Of course, there was furniture left behind in these homes, but it was decades' old when we found it, and not everything was salvageable—time and neglect have a powerful impact.

Thankfully, there's enough skill and experience among the Vultures to allow us all some of the creature comforts we took for granted in our lives before. You never really think about the impact of having a clean, comfortable couch to sit on until the only thing you can find to plop your ass on in the middle of the desert is a fucking rock.

The sunset filters through the double-paned glass French doors and the two picture windows on either side. Shades of light are painted across the furniture in dim strips of yellow and orange. Through the windows, I can see the desert mountains off in the distance—a stunning backdrop to the rows of homes in our gated community. The view is beautiful and deceptive, one that could have fooled me into thinking that the world as we knew it was still within our grasp…

It's not.

Living here in the Gates is the closest we'll ever get to normal.

My head whips sideways at the sound of a door clicking open. Without thinking, I find myself pulling the butterfly knife from my jeans, though I don't expect I'll need it. I don't need a knife to threaten or subdue her. She's a fighter for sure—scrappy, strong, and motivated—but I could overpower her with my bare hands without breaking a sweat.

Has she found the right bedroom yet?

Has she found Angel?

I wonder what will happen when she does…

The unpredictability of what this woman will do as I stalk her through my own house is a little overwhelming.

Thrilling.

Intoxicating.

Naturally, my hand twists to flip open the knife, exposing the blade and locking it into place. I step down into the sunken living room, move across the traditional-style faded black and gray area rug, then step up again to enter the main living space.

To my left is a short hall leading to the laundry room and garage, and just a few steps ahead is the staircase leading up to the second floor. But I find her right in front of me, facing the open door leading to the second of two bedrooms on this level.

Angel's room.

Guess she found her.

Gemma must not see me because she doesn't turn her head or make a sound. I strain my ears and hear Angel's low warning growl. I expect Gemma to step back, maybe run away or simply slam the door shut.

But instead, she steps inside... uninvited.

What the fuck is she thinking?

Angel could bite her, break the skin and draw blood.

My empty hand curls into a fist as the thought catches my dark obsession. She could bleed in my home, alone with me, no one else here to make it stop...

And what if there's no one to stop me *from letting it spill?*

A shudder ripples up my spine as I fight the desire to watch her bleed—desire so unexpectedly heavy that it makes my cock twitch at the thought of cutting her myself. I reach over, placing my hand on the banister to steady myself as the darkness courses through my veins.

But I shouldn't have touched the railing. A glance at my hand sends me spinning back to that night, sparking a vision from nearly a decade ago. I see my palm wrapped around a tan wooden railing—not the black metal railing I'm holding on to now—and it's soaked with blood. It streaks the banister as I climb the steps, gripped by fear for what I might find in Emaline's bedroom...

This isn't her house.

Her bedroom isn't upstairs.

Emaline is dead.

I blink and shake my head, forcefully dragging myself from the bloody memory as I flash back from the past to the present. I glance down and find that I climbed the steps along with my memory. I'm a third of the way up the staircase, though I don't recall making the decision to go upstairs.

I pause to get my bearings.

The feeling of regret gradually fills me.

The vivid memory brought me a sense of shame so powerful that it strains every muscle in my body.

I should've been there for her.

I should've done it for her sooner.

I shouldn't have watched her bleed for so long when it was over.

My grip on the banister tightens as I fight the monster inside me. It craves that final, horrible image in which Emaline was lying on the floor, soaked in her own blood, and smiling up at me before she drew her last breath.

Nearly ten years later, and the memories still live so clearly in my mind. I feel like I'm still fighting the pull of them when I catch the sound of a voice singing sweetly. My head turns in the direction of the sound—it's coming from Angel's room.

Cherry blossom can sing?

Curiosity is strong enough to bring me fully into the present. I take a deep breath and tilt my head from side-to-side, stretching the strained muscles in my neck, trying to convince my tense shoulders to relax.

I back down the steps and slowly move down the hall, my footfalls cushioned by the plush flooring beneath my boots. Stopping beside the open door, I press my back against the wall, stifle my breathing, and strain to listen as she softly sings.

Angel is quiet, aside from the light jingle of the tag on her collar and the gentle huffs of her panted breaths. It's strange, though—she only pants like that when she's been outside in the heat too long or when she's... happy.

It doesn't even seem like she's scented my presence yet.

I should call for her.

I should go in there and make sure she's okay.

Pinky is a violent offender, after all. She could be a cold-hearted dog killer for all I know. The thought is nearly enough to have me charging in, but then I suddenly recognize the melody of the song, and it makes me pause.

The song is *Isn't She Lovely* by Stevie Wonder, but her rendition isn't quite the same as the original. The melody of the song is, by nature, joyful, yet her interpretation is slower and more somber. And there's something about her voice, something about the rich intonation and the velvety, angelic quality that's textured with raw edges...

It's captivating.

She sings it like it hurts her and heals her at the same time.

She sings like she doesn't care if anyone is listening.

But I'm listening, rooted to the spot, unable to move.

The song stops mid-refrain as she laughs—a light, sparkling sound that breaks the spell cast by her voice.

"Aw, sweet girl!" Her voice is deceptively pleasant. "Such a pretty girl, aren't you? No, you're not a mean puppy. That collar doesn't suit you at all, does it? You need a little pink, too." Then, in a baby-talk voice, she says, "Yes, you do. You do, don't you, sweet puppy?"

What the fuck is going on with Angel?

No warning bark, not so much as a growl. For some reason, she's not seeing this stranger in our home as a threat, which goes against all her training.

"Don't worry, pretty baby, I'll get this yucky spiked collar off you and get you a pretty pink one instead. I just need to kill that nasty man holding you hostage here first. We'd like that, wouldn't we? Yes, we would. I'll kill that motherfucker and take you away from here, sweet girl—"

"Over my dead fucking body!"

I shove the door open wide and rush in, a sudden rage tearing through me at the mere thought of her trying to take Angel. I stomp across the room, intent on grabbing this bitch by her pink fucking hair, momentarily tempted to slit her throat for so much as threatening to take my girl.

But then I see them, and it stops me dead in my tracks.

Gemma's sitting on the floor, leaning her back against the far wall of Angel's dedicated room. Her legs are flat on the floor, spread wide to make room for my jet-black, three-year-old pit bull to sit between them. Angel turns her head in my direction, and she spots me. Her ears go down, her tail wiggles, and she lets out a pathetically sweet half-bark, half-whimper in greeting.

This isn't how Angel greets me. And it's sure as fuck not how Angel handles strangers, especially when they enter our home without a proper introduction from me. My smart, obedient, loyal-to-a-fault dog isn't just defenseless and subdued, she's fucking happy... Butt shaking, tail wagging, face-licking happy.

This bubblegum bitch has my Angel defenseless.

The sight of me standing here should be enough of a command for Angel to greet me. Her hind legs lift from the floor for no more than a second, just long enough for her to shake her whole body with utter delight, before promptly sitting again. I nearly lose my shit when she turns her head away and starts licking Gemma's cheek.

Whatever childlike glee I'd heard in Gemma's voice before is gone now. Her expression reflects a ruthless, brutal hatred that's directed at me. She scans me from head to toe, her gaze pausing on the knife in my hand before raising to capture my stare. She shoots daggers with her hazel eyes as she scruffs behind Angel's ears.

"Are you planning to kill me with that?" Her voice is low now, vicious, like my presence turns her into an entirely different person. "Don't you think it would be in poor taste to stab me in front of your dog?" She plants a kiss on Angel's nose, and she shakes with joy, licking Gemma's face with even more enthusiasm than before.

Those are my fucking face licks...

"Get up." My seething voice rumbles with a barely contained growl. "Get up and get the fuck away from my dog."

"Call her."

I clench my fist, my head tilting with silent warning.

"Go on... call her," she repeats. "Call your dog."

My eyes narrow at her audacity, wondering what game she's playing. My stare is scrutinizing as I try to decipher her intentions.

"What's with the hesitation?" She tilts her head to match the angle of mine. "Are you afraid she won't come if you call her? If she'd really prefer you over me, I won't stop her, so... call your dog."

Does she really think Angel won't rip her face off if I tell her to?

With coldness in my eyes, I hold Gemma's stare while I call my girl, "Angel." Angel turns her head to look at me, her demeanor changing instantly at the sharp tone of my command. With my free hand, I point my index finger straight down at the floor. "Here."

Angel hops up without hesitation and trots across the room. Faithfully at my side where she belongs, Angel turns twice beneath my finger before lowering her hind legs to sit.

My eyes remain on Gemma as I reach down to scratch the top of Angel's head. "Good girl."

Gemma suddenly looks uneasy, and that makes me feel like I can finally take a deep breath. Angel's reaction to her was unsettling, and it felt as though it gave Gemma a false sense of power that she certainly won't possess in this house. But the way she pulls up her knees and hugs them to her chest suggests her acknowledgment of the truth—Angel is mine, I'm in control here, and Gemma will only get the power I choose to give her.

"Where are they?" Her voice is still venomous, but it's quieter now than it was before.

"Who?"

"The other women you kidnapped."

"I didn't kidnap anyone."

"You kidnapped *me.*"

"No, baby, I *saved* you."

"Saved me?" Her head jerks back as she pulls a look of disgust. "I didn't need to be saved."

"Trust me, I did you a favor, cherry pie. The Reborn would have destroyed you."

"You can't destroy wreckage." She scoffs, her gaze drifting from mine, and there's an unexpected shift in the tone of her voice. "I'm already in ruins."

It seems there's some depth behind all her rage, and it tugs at my curiosity. I'm tempted to ask her to elaborate, to demand she tell me her story and explain what—or who—destroyed her. I'll bet it has something to do with that Reborn pretty boy she went feral for at the Crevice.

But I won't ask her about it tonight.

"Stay," I tell Angel before slowly crossing the room.

I invade Gemma's space, stopping at her feet. Though I tower over her, standing uncomfortably close, she doesn't cower. She doesn't hug her knees tighter and draw back like I was hoping she would, but she does react. Tensely, she shifts, appearing as though she's ready for the attack without really changing her position. There isn't a quick or easy way for her to slip away from me, but it's clear she's prepared to push me away by force.

"Back the fuck up," she snarls, staring straight ahead between my knees.

I quickly drop to my haunches, and she flinches. "Careful now." I switch the knife to my left hand before resting my elbows on my knees, let the weapon hang from my fingers between my legs with the tip aimed at the floor. "I know I told you to watch your words with me."

Her eyes snap to mine and show me that addictive rage. "You have a death wish, don't you? Go on, keep pushing me..." She flashes a shit-eating grin as her head drops back against the wall. "You have no idea what I'm capable of doing to you."

"I have no doubt, *professor*." My gaze sweeps briefly to the dried blood on her throat. "I can only imagine all the wild things you're capable of doing to me."

"I'd be happy to bring your imagination to life." She holds her hand out over her knees, palm up. "Hand me the knife and I'll show you just how *wild* I can be."

Goddamn.

That pulls at something deep in the pit of my stomach—that dark desire for violent intimacy. The idea is so powerful... A woman who needs me as obsessively as I need her. A woman who would bleed for me and insist I bleed for her, too.

There's something so wrong about the idea of it.

Emaline would be ashamed of me just for thinking it.

But would she?

Emaline never judged me; she never judged anyone, least of all those who hurt her. And in the end, that was her downfall, assuming she'd get the best out of the worst people in her life.

But this pink princess judges indiscriminately. She assumes every person with a dick wants to fuck her and hurt her. Maybe she's right about that. I definitely want to fuck her and hurt her, but that doesn't mean that I *will.*

With a grin, I watch her silently, twirling the knife around my fingers. She and I both know I'm not handing it over, but I'm curious to know what her next move will be when she gets no response from me.

Will she try to take it?

Will she give up and pull her hand back?

It doesn't take her long to decide.

With a sigh, her hand falls, landing on her knee. "It's fine, I get it. I'm too much for you. Maybe some other time."

"Maybe." I can't help my smirk. "Tell me who you are."

Her eyebrows slant toward her nose. "Tell me who *you* are."

"I asked you first, petunia."

"You know my name. I know you heard Seb call me *professor,* so I know you heard him say my name."

"Yeah, I heard it, Gemma. But I didn't ask you to tell me your name. I asked you to tell me who you *are*."

A silent beat passes while she stares me down and wrinkles crease her forehead with her scrutinizing expression. "I'm the Siren."

I lift an eyebrow and tilt my head, wait for her to continue.

"You haven't heard of me? Is it only the Reborn who know who I am, then?" She pauses, and her eyes appear to shift along with thoughts running through her mind. "How did they know I'm the Siren, but you don't? How do they know what I did?"

"What did you do?"

Her expression hardens. "You wanna know what I did? You wanna know who I am? I'm the girl who tortured and murdered three men who fucked with me and streamed it live on social media."

Right. She's a serial killer.

I made the connection when I saw how much the Reborn wanted her, yet that rather important detail must have slipped my mind somewhere between the Crevice and the Gates. For that reason alone, I should've left her behind. I should've found another woman to bring back in her place.

But there was just something about her that I couldn't walk away from, not from the second I laid eyes on her. The way she was standing there in the open desert, her long, pink hair briefly waving as a phantom breeze caught her. I don't think there was actually a breeze, but that's how I saw her—a mirage of all my deepest desires and darkest fears about myself come to life.

I know I'll have to vet her carefully before handing her over to Salem. I've vetted enough lawless to know who can be managed in our community and who poses a threat to our sustainability.

If Gemma killed repeatedly just for the thrill of it, then she'll be too dangerous to keep. If she proves to be a liability, then I can't allow her to stay here. I'd have to send her away to wander Lawless Land alone—maybe that would stop my dangerous obsession dead in its quickly laid tracks.

Except the mere thought of sending her away makes my molars grind, causing an ache in my jaw and tension in my neck.

I could just keep her here, like a pet...

Get her a collar and chain, lock her up in here with Angel...

I could bring men for her to kill, help her satiate the demented appetite of her bloodthirsty soul...

What the fuck am I thinking?

I drag myself from dark thoughts and snap back into reality. With a flick of my wrist, I snap the knife shut. I quickly slide it into the sheath in my boot, and shove to my feet. Gemma's arms drop from her knees, and her palms press to the floor on either side of her hips. She looks up at me, ready to leap to her feet and attack if I make a move against her.

"Get up," I command. "Walk upstairs. Do it yourself, or I'll drag you up the steps if I have to."

Her head shakes slowly, her face twisting toward anger and defiance. "No."

"Gemma—"

"I said *no.*" She jumps to her feet. "You'll have to kill me and drag my dead weight yourself because I'm not going anywhere you ask me to while I'm still alive."

"Final answer?" I give her another chance to make this easier for the both of us.

She shows me both middle fingers, her expression full of malice, though her voice is unnaturally sweet. "Eat a bag of shit."

I chuckle. "Okay, I see how you want this to go. Don't try to tell me later that I didn't give you a chance to do this the easy way."

I stomp toward her, and she side-steps with her back to the wall, moving until she hits the corner, and lodges herself there defensively. She holds out a hand to stop me, but she must know by now that she can't.

Angel barks as I reach out for Gemma, grabbing hold of her outstretched arm and using it to yank her away from the wall. She stumbles in my direction and collides with my chest. I grip her upper arms, keep a firm hold on her as I twist her around, force her to face away from me, and march her toward the door.

She shouts and thrashes as I push her into the hallway. She anchors her feet, sinks her weight, nearly lowers to a sitting position as she shoves back in an attempt to stop me.

It doesn't stop me, though.

I dip and wrap my arms around her waist from behind, spin us both all the way around so I can walk backward, lugging her with me down the hall. I reach the bottom of the staircase and move backward, dragging her up by the armpits.

She screams and shouts, fighting me with each step.

Her fists pummel my forearms.

Her shoes slide off from her kicking and tumble to the bottom.

Angel barks, though I can't tell if it's directed at her or at me.

I make it halfway up the staircase before Gemma twists. She pulls herself around, turning with enough force to corkscrew right out of my arms, flipping entirely onto her stomach. I reach for her with a grunt, but she slips away, quickly sliding down the steps.

"Shit." I race after her.

My boots share the steps with her sliding body, and I reach her mid-section just as her sock-covered toes reach the bottom step. With a quick turn, I lift one foot over her body and straddle her waist on the step. I reach down and grab hold of her, forced to handle her roughly with the way she fights so fucking hard.

It's starting to make my cock fucking hard, too.

I turn her beneath me, violently twisting her onto her back. She kicks her legs and fights to pull them free. When she plants her ass on a step and tries to sit up, I drop to my knees, kneeling on the same step to straddle her waist. To effectively pin her beneath me, I make her take some of my weight, ensure it's impossible for her to slip away, even though she continues to fight.

Fuck, I like the fight too much.

"Get off me!" Her arms swing wildly, and she's bound to land a strike sooner or later if I don't get her under control.

I snatch her wrists and wrestle her arms out of the air, press them back above her head, and put more weight on her hips. "You're not being very ladylike—"

Spit flies out of her mouth and strikes my cheek.

My head twists to the side as I take a moment to process. Then I shift her wrists to my left hand, squeeze them tight enough to grind her bones, and swipe the spit from my cheek.

"You trying to get a rise out of me, pink?"

I bring my spit-soaked fingers to her mouth and press them hard over her tightly pursed lips. I rub them around, give her a nice, glossy sheen with her own saliva as I attempt to pry them apart.

I'm losing control.

"Open up, Gemma. Let me give it back. We're in the middle of the desert, and fluids are scarce. We can't afford to waste a single drop."

Her head whips back and forth as muffled sounds of protest vibrate behind her sealed lips.

"Come on now, baby. One of us is swallowing that spit. Let me keep you hydrated."

I'm really losing it...

I want to hurt her.

I want her to like it.

I dig at the seal of her lips and manage to pry just enough to sink the tips of my fingers inside her mouth. But the second her tongue sweeps across them, she relents and opens wide. Then her teeth clamp down on my knuckles.

I yank my hand away. "Fuck!"

Guess I didn't learn my lesson the first time she bit me.

Unable to fling her arms, she whips me with one infuriated obscenity after another, swearing like a goddamn sailor.

I laugh a little because it's fucking cute.

"I'll string you up by your motherfucking ankles and choke the life out of you with your own shoelaces..." she says, then continues on, blazing with fury as she tells me all the horrible ways she wants to hurt me.

The fight in her is so incredible, the way she refuses to give up is so stunning. It's what I'd always hoped for from Emaline, and while she was strong and found her own way to survive, I never did get to see her become *this.*

Fierce.

Uninhibited.

Alive.

"...slit your throat and piss in it while I cut your dick off..."

I should be hesitant to put digits near Gemma's teeth again, but I can't help myself. I cup her cheek, brushing my thumb beneath her lip. Confusion melts into her expression at my sudden switch to a gentle hand, and it slows the speed at which she flings her words.

"...then shove it up your ass..." she trails off.

"I like your lips, Gemma."

With a shocked expression, she flinches. If there were any space between her head and the step it rests on, she would've jerked it back with enough force to give herself whiplash.

"When you were trying to distract me, and you kissed me on my bike... Felt good, didn't it? Your lips felt so good on mine."

"Excuse me?"

"Do you want me to kiss you now? Are you afraid to admit that you want it? Is that why you fight me so hard?" I dip a little lower.

"Get the fuck *off* me!"

I bend until our noses touch. Her eyes widen and her entire body stiffens, making the quick shift from fighting for her life to frozen in shock.

"Don't you fucking dare," she hisses.

"Do I have your full attention now, princess?"

Her eyebrows shoot to her hairline. "Did you think you had *less* than my full attention up until now?"

I pull back a few inches, give her a little space as I flash a grin. "I'll take that as a yes. Now, listen to me carefully. Your ass is going upstairs whether you fight me or not. Do you see where you are right now? How you tried so hard to fight me, only to end up beneath me, anyway? You're only gonna get hurt."

Absently, I stroke her hair. "And I don't know if you've forgotten or if you've just stopped caring, but you sliced your throat pretty good a couple of hours ago. Don't worry, we have people trained for medical care. Not exactly world-class physicians, but

I'm sure you already knew we don't have hospitals or an endless supply of sterile instruments here in Lawless Land. You're definitely at risk of infection, and you probably shouldn't have let Angel lick all over you like that, but we'll do our best to keep you alive—at least, until you've served your time with us."

"Served my—"

"But let's say you break a rib thrashing around like that and puncture a lung, or hit your head on the wall and get a concussion… How much help do you think we can give you then, Gemma?"

"I'm not—"

"You need medical attention; I have people who can give you that. You need to eat; I have food. You need shelter; I put a roof over your head. You have questions; I have answers. But I can take that all away in a heartbeat if you can't learn to live by my rules."

Golden flames burn a halo of fury in her hazel eyes. "Fuck you and your rules."

I lean over her again, my body pressed to hers as I bring my lips to her ear. "Stop fighting me, Gemma. I can't help you if you insist on hurting yourself."

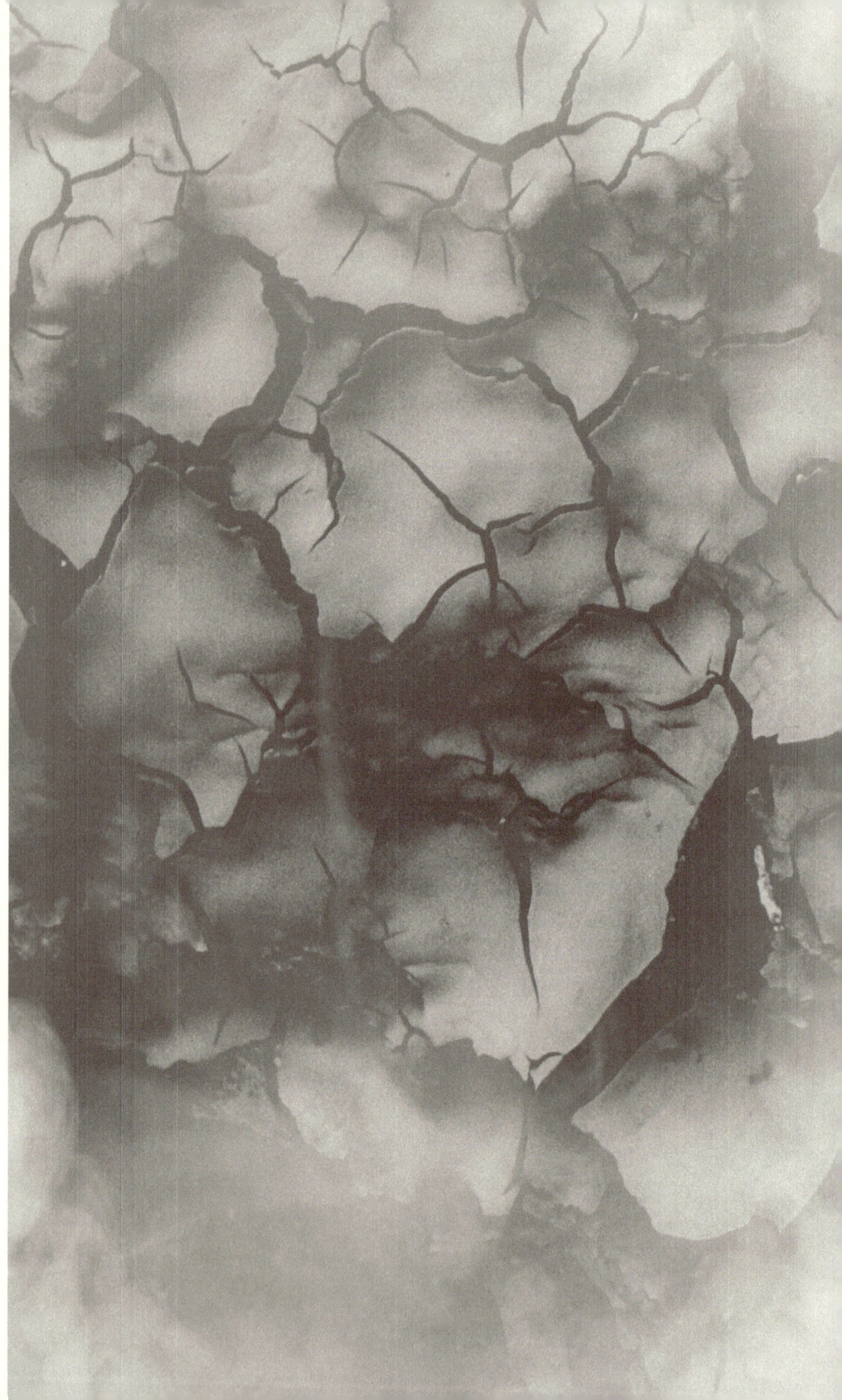

CHAPTER TWELVE
Beautiful and Terrifying

Gemma

HE'S EVERYTHING I hate.

He's all the things that frighten me.

He makes me as furious as the men who left me for dead.

I don't even know his name, but the profile of who he is develops with each passing moment. I'm taking notes in my mind and bold print highlights the traits that scare me the most—powerful, insistent, violent, *magnetic.*

The rage he inspired sparked flames that were burning me alive from the inside out, yet the same heat awakened butterflies in the pit of my stomach. When he pinned me on the staircase, their wings were beating hard against the rising smoke, a flurry of tiny wings whipping around my insides, trying to escape the fury smoking them out. And inexplicably, their fluttering fear caused an uncontrollable clench of desire low in my belly.

I don't know where to begin to process that. It's not the same thing I felt with Seb when he found ways to force my body to betray me. I've found a way to process that, to accept that it was just one of the many ways he abused me. It was never something I liked, never something I wanted him to do again.

But this feeling wasn't the same.

It came then passed quickly, but I didn't hate it.

And I hate that I didn't hate it.

And the way he smiles, the way he grinned at me while we fought really pissed me off. It's annoying that his teeth look so perfect, all straight and pearly white.

How can he keep them so damn clean here in the Territory?

It's un-fucking-real.

As if it weren't enough to be dazzled by the flash of his unreasonably perfect teeth, he had to go and let his grin cut those subtle dimples in his cheeks. His smile altered his face from a smooth scowl to reveal the shape of his cheekbones hidden beneath, drawn from perfectly angled lines that run from either side of his nose to his dimples.

It was beautiful.

He was beautiful.

Beautiful and terrifying... He's a gorgeous, dangerous man.

The contradiction is giving me whiplash. He's drawing me into a treacherous game. One moment, he's got me suiting up, putting on armor, and ready for war. The next moment, he's disarming me, nearly charming me, and I know I can't let him do that. I know I should've kept fighting him on the stairs, but

I'm just so fucking tired. This has been the longest day of my life, and I still don't know when it will end—I don't even know *how* it will end.

Please, just let it end.

On the staircase, I gave him the last burst of adrenaline-fueled combat I could muster, but I knew in my bones I wouldn't find another surge of strength until I slept. I conceded. I guess I should thank Seb for helping me know when to give up for one day so I can prepare to fight another.

I hesitate at the threshold of an open door at the end of the hallway on the second floor. The room is dim without electricity, but there's some light from the fading sunset which must be coming from a window inside.

"Go on," he says, his voice unnervingly close.

I turn halfway, standing sideways in the doorway. I'm afraid to have my back to him any longer. He's standing too close, only inches away from my shoulder. I don't want to be so close to him, but I'm afraid to enter this room. He lifts his arms and places his hands on either side of the doorframe, caging me in, leaving me with only one direction I can move to escape him.

"Go inside." He leans forward, and his chest bumps my shoulder.

I react with an instinctive, backward step, and my ass rebounds off the doorframe.

"Unless you wanna fight me again… I could go another round."

"I didn't want to go the first round."

"But you did, and I think you kinda liked it."

Exasperated, I let out a heavy breath as I glance inside the large bedroom. "You could at least tell me your name before forcing me to bed."

"You wanna know my name, baby?"

"I assume it would be rude to call you whatever the hell I wanna call you, yeah?"

He gives me that damn grin again. "Depends on what you wanna call me."

"I was thinking something like Asshat or Douchebag... Maybe Foul-Mouthed Motherfucker if you prefer something a little more formal."

"Don't sell yourself short, pink. I'm sure you can be a hell of a lot more creative than that."

"Oh, you have no idea."

"I'm sure I'll find out." He tips his forehead toward the bedroom. "Go inside. If you're good for me, I'll tell you my name and answer your questions."

Good for him?

Shit. What is he planning to do to me in there?

The words rush out, "I'm not gonna fuck you."

His eyebrows briefly slant toward his nose before straightening again. "Good," he says with a smirk. "I prefer a pillow princess... vastly underrated."

A spark of anger has me turning to square off, but exhaustion quickly snuffs the flame and drains the heat from my words. "Who the fuck do you think you are?"

"A guy who prefers to be on top." His palms land on my shoulders, and Angel barks from somewhere behind him. "Stop wasting my time, cupcake."

He twists me around and marches me forward into the bedroom. I don't even have the energy for light resistance, so I let him walk me into the room. He moves us straight ahead, stopping me at the foot of his king-sized bed before releasing my shoulders. In the nearly dark room, my gaze sweeps across the unmade bed. The flat sheet is twisted up with the plush comforter—bunched near the bottom right corner of the bed—and the pillows lay askew.

He sleeps here, tangled in these sheets.

He wants me here. He wants me in his bed with him.

My heart leaps, a painful collision with my ribs.

He's gonna rape me. I knew it... I fucking knew he would.

Shit. No... I can't...

"I can't go through this again..."

"Sit on the bed."

I whirl around to face him. "Don't... *Please...* I can't..."

"Sit down, Gemma." He takes a step toward me.

I take a step back.

My thighs bump the edge of the bed—that fucking frightening bed—and I jump away from it, rushing forward again.

But there he is, right in front of me.

Tall and towering, oppressive and demanding.

My stomach lurches with warning, with the sick, sinking feeling that I should've held on to this entire time. I'm in a new world, one without laws and consequences, and it's ruled by violent men.

There's no one to call for help; there's no one who can save me.

There's nowhere to run; there's no safe place I can hide.

How the fuck did I think I could survive here?

"I know I told you twice to sit down."

He did... He did tell me twice, and I'm still standing.

Fear climbs the back of my throat, then drips slowly down my face. Trauma crawls from the pit of my stomach where a thousand black tendrils are clustered and rooted. Their pointed claws scratch my insides, shredding my strength, tearing apart my bravery, ripping at my will to fight.

I blink and see Seb standing before me—the man who carved me out, made room for it to nest. He put this creature inside me, the one I thought I'd conquered, though evidently, was only dormant. It strips my power, makes me an empty shell that can only be filled with fear and the will to survive it. And with Seb, compliance was the only means to survive.

For moments, I feel weak, empty.

I take a step back.

I comply.

I sit on the edge of the bed, helpless.

Don't touch me. Please, don't touch me.

Don't hurt me.

Don't make me do it.

I can't do this.

"Gemma." His voice is commanding.

I blink through tears and lift my eyes to meet Seb's. He's standing right there, then in a flash, he's gone. Seb disappears, and in his place is the nameless man who stole me.

He lowers in front of me, crouching to bring his eyes level with mine. "Where'd you go, desert rose?" His face is cast in dark shadows as daylight escapes, but I can feel his eyes roam my face. I can see the dip of his brow line as his eyes narrow to study my features. "How did I lose you?"

"I'm not gone," I whisper.

"Bullshit." I feel his knuckle touch my cheek and wipe away a tear. "I know dissociation when I see it."

I want to tell him that he doesn't know what he's talking about, but as silent seconds tick past, I know he's right. I've been through this before. When something triggers a flashback, I'm dragged from the present, seized from reality by the clawed and tentacled creature who takes me back to Seb. It hasn't happened for a while, and I hope it won't last long.

When he touches my other cheek to wipe the tears, it makes me flinch. His gentle touch scoops an ounce of fear from the void and lets a spoonful of anger replace it. That's how I know it's almost over, when fear gets out of the way and other emotions fill the space.

I turn my head sideways. "Don't."

He grips my chin and lifts it skyward, leans in so close that, for a second, I almost think he's going to kiss my throat. But as quickly as he grabbed me, he lets me go.

 "First day in Lawless Land is a bitch for everyone. I get it." He sighs, watches me for a beat, then stands. "It's nearly eight. I need to go flip the breaker. I can't see what the fuck I'm doing to clean that cut until we get the lights on."

His hand floats toward me as he speaks, catching a strand of hair and slowly trailing to the end.

"I know we had a good tumble out there, but I have a feeling you're gonna stay right here for me now, aren't you? I'll be back in fifteen minutes with some clean clothes, food, and water, but you have to be good for me or I'll take them right back out. All you need to do is stay right there, and if you do, I'll let you eat, help you get cleaned up, let you shower and sleep. That's it. Just sit and wait. Fifteen minutes. I'll be back. The lights will come on before you see my face again."

He turns and strides toward the door.

I should chase him, attack him while his back is turned, try to escape one more time. Instead, my hazy mind and fatigued body insist I stay put.

He pauses just before leaving, glancing back at me from the door. "I'll take good care of you, baby. Just sit still and wait for me to come back."

I watch as the door closes behind him.

Then I sit silently, think of nothing as I wait for his return.

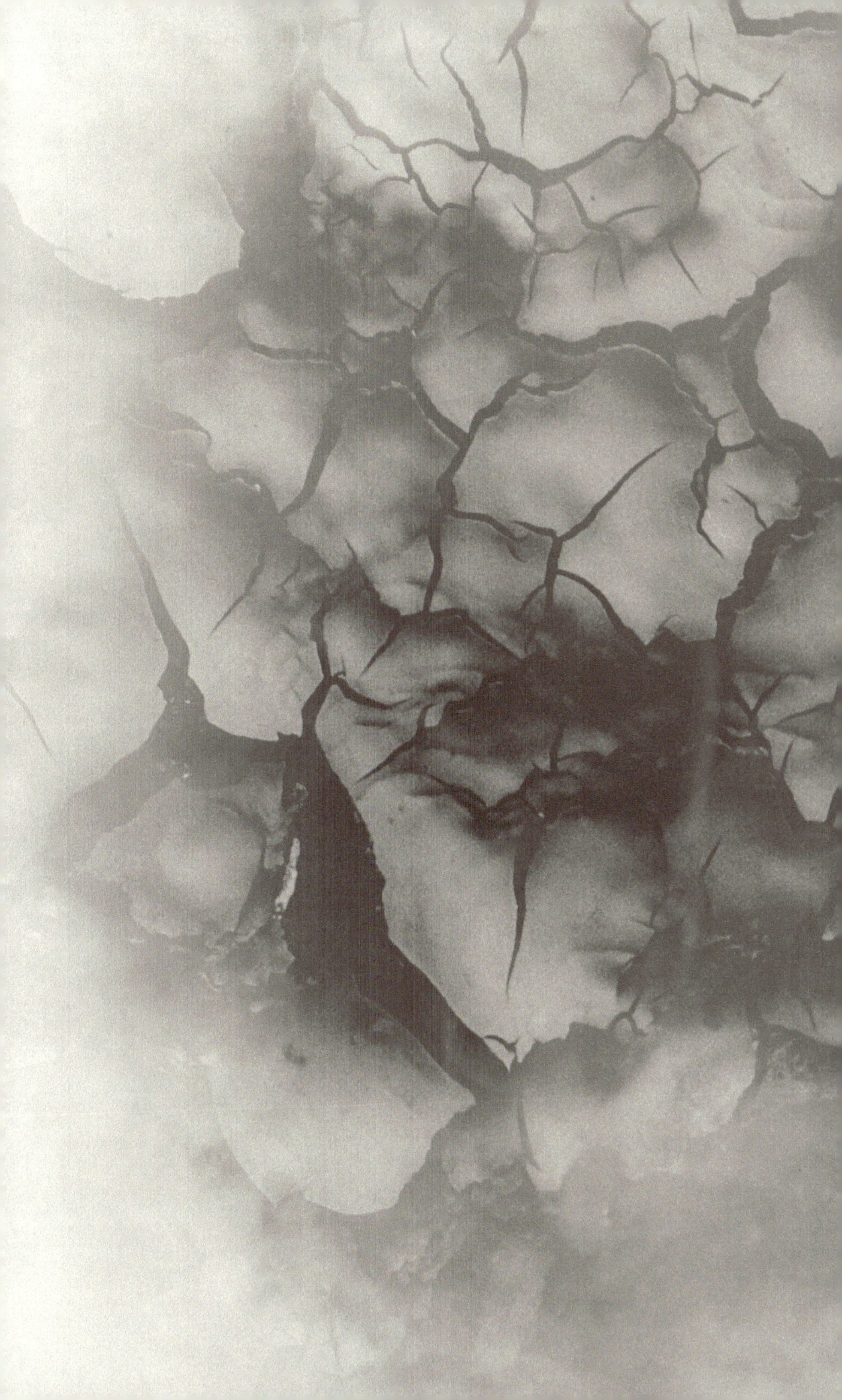

CHAPTER THIRTEEN
Anxious

Oz

THE DOOR CLICKS shut as I step into the hallway. I force the air from my lungs in a rush, then slowly fill them again. My veins are throbbing with a heavy pulse of desire. A steady beat sends bursts of dark lust to flood the smoothly flowing streams of blood, turning them to black rapids.

This woman makes me feel things I'm afraid to feel... Things that are wicked and filthy, dangerous and obsessive, possessive and uncontrollable.

It was a mistake to bring her inside my home, though it's one I could easily rectify. I could still take her to the holding house and let one of my Vultures take over with her. But I know I'm not going to.

Angel nudges my hand, and I squat to give her some attention. Her entire body twists back and forth as she comes between my knees. I cup her giant face in both hands, gently scratching and rubbing the way she likes as she presses close. I let her lap at my cheek as I pet her. I tell her what a good dog she is. I give her the love she deserves.

"You're my girl, Angel. The only one I need."

That's great. Keep telling yourself lies, motherfucker.

I kiss the top of her head before standing, then I point at the floor in front of the bedroom door. "Stay." Instantly, she moves to the spot and sits. "Guard." Her ears perk up at the word, and her back straightens on alert.

She'll stay there until I get back. That's the expectation, and on any given day I would have no doubt she'll do just that. But the way she greeted Gemma still has me wary that she's suddenly forgotten all her training. I still don't know what to make of that, but for now, I have to trust her loyalty and obedience.

I don't know enough about Gemma to leave her alone for long, so I hustle downstairs, make a right, and enter the garage. I pause in front of the breaker to check the analog clock hanging on the drywall above it.

8:03 P.M.

Our negotiated electrical access is granted precisely at eight o'clock, and since it's three minutes past, I know we'll have power as soon as I flip the switches. We have a strict rule against drawing electricity to more than two circuits at a time in each personal home, so I only switch on power to the master suite and to the kitchen and living room, which runs on the same circuit. Our contract with Prosperity requires us to guarantee full electrical access to Eden during the negotiated hours, so following this rule ensures we don't overflow the system.

I feel a bit of relief knowing Gemma's no longer sitting in the dark, all alone. She was probably fine, but somehow it makes me feel better knowing she can see her surroundings. Hopefully, she'll realize there's an en suite bathroom and make use of it if she needs to. She didn't seem so detached from the present that I should be concerned about her sitting there in a vegetative state, pissing herself because she couldn't think to get up and use the toilet. I don't even know if that's a thing that happens with dissociation. Never happened to me, though that doesn't mean it hasn't happened to anyone.

I don't know what made her slip away, what shifted her from an all-out brawl into docile submission. All I remember is the feeling of it, the shift of her energy as she drew back inside her mind. And it was something I did or said that triggered it.

Maybe it won't happen again if I keep giving her reasons to fight me. Maybe I just like the fight and want to justify poking the bear. As if I've flipped the switch myself, I feel a surge of electricity shoot through me, a sizzling flow of sparking heat that rushes through my cock.

Goddamn.

I need to hurry so I can get back to her.

I rush back through the house and exit through the front door, locking it behind me, and then head down the street toward the holding house.

Most of the Vultures selected homes closer to Eden, though there are a few outliers farther out from the noise and chaos. Aside from mine and the holding house, there's only one other occupied home on this cul-de-sac. These three houses glow with light from within, but otherwise, the street is dark.

All the other unoccupied homes are shadows of what they might have been, dark blemishes that stain the night. For me, they're a haunting reminder of all the dark nights I spent alone in the desert with only the stars to keep me company.

I'm lucky to be here. The girls we picked up are lucky to be here. Gemma's fucking lucky, and she'll show me gratitude before long.

I follow the guiding light of a single streetlamp illuminating the intersection of the cul-de-sac and the cross street up ahead. We only use streetlamps in a few places. A little bit of light helps us move safely through the Gates at night, but we also don't want to attract too much attention from outsiders—not that I'm particularly worried about a barrier breech, but it's always a possibility.

I reach the holding house near the end of the street and make my way up the driveway, turn to follow the walkway to the front door. I hear voices from within as I step onto the portico landing, and though the curtains are drawn over the large window to my right, the living room lights cast a glow from behind them.

I have my own key, so I let myself in and lock the door behind me. A few steps ahead, the entryway wall opens around a corner to reveal the living room on my right. Hayes sits in a brown leather armchair that's angled in my direction. His elbows are on his knees as he leans forward, watching the girl sitting across from him on the matching sofa.

"… and that's fair," Hayes says, mid-conversation, "but it still doesn't answer the question. Why did you do it?"

I glance at the girl. She's got one foot tucked beneath her as she leans an elbow on the armrest. She's still giving him eye contact, though she anxiously picks at her fingernails.

Hayes glances in my direction, but quickly returns his attention to her—exactly as he should in the middle of questioning. Maybe I'll tell him later that I've noticed he's doing better, but not right now. It's clear the girl is anxious as fuck, and I don't want to distract him. He needs to watch her carefully to get a good sense of whether she's lying. I rely on these men to help me determine whether someone's right or wrong for our community.

"Zuri?" I ask.

The girl on the couch swivels her head at the sound of my voice.

"With the girl," Hayes says quickly. "Last room on the left."

I give the girl a severe look. "Don't lie to him. He'll know. Then you'll have to answer to me."

Her eyes widen as she bobs her head.

Hayes snaps his fingers in front of her. "Hey, answer the question. Why did you do it?"

She turns her eyes back to Hayes and starts talking. Her speech is quiet and slow, but she's talking.

At least we got one obedient girl today...

I head past the living room and turn down the hall. On my right, there's a bedroom with the door cracked open, and voices filter out from within.

"I can take a shower? Seriously?" The girl inside the room lets out a laugh. "I don't even know what to say. Here I thought I'd be fighting to survive the night. Do you know how much I've dreaded this day? I can't believe it..." A pause. "No. I really don't believe it. Shit. Hot guys don't just show up in the middle of the desert and take women for no reason. Fuck!" Panic rises in her tone. "What do you want from us? What do you think you're gonna get from me?"

"First of all, thank you," I hear Santi reply. "I *am* hot, and I appreciate the recognition. But let me be clear that, personally, I want nothing from you. Don't take that the wrong way; there are plenty of Vultures who'd be happy to fuck you, but I'm just not one of them. I have eyes for one woman and one woman only. And a quick piece of advice? Don't let my girl Maizie hear you say I'm hot, she'll fuck you up. I mean it. No disrespect to you, but she will knock your fucking teeth out."

"What the fuck?"

Amusement tugs at the corner of my mouth as I continue past. We all know Santi's dutifully attached to Maizie, but there's something about him that new girls always seem to be drawn to. I guess he's a handsome guy—black hair, dark eyes, bronze skin—though I think it's more to do with his charm. He flirts without realizing he's flirting, and for obvious reasons, that's a big problem with Maizie. Thankfully, it's a manageable problem, but part of that management involves Santi stopping it before it starts.

I continue down the hall to the last door on the left. It's closed, but I can hear Tucker on the other side.

"I didn't hurt her, right?" He sounds distressed. "I swear, I was really gentle about it—"

What the fuck did he do?

I whip open the door and charge inside. "Tell me what you—"

"It's okay, Tuck. Really. You did great." I spot Zuri sitting on the bed, one knee tucked beneath her, the other leg dangling off the side.

The unconscious girl we picked up from the two wandering lawless is prone on the bed beside her, laid flat on her back. Zuri glances at me before lifting the girl's arm to check her pulse.

"Go wash your hands," she tells Tucker. "Then, don't touch anything. I might need your help again and we don't want to risk infection."

Tucker's eyes anxiously dart between us before he nods, turns, then disappears into the attached bathroom.

I approach Zuri. "Did he do something to the girl?"

Her hair is growing out—the styled ringlet curls of her short Afro hairstyle bounce with the movement as she shakes her head. "No, he didn't do anything other than help me roll her over. He's fine, Oz. He's a good helper."

"Good." I let out a breath. "That's good."

"But you're gonna have to go."

"Why? What did I do?"

"Your vibe stresses him out. I knew the second you came in the house because that's exactly when his anxiety kicked in."

"I don't know what the fuck I did to make him so anxious."

She admonishes me with a look. "You acted like yourself."

"I don't make *you* anxious."

"This whole situation is making me anxious right now. She's not in good shape, Oz."

"What do you need?"

"A hospital. A lab. An OR. A surgical team—"

"If I could give you all that, you know I would. Tell me something you need that I can actually get."

Zuri gently lays the girl's limp arm on the bed as her dark brown eyes scan her body. "Then I guess the only thing you can give me is time." She sighs before she looks at me. "I don't know if she's going to make it."

"What?" Tucker appears in the room, holding up his freshly washed hands like a surgeon who's just scrubbed in. "Is she gonna die?"

"I don't know, Tuck," Zuri tells him. "I'm going to try my best not to let that happen, but I really need your help. You're going to stay and help me, right?"

His eyes are wide, filled with fear as he stares at the girl. "If she dies, it's not my fault, right?" He pauses, then his head turns, and he looks at me. "I didn't… I'm not the one who hurt her."

I start moving toward him as he stammers through fear.

"She's my responsibility. If she dies, is it my fault?"

"Tucker, listen to me—"

"And then what happens to me? What do you do to me then?"

I place my hands on his shoulders and dip down a bit to level our eyes. I lean in to make sure he has nowhere else to look but at me. "Did you hurt her? Are you the one who did this to her?"

He shakes his head. "No, but I'm responsible—"

I grip the back of his head with one hand to make him stop. "Tucker, yes or no. Are you the one who caused her injuries?"

"No..."

"So, is it your fault if she dies from those injuries?"

He doesn't respond, just blinks at me with glistening eyes that tug at a heartstring.

Yeah, okay, I get it.

Something about me makes him too anxious to think straight.

I lay it out clearly for him, speaking slowly. "If she dies from injuries that someone else caused, that is not your fault. Yes, you are responsible for her in the holding house, and no, she's not okay right now. But that's not because of *you*."

I give a quick squeeze to the back of his neck as reassurance, then let go and turn to Zuri. "If time is what you need, then that's what you've got. I'll let Salem know you won't be at Glimmer this week."

She nods. "Okay."

"And I'll have Brady come back to help you out."

"I won't turn down the extra hands, but honestly, Whitney's help would be even better. She has a nursing background, and she seems to have an interest in helping more."

"Fine. Done. She'll be off for the week, too."

"And Tuck's gonna stay to help out, too." She looks at him. "Right, Tuck? I really need your help."

Tucker starts to open his mouth, but I speak first.

"Yeah, Tuck's gonna stay. He's responsible for her in this house."

"You swear you're not gonna kill me if she doesn't make it?"

"Not unless she dies because *you* do something stupid, like wrap your hands around her throat and choke her to death. Just do your best, Tuck. Don't touch the girl unless Zuri tells you to, and there won't be a problem. Got it?"

"Okay." He nods slowly. "Yeah, okay."

"Where's your kit?" I ask Zuri.

She tilts her head. "Over there, on the dresser. How's the girl at your house?"

"Small cut." I spot Zuri's med kit on the dresser beside the door. "I'll clean it myself."

"Does she need stitches?"

"I don't know." I open the kit and take out some alcohol pads, sterile gauze, and bandages. "I don't think so. I'll bring her over tonight if it looks concerning, otherwise, it can wait until morning."

"Fine, just clean it well. Infections are no joke. We have a few rounds of antibiotics left, but this girl is gonna need some, and I don't know when we'll get more."

I close the lid on the kit and turn to face her. "Use what you need. Let me and Salem worry about getting more."

"They're hard to get."

"I'm aware. Don't worry about it." I wave the supplies at her. "I've got what I need, and I promise I'll be thorough."

She thanks me, and I move quickly to the empty bedroom next door—the room Gemma should be in now. I pull some random clothes from the drawer to bring back to her. I make a brief stop in the kitchen to grab a bottle of water and some pre-packaged food items for Gemma.

Then, on the way out, I pull Hayes from questioning the girl on the sofa. I relay instructions so he can ensure Zuri has her helping hands and anything else she may need.

And then I hurry back to my house.

I go inside, lock the door, then pick up Gemma's backpack from the entryway floor. As I slowly ascend the staircase, I wonder again why I'm doing this, why I'm keeping Gemma here in my house when it's not serving anyone. I should right this wrong by taking her back to that room in the holding house. I could still stay with her; I'd still be responsible for her. And Zuri would be right there to check her cut without leaving the other girl's side.

That would be the *right* thing to do...

That's what I *should* do.

But as I approach the bedroom door—which Angel still guards obediently—my veins begin to throb with the heavy darkness that drags me in.

The pounding rhythm says she's mine. It tells me to keep her for myself. I know I can't keep her here forever, but a part of me wants to... That desperate, aching part of me *needs* to.

I search my mind for justifications to keep her, grasp at untenable thoughts, and pull at threads of weak rationale. Eventually, I settle on following the same kind of compulsive stupidity I'd expect my Vultures to weed out through vetting.

I convince myself that continuing this way is fine. After all, it'll only be for a few days of vetting before Gemma's sent to Eden.

I can manage her for a few days.

I can hide the darkness until she's gone.

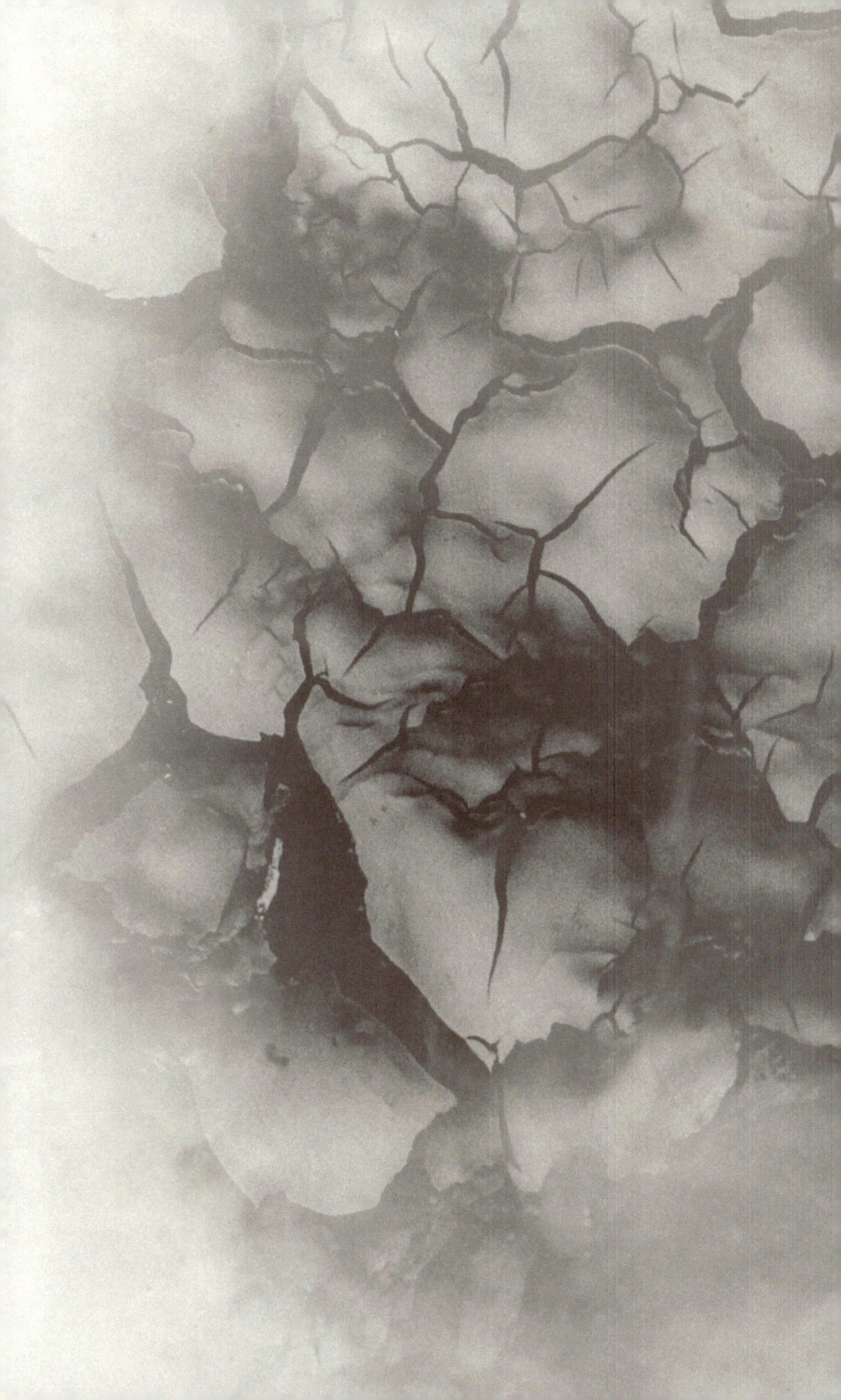

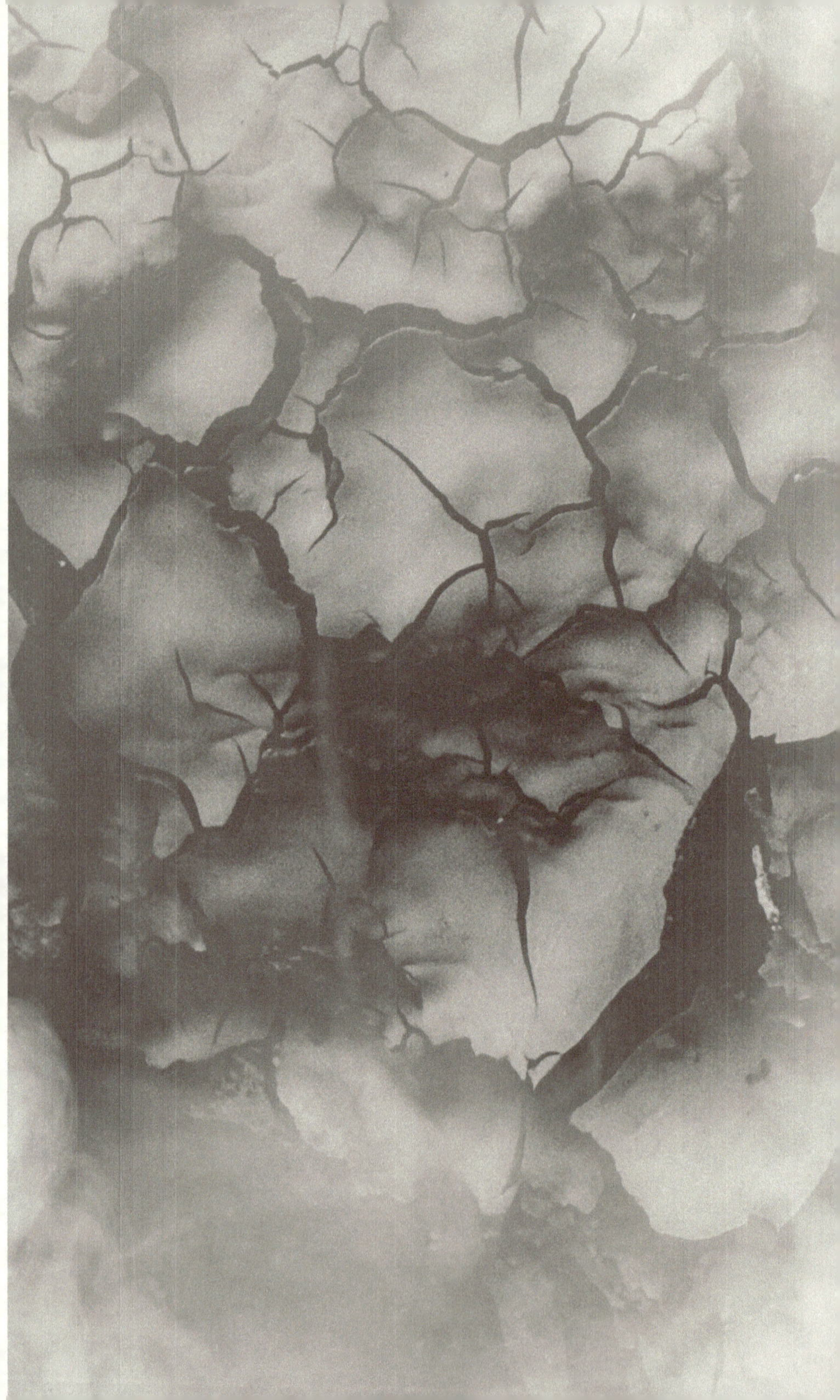

CHAPTER FOURTEEN
Siren Song

Oz

I'M NOT SURE what I expected to find behind the bedroom door, but I'm surprised to find Gemma exactly where I left her, sitting on the edge of my bed. Her gaze sweeps my face as I step into the bright room, then lowers to take stock of the items I brought with me.

I set everything on the dresser beside me to free my hands, then mutter a quick command for Angel to stay outside the room before closing the door. I leave the clothes, food, medical supplies, and her tan backpack from Eviction where I set them and pick up the plastic water bottle. I twist off the lid as I walk over, holding it out for her to take.

She throws me a suspicious look. "Did you put something in that?"

"Does it matter if I did? You need water. Drink."

Fuck, she looks tired.

She seems to have come back from wherever she mentally retreated, though she looks like she'd pass out if I gave her a little nudge to make her fall back on the bed.

I'm half-tempted to try it.

"Take it, pink. I'm not trying to drug you. I just don't want you to die of dehydration on my bed."

Her pretty eyes are on the bottle in my hand. She wants it.

I have half a mind to grab her by the chin, pry her lips open with my fingers, and force the water down her throat myself. But I need to have some self-control if I want her to trust me.

Like the self-control I had throwing her around on the stairs...

I wait, and eventually, she reaches out to take it. She holds it in front of her, looking down at it distrustfully.

"Earlier, you said something about taking a shower. So, you have running water?"

"Yeah."

She stands, walks across the bedroom, and enters the attached bathroom. I'm confused for a moment, but then I hear the crackle of the plastic water bottle being squeezed, and the *glug, glug, glug* of water being dumped out.

I move to stand in the doorway between my bedroom and the bathroom, crossing my arms and leaning against the doorframe to watch her. When the bottle is empty, she turns on the faucet, watches the water sputter for a few seconds until the flow smooths out and steadies, and then she refills the bottle from the stream.

I look at her reflection in the mirror behind the sink, watching as she turns off the faucet and raises her chin. She lifts the bottle to her lips, tilts it up, and drinks. The reflection of her stare meets the reflection of mine. The heat behind her eyes burns with defiance for her minor act of rebellion, and she holds me there for seconds as she sips.

But then, the relief of sated thirst washes over her, and her eyes fall shut. I watch the way her throat works as she swallows each satisfying drink. She quickly downs half the bottle before lowering it, then lets out a pleased sigh.

Goddamn, this woman is dangerous for me.

I haven't had such a strong desire to fuck a particular woman in almost a decade. Of course, I've wanted to fuck women in general, but this need to fuck one in particular is throwing me off. I'm intensely physically attracted to her—and that's really something, considering the fact that she's probably the least attractive today than she'll ever be again.

The orange jumpsuit doesn't exactly suit her, and though she was likely required to shower at the Transition Center, that may as well have been a lifetime ago—she's been out sweating her ass off in the desert all day. A light dusting of desert sand and dried blood coats her skin, and her pretty pink hair is twisted and tangled in knots from all our tumbling and fighting.

And I still find her breathtakingly stunning.

I'll probably have a heart attack once Salem cleans her up.

But there's also this other kind of attraction—something deeper than the physical. There's a magnetic draw to engage with her, an insistent obsession for the way she hates me. I would never tolerate the way she speaks to me from anyone else, so I don't know why I like it when it comes from her. The way I'm enjoying the power struggle is a total mind-fuck.

"For the record, I didn't put anything in your water."

"I wasn't willing to take that chance."

"So, should I get rid of the food I brought you, too? I don't want you tossing that shit in my bathroom sink."

There's a slight pause before she asks, "What do you have?"

"Turn around."

Something flickers through her expression, not exactly a flinch, but some brief twinge of pain as she acknowledges my command.

Did someone she know before give her commands?

Did they tell her to turn around?

Did they hurt her once she did?

She lifts the bottle to her lips, takes her sweet time swigging down another long drink. Once she's nearly emptied the bottle, she places it on the countertop and turns to face me with a relenting sigh. "So, this is where it starts… You command and I obey in exchange for food? I'm honestly too tired to play these games. Just tell me what you expect me to do so I can eat."

I push off the doorframe and move in front of her, slowly filling the space between us. She backs up as I close in, but there's nowhere for her to retreat. Her ass collides with the edge of the counter behind her, and I take advantage of her position to cage her in. I stretch my arms around her, placing both palms flat on either side of the countertop.

I wasn't gonna make her do anything for the food, but if she's gonna insist on me being another villain in her story, then I'm gonna have a little fun letting her think she's right.

She might not be wrong...

"What would you be willing to do for me, Gemma?" I tilt my head and watch her carefully. "How badly do you wanna eat tonight?"

Her gaze briefly drops to my lips before she gives me her eyes, showing me all the intensity she can muster despite her exhaustion.

With a steady, quiet voice, she says, "I can go without."

"Not forever."

"Long enough to get away from you."

"You think denying yourself food is gonna keep you strong enough to escape me?"

She lets a vicious, adorable smile tug at the corners of her lips. "I'll be stronger than you when you're dead."

"No, you won't, baby..." I lean close and her hands shoot up between us. Her palms brace against my chest, though she doesn't push me back. With my cheek pressed to hers and my lips brushing the shell of her ear, I whisper a promise—one I have no business making, "When I die, I'm taking you with me."

I expect her to shove me or scream at me, so I grip her hips with both hands, hoisting her up to sit on the counter before she can react. I press in close and stand between her knees so she can't escape me.

Surprisingly, her fingers twist, bunching the fabric of my shirt as she uses it to pull herself up against me. Her spine stretches as she lifts her chin over my shoulder, bringing her lips to my ear to speak, just as I did to her.

"I'm already a ghost," she whispers. "You can't kill someone who's already dead."

She leans back, pauses just long enough to show me how easily I inspire her tears; a glossy sheen has appeared over her hazel eyes, and it makes the bronze hues glimmer like gold under the sun's glow. Her hands glide down my chest. Her fingertips brush lightly, though they burn like fire, trailing down through the trenches of carnal lust already etched into my soul.

And then she relents.

She slumps as her hands fall away. She lets her head drop back against the mirror. Her palms rest on the counter, one beside each hip, and she turns her eyes away from me, gazing off at nothing.

She's entirely at my mercy. I could do anything I want to her. I feel my self-control slipping, falling away to make room for depraved urges that insist on thoughtless action. I dig my fingers into her hips, drag her ass to the edge, and push my cock against her pussy. My body shudders at the mistaken perception that relief is coming for the throbbing ache in my cock.

Relief isn't coming.

I'm not fucking her.

I can't... not like this.

In a vain attempt, I take a deep breath to steel my resolve, then try to get her talking.

"So, they call you the Siren." My eyes wander, roving across her face. "I have to assume that's a reference to mermaid lore. Sirens would sing to lure sailors to their death, right? The men you killed… Did you sing them a song before you ended their lives?"

She's dead in the eyes—resigned. But she hasn't fully retreated like before. I can still sense her fighting spirit there, only shielded behind a wall of glass.

She doesn't speak, but slowly grants me a subtle nod.

"What song did you sing?"

Muted amusement rolls through her features. "I'll sing it to you one day, I promise." She holds my stare for a beat, and then she looks away. "Just do it, okay? Use me if that's what you want. I just can't…" She sighs, and her heavy eyelids fall shut. "I don't have the fucking energy to fight you anymore tonight."

"Is that what you want, Gemma?" I drag my palms down her thighs before running them back up again, sliding them over her hips and reaching around to grip her ass. "You wanna be used?"

My cock thickens, straining against its denim cage.

My self-control is fading quickly. The darkness I've been hiding within me for so long is rising to the surface, and it begs me to give in.

It tells me to forget all the rules.

It tells me I could use her if I wanted to.

It tells me I could fuck her right here, right now.

It tells me I could do whatever the fuck I wanna do to her. I could be the vicious annihilator the judge and jury claimed me to be. I could live the lawless life they sentenced me to lead.

Fuck.

My stomach twists, wrings out knots of lust that send a flood of need rushing straight through my cock. One hand remains on her ass while the other sinks into her hair, my fingers catching in tangled strands as they reach around to the back of her head. I cradle her skull in my palm as I pull her away from the mirror, drawing her close against my chest.

I twist her knotted hair, tightening my grip around a dense section, and jerk her head sideways. She lets out a whimper, but she doesn't cry out, she doesn't fight the pull. She just lets me do it. I search her face for a few seconds, but all she gives me are quiet tears, and even those seem to be drying up.

Come on, cherry blossom... Give me something.

I hold her in place by her hair and bend down to run my tongue along the tender flesh just beneath her jawline. I start beneath her chin, and lick all the way up, sweeping behind her ear until my tongue reaches her hairline. I taste her skin, her sweat, the iron-tang of dried blood.

Fuck, her filth tastes good.

There's a bloodthirsty beast inside me, and he howls at her raw taste. It makes me move. It has me grinding my cock against her softness. It wants me to let go and say my final goodbye to my self-control.

I can't lose control... not now.

I'll lose everything I've built.

Stop.

Step back.

I fight for power over this pure, carnal lust. Somehow, I manage to drag my hips back, but another shudder of desperate need ripples through me. I thrust, slamming my dick so hard between her legs that it's nearly painful. A strangled groan escapes her, though she's still limp in my hold, lifeless and disengaged. Her lackluster response only tempts me to be rough with her.

I trail down the beautiful slope of her neck, kissing and nipping at her flesh as I follow the curve toward her shoulder. She tenses at my scraping teeth, and the subtle protest is fuel to the fire. It has me groaning, pressing hard, kneading her flesh with grinding thumps.

"Goddamn, you feel so good, baby."

I get nothing in response.

I lift away from her neck, shift my grip in her hair, and yank it straight back to aim her chin at the ceiling.

I'm fucking panting.

I don't remember the last time I was this stupidly desperate.

"Tell me to stop," I plead.

She doesn't speak. She just looks at me, blinking away the remaining tears from her unfocused eyes as my hips work.

Shit. Have I lost her again?

"Tell me to fucking stop, Gemma."

"What would be the point?" Her voice is low-pitched and flat, but there's enough movement in her expression to tell me she's still present.

If she's mentally present, then she's capable of telling me to stop if that's what she wants… And if she tells me to stop, I'll stop.

Fucking liar.

A baneful laugh crawls out of me from the darkness within, rumbling across her skin as I dip to press a kiss to her throat. My hand falls from her hair to wrap around her back, and I hug her to my chest. I burrow my fingers into her ass with the other hand and lift her off the counter. Her thighs instinctively squeeze around my hips, which helps me move her, though I only make it through the doorway into the bedroom before desperation begs me to get her on her back.

I fall to my knees, drop her on the carpet, and climb over her.

The rough motion seems to have woken her up a bit. She tries to slip backward and get out from beneath me, but I grab her wrists, slam her arms to the carpet above her head, and pin her body beneath the weight of mine. Her legs are spread on either side of me, and she moves them with slow kicks, almost lethargically testing her range of motion. There isn't much. She can bend her knees and draw them back or stretch them out straight, but my insistent hips hold hers in place.

She starts to shake her head, but the beast doesn't want her protests. I shift to hold her wrists in my left hand, bringing my right hand to her throat and squeeze.

Gemma stills.

Her eyes widen, but only just a little before she forces her eyelids to stop mid-rise, as though she's attempting to hide her fear. I don't actually want her to fear me in this way, but my intolerable appetite for sparring with her takes a bite of her unease, and it finds that satisfying enough.

My hips grind, pulsing against her.

"Are you gonna tell me to stop now, *professor?*"

Something inside her snaps at the nickname—I feel it crack and ripple like an earthquake between our bodies.

She punches me in the gut with a single syllable. "*Don't.*" The word is scolding, intense, scorching me with the heat of a thousand suns.

The pain of that alone should stop me...

It doesn't.

"I couldn't hear you." I slip my right hand up her throat and over her chin to cover her mouth. "Say it louder." I feel a grin pull at my cheeks, though I didn't call for it to appear.

She comes to life beneath my hand. Her face scrunches in anger as she thrashes. She tries to scream, but her sounds are muffled as I stretch my palm wide across her face. I dig my fingers into her cheeks and press down, holding her head in place so she can't turn away from me.

And with my hand over her face, I see how flawlessly we fit.

I turn my palm and lift it higher, aligning the tattooed image of a partial skull on the back of my hand with her face. Two blacked out voids inked across the knuckle of my index finger represent the vacant nasal cavities of the skull which lays perfectly over the tip of her nose.

My index finger rests over the bridge of her nose, aimed straight up, and resting on the center of her forehead. I slide my other three fingers down toward her cheek, creating a gap between the middle and index finger, framing her eye between them.

With my palm stretched wide, and my thumb pressed to the opposite cheek, the tattooed grin of a skeleton spreads beautifully over her lips.

I can feel her thrashing beneath me.

I can hear her whimper and moan under my grip.

I can see fire in her eyes, the anger returning with such ease, despite the way she thought it left her.

And the way her pretty pink hair creates a halo of femininity to frame the masculine lines and edgy style of the black-ink tattoo... It stops my heart.

I'm mesmerized by the image.

Her hands grip my forearm, and she's pulling hard, but I'm not ready to look away yet. I press harder, though I can sense her gasping, tugging my arm, flinging desperately as she gasps for breath. It's not my intention to take her breath away, but I'm captivated by the wild beauty of the woman beneath my palm.

My mind fuses her skin with the image etched in mine, making her appear as though she's half dead and half alive.

But I don't just see it... I *feel* it.

Her feral pink soul is hovering between life and death, and I think that was true before I found her... She's hovering between life and death now as she fights for breath beneath my palm.

I blink.

Gemma disappears, and I see Emaline lying beneath me.

She's half dead, too.

She's looking up at me and smiling, though the grin is her own—not placed there by a smiling skull drawn on my hand.

There's a halo around her head, but it isn't pink.

It's red, and it's ever-growing.

It's blood, and she's dying.

She's dying.

Emaline is still. Her eyelashes flutter as she fights her heavy lids.

They flutter shut over dark eyes, and then...

They open wide to hazel shades of swirling green and bronze.

Fuck, she can't breathe.

I tear my hand away from Gemma's face and climb off her, scrambling to move away as she gasps for air, struggling to take a deep enough breath to satisfy her lungs.

I sit with my back to the wall, place my elbows on my bent knees, and drop my head into my hands. I watch her from beneath my lashes as she rolls to her side. Panting, she curls into the fetal position.

Minutes pass while she lies still.

Her breathing gradually slows to a normal cadence.

She doesn't move, she doesn't look at me, she doesn't speak.

Nothing happens until, softly, she begins to sing.

I lift my head and let my hands drop between my knees. At first, she sings so quietly, I can hardly understand the words, and there's nothing immediately familiar about the tune. I sit still, and I watch as she spellbinds me with her song. I know she's not singing for me, but I'm compelled to listen all the same.

She reaches the chorus, and I recognize it now...

Angel of the Morning by Juice Newton.

It's interesting because I think that's the same song the man with the Reborn was whistling at the Crevice—I remember how it caught her attention.

It must be her Siren song.

She cycles through every emotion as she sings the rest. Tears fill her eyes, run down her cheeks, and a sob cracks her voice during the refrain. Then emptiness follows, making the melody hollow, void of emotion. Next, she's struck by humor, and an oddly placed laugh breaks through her words. The rest is sung sorrowfully, mournfully, her sadness reframing the lyrics as a recollection of haunting memories.

And then, silence falls

It's deafening.

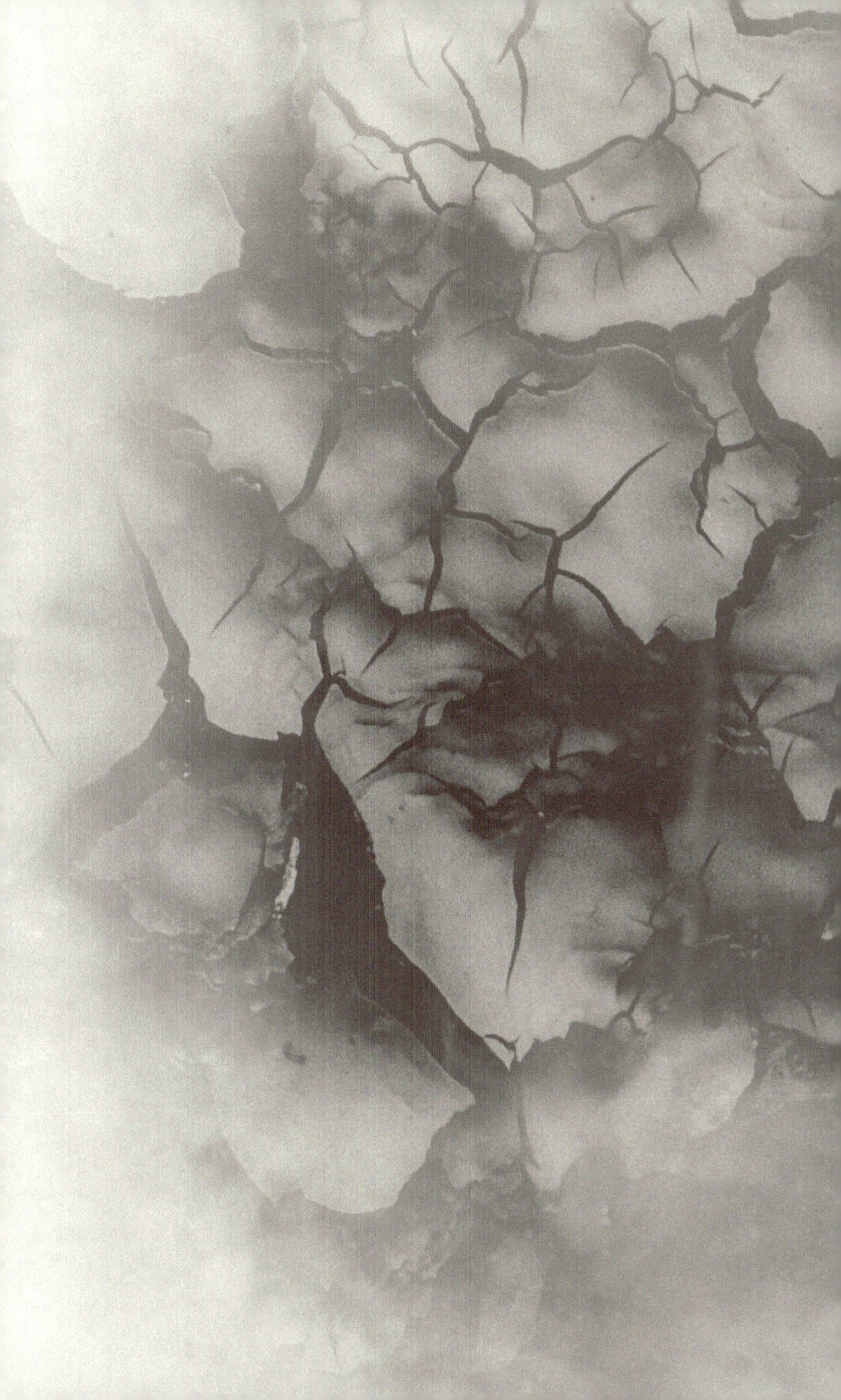

CHAPTER FIFTEEN
Shiver

Gemma

HE WAS ON top of me, suffocating me, and all I could hear was the song, the one I thought I'd conquered, the melody I thought I'd reclaimed in the name of vengeance.

I was wrong.

I haven't mastered the song at all; I haven't overcome its power. It still dominates me, still holds my mind captive, puts me back in a cage only Seb can open.

The melody started to play in my mind the moment he covered my face with his palm, and it started to loop again when he finally let me breathe.

I had to sing it out loud.

If I'd let the song whisper quietly in the mental darkness, it would have looped forever. It would've stolen my breath again and again as it played. It would've held me prisoner in the past, dooming me to relive that horrid, breathless night with the plastic covering my face—

No, Gem...

"No. Don't go back there..."

Did I say that out loud?

My head turns with my eyes sweeping skyward, searching for stars I know I won't see on the white ceiling. I slowly roll to my back, staring up at the blank white canvas above me. I imagine painting it black, splashing it with flecks of silver-white light, and watching them fall into their places like stars in the night sky.

Rastaban.

Eltanin...

"Deneb. Altair. Vega."

Naming the stars gives me the illusion of peace, lulling me into a trance-like calm.

I'm neither here nor there, present or past, connected or disconnected. I simply exist in this realm of space, floating among the stars, waiting for my time to die.

Heavy hands slip beneath me, raise me higher, closer to the stars.

"Take me to Tabby's Star," I tell the hands guiding me through space. "I wanna see for myself what keeps dimming her light."

"Did I break you, baby?" His voice floats along with me. "Goddamn. I didn't mean to break you like this."

I wonder if he tacks on the words, "Not yet," in his mind.

"Liar," I whisper at the vision of stars.

An abrupt change in the light above me wipes away the illusionary image of peace—my imaginary night sky is blown away by the harsh lighting in the bathroom, and I soon find myself back where we started. He plops me down on the counter, rushes back to the bedroom, and returns seconds later. His hands are full, but he empties them quickly, placing some items I don't bother to spare a glance at on the opposite end of the counter.

I hear something rip, then his fingers gently tap beneath my chin before he tilts my head back. Something cold and wet touches my skin, some soaked paper-like cloth he rubs over my cut in light, diligent circles while—

"Fuck!" I draw back sharply at the fire suddenly searing my flesh, the sting of alcohol sparking a tiny blaze that burns through the small slash.

"I know it hurts, baby, but you can take it."

I lean my head back against the mirror and shut my eyes. I know that getting an infection would be so much more painful than this temporary burn—painful and potentially life-ending. The risks are so much greater out here in the Territory... in *Lawless Land...*

"Why do you call it Lawless Land?" I ask quietly as he swipes the alcohol pad across the cut again. I hiss and flinch at the fresh sting.

"Because that's what we all call it."

A cool breeze flows over the burn.

I open my eyes to find his head lowered in front of me, lips puckered, blowing air over the cut to soothe my pain. His head moves as he blows, tracing the line twice before pausing to inspect the area with scrutinizing eyes.

"The country that banished us can call this place whatever the fuck they want beyond the borders," he says, then lifts his eyes to meet mine, "but this world is ours, so we claim it with our own name." He steps back. "Stand up."

I forget to protest, hopping off the counter at his request and landing on my feet. I'm too tired to think beyond the way he's triggered me, the way he's flipped the switch on every instinctual mechanism my trauma developed to protect me.

I flinch as he reaches forward to unfasten the buttons of my hideous orange jumpsuit. My hands rise with the urge to smack his hands away, but instead, my palms land on his forearms. "What are you doing?"

"I'm helping you undress so you can take a shower."

"I can do that myself."

"Can you?"

"I…" I pause because I actually need a moment to decide whether I *can*, whether my hands are too unsteady, or my mind is too foggy to remember what I'm doing halfway through. "I don't know."

He unloops the first button, then looks up at me from beneath his lashes. "Then just stand still and let me do it."

"Are you ever gonna tell me your name?"

"If you'd given a bit more attention to the details when you read that note you found in the entryway, you would already know my name by now."

I feel my cheeks flush. I almost feel embarrassed for not realizing right away that the note was referring to a dog and not a human woman. He probably thinks I'm fucking stupid. I don't know why it bothers me to assume he thinks that; I don't give a fuck what he thinks of me.

At least... I know I *shouldn't* give a fuck about what he thinks of me.

This has always been an issue for me as a woman in science. Every man I ever met in the field has demonstrated how stupid they initially thought I must be, though I proved every single one of them wrong, outperforming them all on every measure. But the initial assumptions always stuck with me, always bothered me. It disgusts me that so many men assumed I must be dense, all because I'm a decent-looking girl who likes to dress cute and do her hair and make-up...

"I was top of my doctoral class in astrophysics at Yale, for fuck's sake."

Goddamnit. I didn't mean to say that out loud!

He pauses, lifts his head, and stills his hands. "I'm not intimidated by smart women. And I already knew that. Your man with the Reborn said as much."

He works the button that's fastened right between my tits. His knuckles graze the sides of my breasts, and I accidentally gasp. He smirks, but he doesn't say a word.

"He's not *my man*. And I wasn't exactly reading for the details when I saw that note."

He chuckles. "No, shit." There's a long pause as he moves to the next button. "My name is Oz, by the way."

"Oz," I repeat. "As in, *The Wizard of...*?"

"As in Ozlo. Ozlo Kincaid."

"Ozlo Kincaid." I commit it to memory.

He doesn't speak again until he's unfastened all the buttons. His hands skim my shoulders to push off the short sleeves of the jumpsuit. I let it slip down my arms, and the ugly thing drops right to the ground, pooling at my feet.

"Step out."

I feel exposed, entirely vulnerable.

My pulse quickens, making blood race through my veins.

I step out, and he kicks the jumpsuit away. My arms naturally rise, crossing to cover my chest. All my naughty bits are still covered by the plain white bra and matching panties, but I still feel bare, accessible, on exhibit for this vicious man.

His eyes wander over me. "Do you need me to help you remove the rest?"

I assume that's a thinly veiled demand for me to remove the bra and panties. I shake my head. It takes all the strength I have, but somehow, I manage to pull my arms away from my chest. I start to bring them behind me so I can unhook my bra, but then his hands shoot forward, grip me just above my elbows, and stop me. He tugs my arms forward and pins them to my sides.

"Do you need help in the shower?"

I lift my head and meet his stare. "Are you *asking* me?"

His forehead wrinkles. "I don't know what that means. Do you need help taking a shower right now? Yes or no."

I let out a heavy breath, making room for the quick draw of another as anxiety stutters the rhythm of my lungs. "I don't— How do you want me to answer that?"

I don't know if he wants me to say yes or no. Maybe he needs me to say yes so he can feel like I gave him permission to get in with me. Maybe he wants me to say no so he can force himself on me, given the way he seems to enjoy fighting me so fucking much. I don't know which answer is gonna lead to hurt; I don't know which one will ease my future suffering.

The wrinkles creasing his brow slowly disappear as he watches me, then he lets go of one of my arms to cup my cheek, brushing his thumb across my skin. "Someone really fucked you up, bubblegum. Who was it? Was it the man you knew with the Reborn? What did he do to you?"

I don't wanna talk about it.

I subtly shake my head against his palm.

He brings the other hand to my opposite cheek, firmly but softly gripping my face, and dips to level our eyes. "I won't lie to you, baby. I'm not gonna stand here and tell you I'm a good man. You already know what I am. We've all been banished for the same reason."

I swallow hard at that reminder...

He's a convicted Class A violent felon—the same as me.

What the fuck did he do?

Just how dangerous is this man?

"I'm not gonna tell you I'll never put my hands on you, because we both know I will. I can't even tell you I won't hurt you." He widens his stance, and his body shifts closer. "I know it, Gemma—I feel it deep in my *gut* that you want the kind of pain I can give you. So, I *know* I'm gonna hurt you. I *know* I'm gonna cut you, make you bleed, taste you, fuck you, make you come. I'll never promise you that I won't, but I will promise you this… Unless you make it necessary, I won't do anything until you're begging me to do it."

His lips brush the apple of my cheek, just beneath my eye, then he peppers deceptively soft kisses across my face. "And one day, pink… you *will* beg me for all of it."

Though his words make me shiver, there's a reverent warmth spreading from each point his lips touch.

I hate the shiver.

But I want more of that warmth. It heats my soul in a way I've never felt before, in a way I never expected.

You feel nothing, Gem.

You're exhausted, delirious.

Oz pulls away from me, then disappears.

The bathroom door closes behind him, and I'm left all alone.

My fingers press softly to my cheek, and I think I still feel some of his warmth linger on my skin. I curl my fingers into my hand, hold the warmth in my fist—it's something to cling to in the dark while his violent coldness makes me shiver.

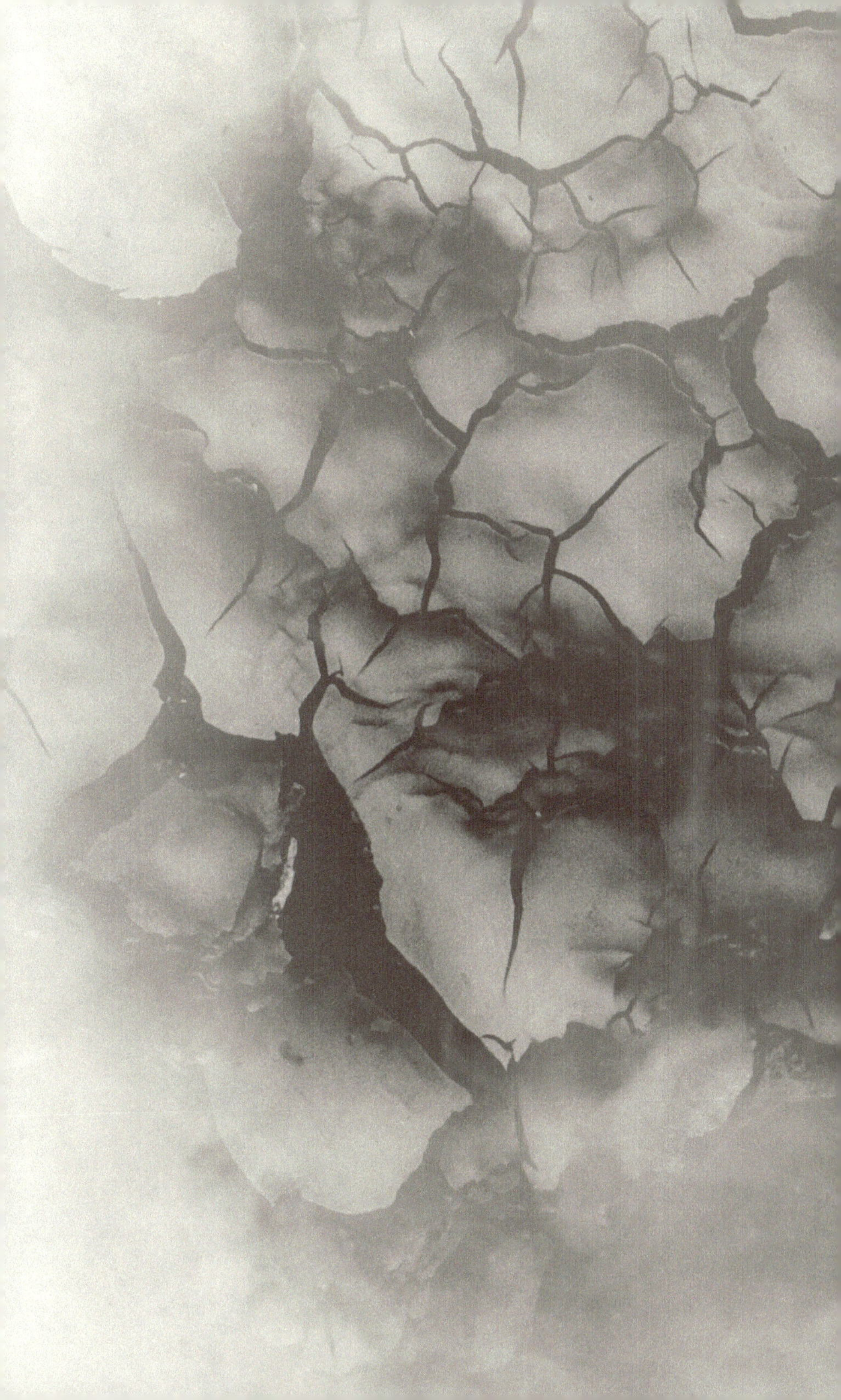

CHAPTER SIXTEEN
The Point of No Return

Oz

I'M NOT A liar, and I never make promises I can't keep.

Except for the fact that I am, and I just did.

Fuck.

I don't know what it is about this girl that has me so fucked in the head that I can't think straight. When I'm near enough to touch her, I forget there's anything else worth thinking about. That's why I left her alone in the bathroom. I meant to leave, put some distance between us while I get my mind right, but instead, I pace the bedroom. I'm so fucking reeled in, and she doesn't even know how deep her hook has punctured me.

I could stop doing this, send her away and make her someone else's problem until I've cooled off completely. But she's not a problem I want to offload—the fact that I'm not willing to offload her *is* the problem.

I don't wanna stop this.

I don't wanna be the good guy right now.

I don't wanna be the man who tries to make something decent out of his life sentence in Lawless Land.

I don't wanna be the community guy, the one who has to hold his shit together just so everyone else doesn't fall apart.

I wanna lose control. I wanna forget that everything we have isn't riding on following the rules.

I hear the shower water turn on, and I stop.

I take a step toward the bathroom door when I hear the familiar sound of the glass shower door opening, then closing again.

I need this... I need this obsession.

I need this craving.

I need this rush of knowing I'm dangerous for her, knowing I might actually hurt her, which would destroy everything I've built.

I need *her.*

Fuck the rules.

I wanna be lawless.

I rip off my clothes in a hurry, strip naked, then burst through the bathroom door. Gemma's form is blurred through the frosted glass enclosure, but I can easily make out the way she twists around to face me. Her arms rise, crossing to cover her naked chest as I charge directly for the shower door. I jerk it open, and without preamble, I step inside. I almost expect her to scurry backward, to press her back into the corner, but she doesn't.

She doesn't even look surprised at my return.

She only stands still before me, her chin raised as she gazes up at me with a thousand questions in her eyes.

I take a step closer. "I'm not a liar. I've never been a liar, and I've always done everything in my power to make good on my promises." Another step. "But I will stand here before you and become a liar, Gemma. I'll become a man who breaks his promises if you don't *beg* me to make you come right now, because I can't wait another fucking day for you to beg me and actually mean it."

"Why me?" There's no emotion in her expression—no sorrow, no anger, no humor. She only looks at me with sincere confusion. "Of all the women you could have chosen today... why the fuck did it have to be *me*?"

Warm water pours from the waterfall showerhead above her, dripping down her back, heating the air around us into swirls of disorienting steam.

"Is there any answer that would be satisfying to you?"

Her eyes narrow, and she seems to honestly consider it. "No," she finally answers.

I close the distance between us, grab her wrists, tug them away from her chest, and force her to move backward until her spine hits the tile wall. I shove her arms against the wall on either side of her head, my hands easily wrapping around each of her wrists to pin her in place.

"Then tell me, baby, what's it gonna be?" I push my rock-solid cock against her lower stomach. "Are you gonna beg me to make you come or are you gonna make a liar out of me tonight?"

She slowly blinks, then shuts her eyes. They stay closed for so long that I almost think she's fallen asleep until she speaks. "If I beg for something I don't want," she finally opens her hazel eyes and stares right at me, "will it be any better for me? Will it be any better for *you?*"

I sense the spark of heat rising within her, and then I feel it through the intensity of her words. "Will it absolve you of the pain you cause me? Will it make you feel like more of a man and less like a lying sack of shit?"

Her tone takes on a mocking quality that makes me throb. "Oh, *please…* let me have your thick cock. I've never seen one that big. I *need* it." She thrusts her hips forward from the wall, sarcastically seeking my dick between her legs.

"I didn't ask you to beg for my cock." I slam my hips forward to push hers back and pin her ass to the wall with my weight. "I asked you to beg me to make you come."

I release one of her wrists to grip her chin, twisting her head sideways to force her cheek to the wall.

"Make me come." Her mocking tenor is still present, though it's dulled by the forced monotone quality and staccato rhythm of her voice. "Oh, please, oh, please. Make me come."

""Atta girl." I grin, then lean in closer so I can lick her cheek. "Keep begging, cupcake. I love it when you give me attitude. The day I finally fuck you so hard you can't breathe—let alone tell me to stop—will be *so* much more satisfying after a round of your false bravado."

"You're so fucking sick."

"You love it." I kiss her neck.

Her body thrashes against mine.

I twist her head, forcing her to look at me.

I watch the heat rise in her cheeks, tinting them pink.

She's so fucking aroused, and it doesn't really matter whether she's aroused with anger or lust because the reaction to each of them is the same: violence.

All sex is violence.

Whether it's consensual, sweet, forced, or rough, it doesn't make a difference. The end goal still requires vigorous, intentional friction and a hedonistic resolve. It's all about that moment on the brink of release, when you reach that peak you can't back down from, the point of no return... That's when the carnal urge to achieve the ultimate pleasure is so vicious that someone could stab the girl you're fucking and you'd still thrust inside her to spill your goddamn load while you watch her scream, suffer, bleed out, and die beneath you.

That desperation, that inherent need, that primal *violence*... It lives in all of us. It's the basis of humanity. It's what keeps us reproducing. We're all capable of doing terrible things for the promise of momentary freedom.

And she makes me that promise with every hateful word.

She parts her pretty pink lips to spew more hatred, but I swiftly silence her as I bend and kiss her hard, my mouth meeting hers with bruising force. I hold her in this kiss, keep her lip-locked through the perfect tension she'd like to pretend we don't share.

And when I finally slip my tongue inside to move along hers, a deep, guttural groan rumbles through me.

She makes a strange noise as her free hand smacks my chest—the inflection of the muffled sound makes me think she's trying to say, "Get off me!" through our twisted tongues.

I chuckle into her mouth, lean my body against hers, and rub my cock against her lower belly. The feel of her skin against my shaft is intoxicating. Moving it in small strokes along her dewy flesh offers a subtle reprieve from my violent desperation. The reprieve helps me slow the pace of my kiss, ease back on the pressure, and find a steady rhythm. It gives me a chance to grant her some softness—though it may be fleeting—and use my tongue as a tool for sensuality to gradually draw her into wanting me.

I kiss her like a man in love would kiss his woman.

Obviously, I'm not in love with a woman I just met today...

But I *am* obsessed.

And that's far more dangerous.

Regardless, this deep kiss with long, languid licks seems to be doing it for her—whether she wants it to be doing it for her or not.

Her shoulders lower as the tension holding them up begins to melt. A soft whimper vibrates between our mouths; it's a pleasure-filled sound that escapes her unwillingly. The hand she smacked my chest with gradually slips upward, follows the curve of my neck, and comes to rest with her fingers curved gently around the side.

Then—inexplicably, unbelievably—she kisses me back.

Her limp tongue comes to life, lifting to meet mine, and *fuck*, the way it feels could strike me dead, here and now.

And I'd die a happy fucking man.

I practically growl against the sweet little moan that comes out of her, and it's a struggle against every fiber of my being to restrain myself at this slow pace.

There's the part of me that wants her to fight me so hard that I have to force her to fuck me—the part that wants her to spew hatred and malice, scream and claw at me until I shove inside her and make her come, despite how hard she tries not to.

Yet, all the decent parts of me know doing that to her isn't right. Regardless of the rules in our community or the lawlessness that runs rampant all around us, this small, unbroken piece of my soul wants me to care for her. It wants me to protect her the way I'm supposed to, in the way Salem and I protect as many women and children as we can support with our resources.

But *fuck,* the taste of her, the feeling of her skin against mine, the sleepy, lazy, sexy way she laps her tongue over mine...

Goddamn, I need this woman.

I release her chin, lightly trail my hand down her chest, and cup her perfect little tit in the palm of my hand. Her spine arches, pressing it firmer into my grip. I give it a light squeeze, and I feel the muscles of her stomach tighten beneath my cock. I turn my hand so I can brush my thumb across the peak of her nipple.

She breaks the kiss with a gasp, and I brush it again, causing a shudder to ripple through her entire body. Her head falls back against the tile, her eyes drift shut, and her lips part as she drags in heated breaths.

I draw my head back enough to look down between our bodies. My thick, raised cock visibly throbs where it's pressed to her stomach. I watch her nipple thicken and rise as I continue to play with it. I start to move my hips, watch my dick slip up and down, as I rub the backside along her midsection.

"Oz," she whispers.

Fuck.

I nearly come right then.

I bring my hand down between her legs, trailing my fingertips up the inside of her thigh.

"Yes," she moans. "Oz, yes... *Please...*"

Yes? Please?

I watch her face with skepticism as I drag two fingers along her slit. Though touching her there is enough to have me dripping with pre-cum, it's barely a graze, and it isn't exactly a spot that would elicit the reaction she gives me. I see where this is going now. I understand the game she's playing.

I can play it, too, bubblegum.

Intentionally, I rub all over her outer bits, like a horny teenager who's never actually pleased a woman before. I don't slip inside her, and I don't go anywhere near her clit. I avoid touching anything that would actually make her feel good.

"So good, right?" I eye her suspiciously. "Doesn't that feel so fucking good?"

Dramatically, and with her eyes still closed, she arches her back. "So good," she says in a breathy voice. "Don't stop, Oz, please."

She's truly committed to the performance. She squirms, wiggling her hips, though all I'm doing is probably making her chafe. I might as well be stroking the top of her foot for the amount of pleasure my touch could possibly be giving her.

"Oz—"

"Open your fucking eyes, Gemma."

She does, and I'm certain that when she looks at me—as soon as she realizes that I know she's faking this—she'll stop.

She doesn't stop, though.

She flashes a brief, twisted little smirk, and then she steps it up a notch.

"Oh, God, Oz! Yes, *yes*... Ozzy... Baby, *please*..."

I've already pulled my hand out from between her legs, yet she's still writhing, squirming, rocking her hips as though it were still there for her to fuck.

This is wildly entertaining...

She assumes she's won something.

She's certain this is turning me off.

But if she thinks for a second that this will stop me from using her to get off, then she's lost her damn mind.

I let go of the wrist I still have pinned to the wall, and she theatrically tangles both hands through her hair. "Ozzy, baby, make me come, *please*. I don't know how I'll survive if you don't rub my pussy raw."

I draw my body away from hers, but only just enough to take my dick off her torso and aim it right at her belly button. I place my palm on the wall above her head, and I lean on it, grip my cock with the other hand, and give it a stroke.

Right in the middle of her spectacular and obscene faked orgasm, I give her a grin. "That's right, baby. Fake it for me. That's so fucking hot."

She falters instantly—her body becomes as rigid as a statue, and she's as silent as a mouse.

It's the way she suddenly stops when I call her out... As though she was hiding from the world to pleasure herself to some secret, perverse idea when I caught her filthy hands in the act.

Naughty little thing, isn't she?

Now, the idea of her hiding some dirty little kink shoots sparks of pleasure through the tip of my weeping cock. I stroke myself faster, my hips thrusting erratically. She drops her angry eyes and looks away from me as she realizes her performance didn't give her what she wants—that I'm still hard as fuck and insistent on chasing my release.

I let her look away, but I lay my forehead against hers. My chest heaves as I edge closer, and I want to make sure she can feel each breath fall across her face.

"I wanted you to come, Gemma, but if you're only gonna fake it to try to get me to stop, then I guess you've made your choice, and you can go without."

I stroke myself through her silence, and *fuck*, it feels good.

"Baby, I'm gonna come for you," I pant. "I'm gonna come so hard just for you." I groan and shudder, sharply rising toward that peak. "I'm gonna mark you with my cum so you *never* forget who you belong to."

Fuck.

This is filthy.

This is wrong.

I'm only damaging her further... but I can't stop.

I reach the point of no return, the moment I can't back down from, and a look of defeat sweeps across Gemma's features. She may as well have been stabbed—even if she had been, I know I'd still be thrusting toward relief, willing to watch her scream, suffer, and bleed while I chase the promise of it.

All sex is violence.

Fuck, I'm gonna come...

I breathe heavily down her cheek and groan loudly against her ear. I lose myself in the violent need as I come undone, and I watch with sick pride as my release splashes across her stomach.

ONCE I'D FINISHED painting Gemma with my filth in the shower, I washed both of us with soap as though nothing had happened.

I dried her off with a fresh towel, then dressed her in an oversized T-shirt and undersized panties. I'd either misjudged the size when I pulled the undergarments from the drawer in the holding house, or my subconscious decided that she should show a little extra cheek.

I have shorts and sweatpants she could wear, but I didn't present them as an option. It was a dick move, but I'd already gone so far past giving a fuck, I couldn't even see it in the rearview.

Gemma didn't say a word to me after the shower. She was completely silent as I dressed her, then watched her eat. She didn't speak as I changed my bed sheets before tucking her in.

It seemed she wanted to be left alone, so I left her alone, but only for a short time. I let Angel go outside; I played with her for a bit and then I got myself something to eat. Before long, I started feeling antsy about Gemma being alone upstairs. Though I'm normally a night owl, I decided I was tired enough from this exhausting day that I could probably fall asleep if I laid down.

I gave up on trying to occupy myself to stay away from her.

I put Angel in her downstairs bedroom—one I'd designed specifically for her. Angel's room is equipped with everything a dog could ever want or need. She has several unbearably fluffy dog beds, access to water, more toys than she knows what to do with, and a damn faux grass pee pad in the corner, which she almost never uses. If she's not out with me, then she's with Salem over in Eden, getting spoiled rotten. Angel's really only alone at night, and that's because she prefers sleeping in her room.

Angel steps onto her favorite plush, round dog bed, spins three times in a circle, then collapses with an exhausted huff. I rub her head for a minute before I head to the door, and she's asleep before I leave the room.

I quickly sort through the logistics of our sleeping arrangements as I head upstairs. I know Gemma won't want me to sleep in the bed with her, and I actually think that's fair, given my behavior. But I'm not about to let her sleep alone in my room.

On the second floor, I pop inside a smaller bedroom down the hall from the master. I lift the twin mattress off the frame and drag it down the hallway. Inside my room, the lights are how I left them; the bedroom light is off, but the bathroom light is on with the door left open a crack—just so Gemma can see if she needs to get up. In case Gemma's already asleep, I try to be quiet about hauling in the mattress, but that quickly becomes an exercise in futility.

"Oz?" she says from the bed.

With a final drag, I clear the threshold, then close the bedroom door behind me. "Yeah," I respond as I position the mattress. I place it sidelong against the door to block the exit, ensuring there's no way for her to escape without waking me up.

I walk to the end of the bed as I wait for her to say whatever she wanted to say. The light from the bathroom casts a glow in the room, enough that I can see she's still laying in the exact same position I left her in, flat on her back beneath the covers.

"Will you do me a favor?"

There's an unusual twinge in my chest that nearly makes me say *yes*—compulsively and without conditions. I scoff at the impulse because I've never had one like it before.

"I don't do favors," I tell her.

"This one would save you a lot of trouble in the end." Her voice is odd, distant, almost pleasant, with an ethereal quality; yet at the same time, it's eerie... foreboding.

"I know you're baiting me, pinky, but I'll bite. Ask me your favor."

I hear her take a stuttering deep breath, then blow it out with resolve. "I know I asked you this before when I tried to run away in the desert, and you told me I was no good to you dead, but..."

Where is she going with this?

She sits up, pushing back to rest against the headboard.

"Go on."

"I've been through this before. I know how this will end."

No, you don't.

You have no fucking idea.

I bite my tongue and let her finish.

"Somewhere along the way, you'll decide to kill me, and I don't think I have it in me to survive again."

My head tilts to the side as I bend forward, place my hands on the mattress near her feet, and lean on my palms. "What are you asking for?"

"I want you to kill me now. Just get it over with. If you won't let me go, if you won't take me back—"

"Take you back *where?*"

"To that spot between the mesas. The place you took me from."

"The Crevice? You want me to take you back to the Reborn?" I flash a look of annoyance as I push off the bed to stand. "Get fucked, Gemma."

"Then *kill* me. If I can't do what I came here to do, if you're just gonna keep me here to rape and torture me before you end my life—"

"I didn't bring you here to rape and torture you—"

"Right," she crosses her arms, "like I asked you to jerk off in front of me and come all over my stomach."

I open my mouth to respond, but nothing comes out.

I don't know what I could possibly say in response to that.

Silence clings to the air for too long, thick and suffocating.

Gemma sighs, uncrosses her arms, then softly pleads, "Please… If I can't kill the man who destroyed me, then I don't wanna be here. I don't wanna keep fighting. I don't wanna relive their torture through your hands. *Please*, kill me. Just end my life now."

Her request sounds so sincere that it's like a thorn in my side— just painful enough to be annoying.

"You want me to kill you? Really, Gemma? Right here? Right now?"

She nods.

I shake my head. "Go to sleep. You're fucking delirious." I start to turn away.

"I can't. I can't keep doing this. I can't fight anymore..." Her voice hitches, the sound of some deep-held sorrow climbing up her throat.

I rush to the side of the bed and grip the top of the headboard with one hand. I reach across her with the other and plant my palm on the mattress beside her hip. Trapped, she's forced to twist sideways and tilt her head back to look at me. I bend closer, leaning in until I've fully captured her gaze.

"Are you really gonna try to convince me that you can't fight anymore? Because that's bullshit. You haven't stopped fighting me from the moment I laid eyes on you." I lift my hand off the mattress, place my knuckles beneath her chin. "You're the definition of a fighter. It's imprinted on your fucking soul, and I doubt even death could get you to stop. Besides," I glance at her lips, "I like fighting with you, baby. You might be over it, but I'm certainly not."

As if to prove my point, she completely loses her shit. Suddenly furious, she raises her hand, and before I can catch it, she slaps my cheek. "You don't *fucking* know me."

Still gripping the headboard with one hand, I bring the other away to touch my cheek, and I straighten my spine. "You're gonna have to hit me harder than that if you—"

Her fist strikes me in the gut, punches out a groan and makes me double over.

"Of course, your delusional ass would think fighting is *my* thing..." she rants. "You've given me nothing but reasons to fight since I met you, and I haven't even known you for twenty-four hours. Literally. The Earth has not made a single goddamn rotation in the time I've known you, and you're gonna stand here and tell me you know what's *'imprinted on my fucking soul'?* Christ, you're the worst!"

I knew she wasn't done.

I wonder if she'll ever be done with indulging her rage.

I like watching her indulge.

I want to indulge *with* her.

I almost want to hand her my knife and see what she does with it… Let her destroy us both.

She climbs to her knees on the bed, kneeling in front of me where I'm bent over, still clutching the headboard.

"Kill me," she demands.

I huff as the pain of her strike eases. "Say it again."

"*Kill* me."

My head snaps up, and I glare at her. "How?"

"What?"

"How do you want me to kill you? Do you want me to stab you? Make you bleed to death? Maybe toss you off the balcony? Or do you want me to make it quick and shove your little kill pill down your throat?"

She draws back, and her head inclines at the mention of her kill pill.

"Did you forget this whole time that was an option? Your backpack is sitting right over there on the dresser. Want me to get it for you?"

She turns her head to look at the dresser beside the door.

I push off the headboard and stomp across the room. I flip on the bedroom light before I grab her backpack off the dresser. I walk it to the end of the bed, set it down, then unzip the front pocket. I easily find the small, translucent packet, lift it up between us to show the deceptively innocent-looking neon green pill.

"Here." I toss it carelessly, watch it hit her chest before it lands on the bed beside her knee.

"Take it. Go ahead. Rip it open and swallow it if you really wanna die. Do you want me to get you a glass of water?"

She reaches down to grab it, slowly lifts it in front of her face. She stares at the pill that could end her life for too long, unnervingly still and quiet.

I thought I was calling her bluff, but there's genuine conflict in her expression. She's considering taking the pill.

She's actually thinking about taking it.

My pulse quickens.

Tension pulls at my shoulders.

Fear that she'll swallow it before I can stop her sparks a flame, a fire that nearly has me leaping across the bed to snatch the damn thing out of her hand, but then… Her face scrunches, and her adorably furious expression breaks the tension.

Her head whips in my direction. She draws her arm back. She hurls the packet at me as though she could actually harm me with it.

"Fuck you. You're a coward, giving me that. Be a man and do what men do—kill me your fucking self."

I pick up the packet from where it landed beside me on the floor. "This pill is yours, Gemma. They give them to the female outlaws on Eviction Day for a reason." I stuff it back inside the pocket of her backpack. "If you really wanna die, that's your way out; I won't stop you. But you'll die on your own terms, not mine."

I watch as she slumps back, lowering from her knees to sit sideways on the bed. Then I pick up the backpack and return it to the dresser.

"I suggest you sleep on it before making any life-ending decisions. Like you said, it hasn't even been a full day since you arrived in Lawless Land. Let the Earth rotate or whatever, then see how you feel." I flip off the bedroom light and move toward the twin mattress on the floor. "Get a good night's sleep, baby. I know you'll need the energy to tell me how much you hate me tomorrow."

CHAPTER SEVENTEEN
Lucky Bedsheets

OZ

I DREAM IN black and white. My mind replays the day like one of those old western films—in grayscale moving images behind a filter of flickering dust and scratches. From afar, I watch myself riding my motorcycle down the highway. The entire world around me is dull in the monochrome gray.

And then Gemma appears, standing alone in the center of the open desert landscape.

I see her from far away and from high above her with a bird's-eye view. Abruptly, my perspective changes—like a vulture diving toward its next meal, I swoop low, dropping until she's central in the frame of my mind's eye. A slow zoom gradually brings me closer, closer… and then it quickens, shooting me toward her with haste.

I stop directly in front of her.

She's just this beautiful thing, standing still, all alone.

Dark speckles in the film-like dream burst in clusters all around her hair, appearing as black splotches that erupt into spatters of pink, which color her hair. They continue to appear and burst, landing as a light shade of pastel pink that slowly darkens.

She closes her eyes, then slowly tilts her chin toward the gray sky. She gently lays her hand over her throat, encircles her neck, gradually slides her hand up as the blasts of color appear more powerfully and with more frequency. The eruptions of color begin to stutter the movie in my mind, morphing her movements from a smoothly captured film into a series of still images punctuated by each explosion. Frame by frame, her hand inches up, then finally stops at the cut beneath her jaw.

And then, she's motionless—a single still image frozen in time.

She's still gray.

The whole world is still gray.

But her hair is vibrant pink.

Everything remains still except for the color—it moves through her hair in all directions. Dark and light shades of pink swirl and slip through her strands.

Twist and twirl.

Dance and drip.

I'm mesmerized by the moving colors.

I'm drawn into a trance.

I remain there for hours of peaceful, deep sleep.

Then, all at once, the world changes.

Gemma parts her lips.

She gasps.

Her eyes snap open.

Red seeps from the crown of her head, spilling down, and soaking her hair. Though the pink moved softly, the red is harsh. It's a thick, viscous substance that clings to and stains all it touches.

It quickly coats her hair, but it doesn't stop there.

It pours down her body, spilling onto the desert sand beneath her feet... and then it's falling from above, raining over everything from a cloudless, gray sky.

Her head levels, and her eyes find mine.

She grins.

Her voice echoes all around me as she says, "Cut me, Oz. Make me bleed. I mixed the color just for you."

With a jarring tug, I'm dragged back, zooming out and away from her as quickly as I might drive away on my motorcycle. The whole world is turning red—a captivating shade of raspberry from the meld of pink in her hair tinting the blood. When I'm so far away that she's merely a spec on the horizon, I'm lifted straight up, sucked into the sky, and drawn back to reality.

I drag in a sharp breath as I awaken in the dark.

I blink through the haze, trying to get a grasp on where I am.

I'm on my back on the twin mattress, blocking my bedroom door. The room is dark, and there's no light filtering through the window, though there is a glow from the bathroom as the light is still on. We lose power at 4:00 A.M., so it must be sometime before that.

The covers are bunched around my legs, leaving one covered and the other exposed, and I'm wearing only my black boxer briefs. One arm is raised, resting on the pillow above my head. The other is beneath the sheet, and my fist is closed, clutching... something.

Not my hard cock, which is as thick as a goddamn redwood.

It's my butterfly knife. I remember thinking I should have it close at hand before I fell asleep. I lift it out from beneath the sheets and find that it's been flipped open, the blade pointing outward, ready for action rather than being neatly and safely shut in between the handles—though I know it was closed when I fell asleep.

I flip it shut.

It *clicks* as it closes—a sound that would normally be insignificant, though it echoes in this quiet room in the dead of night.

I hold still, wait, and listen to see if it woke Gemma.

At first, I'm met with silence, but then I hear her snore. It's light, though, barely audible. I probably wouldn't have noticed it if I hadn't been wide awake and straining my ears.

The sound of it verges on cute.

Fucking adorable, actually.

Everything she says and does is so fuckably charming.

I bet the shade of her fresh blood is adorable, too.

I'd seen her fresh blood when she cut herself at the Crevice—I'd touched it, pushed it back inside her mouth, and rubbed it across her tongue. But I didn't really have the time to look at it and examine the color. I know what it looks like dried and stuck to her skin; I just wish I could remember the shade of it while it dripped down her neck... I wonder if it's the same blend of red and pink I saw in my dream.

Vibrant raspberry pink.

I have to know. I need to see it.

A torturous, throbbing need pulses through my veins, pumping this urge through every inch of my body. The need to see her blood pools low in my stomach, where it rolls, tumbling a mixture of arousal and shame that twists together into a feeling of forbidden filth. The immoral sense of wrongness heightens my senses, deepens my desire, and it feels so fucking good.

I'm too hard and too desperate to be alone with her in a dark room. I can't ignore the way her mere presence tugs at the thread of my obsession, drawing me toward the compulsion to make her bleed.

I cling to the closed knife—an extension of my hand—as I shove at the elastic waistband of my boxer briefs. I free my cock, marveling at the rise of it as I shimmy the underwear down my legs, then kick them off. I don't think I've ever seen my dick this thick and long, but it can't stay this way.

Relief is a necessity at this point.

I get up and walk to the bathroom. I push the door open wider until the glow shines across the back of her thigh and over the curve of her ass cheek, which peeks out from beneath the underwear that's just a little too small for her.

Then, I move to the foot of the bed.

Stark naked, I stand and watch her sleep.

She's sprawled sideways across the center, face down, and sound asleep on top of the covers.

With a smooth trick, I flip open the knife.

I should be searching my mind for good sense, but the longer I look at her, the stronger the sick urge becomes… and that urge was pretty strong to begin with. My free hand naturally floats to my cock, and I enjoy a few light, lazy strokes as I watch her sleeping atop the tangled comforter and bedsheets beneath her.

Lucky bedsheets.

A shudder drives anticipatory pleasure up my spine.

I carefully place one knee on the foot of the bed, and then I pause, waiting to see if she feels my presence.

She doesn't stir.

I bring my other leg onto the mattress and slowly inch closer. My pulse quickens the closer I get. When I stop, I'm kneeling so close against her body that I know I'm pushing my luck. I feel her hip against my left knee, and my right is near her breast.

Her arms are raised, bent to frame her head. Her hair cascades down her back, and hides her pretty face, which is turned away from me. I hook my finger beneath a strand and lift it from her cheek. I can't stop myself from stroking her hair, which is unbelievably soft now that it's clean. I don't want to wake her, but I'll risk it to enjoy this bit of softness from a girl who's mostly sharp edges and harsh lines.

I pet her for more than a minute, and she doesn't stir—she's a heavy sleeper. I wonder if I can draw her blood and have a moment to paint her with it before she wakes up.

Shit.

I have to stop stroking her hair so I can stroke myself.

My cock juts high and proud over her backside. It's part of the view as I look down at her, as I study her curves, as I grow more and more desperate to see her bleed. I give myself one more stroke, stifling a groan before I force my hand away. I reach down, gently sweep my finger beneath the hem of her T-shirt and lift it up to clear her perfectly rounded ass and lower back.

I expect to see smooth skin like the front of her, but I quickly spot a scar. It's only a few inches from her spine, at least an inch long, and… it's not the only one. There are several scars on her lower back, and I suspect I'd find more if I could lift her shirt higher. I suppose anything could have made these scars, but they look like puncture wounds—like she was literally stabbed in the back.

Seeing this should be enough to make me stop.

It *should*, but it *doesn't*.

If anything, it makes me wildly possessive.

It infuriates me.

Someone else hurt her. Someone touched her, caused her pain, made her *bleed*… Someone else knows the color of her blood and didn't have the decency to preserve it. Whoever gave her these scars wanted her dead.

They didn't know what they had.

They didn't know that she's mine.

Now that I've seen her scars, a more powerful sense of shame swirls in my stomach, a heavy sinking feeling of guilt over this insatiable lust to make her bleed. It should turn me off; it should be the cold shower I need to bring back my self-control. Instead, it makes me harder, thicker, even needier with the thrill of dropping into darkness.

I move gently, but quickly, straddling her body and hovering over the backs of her thighs. I stay high on my knees, keep them wide, and pause to see if she wakes up...

She doesn't.

Damn, this woman could sleep through a hurricane.

Smoothly, I bend over her. I place my hand gripping the knife on the mattress above her head. The fingers on my free hand curl around her hair near the side of her neck, gather it softly, and drag it back so I can see her face.

She's gorgeous.

Her features are so soft, so pink, so sweet.

Her plump lips are slightly parted, and everything about her expression is loose, relaxed, and calm.

I drop lower, bring my nose close to her neck—as close as I can without touching her—and breathe deeply to draw in her scent.

Goddamn.

I can smell my soap on her skin.

I inhale again to savor a heady mixture of fresh, scentless soap mingling with her sweetness.

Watermelon...

She smells sweet, like sugar and melon.

She's a fucking delicacy in our resource-limited world.

I could cut her here, press the tip of the knife into the crook of her neck...

Except, I know that's too dangerous. Any strong reaction from her would cause me to slip and seriously injure her. That's not what I want.

So where do I slice my sweet little watermelon?

I take one last sniff of her tender neck before I climb off her, shifting to kneel at the side of her that's closer to the headboard. I can watch her pretty face now as I slip down along her body, stopping when my head is near her ass. I prop myself on my side as my eyes trace the back of her thigh.

Perfect.

I lift the knife above her exposed skin, turning it in my hand and holding it like a paintbrush. My hand is steady as I hover the tip above the crease where her cheek meets her thigh. I only slice through air as I draw an imaginary wavy line from that spot to the back of her knee, trying to decide where to make a small cut.

I was thinking somewhere between the knee and hip—she's got plenty of thick, luscious flesh to protect her veins and arteries. Yet my gaze keeps tracking upward, drawn to the tempting bulge of flesh that peeks out beneath the hem of her panties.

If I wasn't so worried about her moving, I'd slice them off first, maybe keep them for myself. I know she put them on fresh from the shower, but I'm sure the scent of her pussy already clings to the fabric. And she must have left the dirty pair she wore all day in the bathroom...

Fuck.

My entire body tenses, knowing there's a delicate piece of fabric somewhere close that holds all of Gemma's filthiest secrets. I can't help but believe she must have had a moment today where she felt some sense of attraction to me, even just a brief flash of something that was gone in less than a second. Maybe—just maybe—that moment made her damp between the legs.

She held so much rage for me. She fought me so fucking hard. She bared her hatred for me with reckless abandonment.

Hatred that raw requires passion, and passion drives desire.

I wanna know the scent of her desire as much as I wanna see her blood. I wanna bury my face in her pussy, know the scent of her arousal, commit it to memory until I know with a single inhale when she's needy.

I wanna be the only man who will satisfy that need.

I wanna claim her, know her intimately—inside and out.

I need her to want me as madly as I want her.

And I want her so fucking madly...

My body shudders in the fight to control myself.

I can't control this anymore.

I need this… I need it *now.*

I lower the knife and press the tip into soft flesh.

It's a small, shallow puncture—a little more than a pinprick in her cheek where it peeks out from the bottom of her panties.

She feels the pain of it all the same, and it startles her awake. She makes an involuntary sound, a high-pitched whimper of surprise and protest. Her head sharply rises from the mattress but drops again immediately with the heaviness of sleep. She barely moves, her tired limbs betraying her as she shifts a little, whimpering as she fights sleep.

Poor thing is exhausted.

How many times has she been triggered in the last twenty-four hours?

I should stop and let her sleep...

I lift my right leg over her left and straddle her calf, pinning her leg to the mattress with my weight as I let my thick shaft press down on her muscle. I groan at the pressure, rock my hips a few times just to enjoy the feel of her.

She gasps, forcing herself awake, and I go still.

Her head snaps up from the bed, twists sharply, and she attempts to scan her backside over her shoulder. She seems disoriented, blinking slowly with wide, startled eyes as she searches for the source of her pain. Her pink lips are still parted—the same as when she slept—but her expression is frozen like the rest of her... as still as a statue and paralyzed in shock.

But then, her eyes sharply rise and meet mine.

Fuck, that feels good.

I feel high when she gives me her attention.

She puts me under her spotlight, and it shatters me.

"Just hold still for me, baby."

With a flick of my wrist, I make a cut. From the shallow puncture in her cheek, I merely draw a small line with a sharp stroke. The nick is short and shallow, a cut that's deep enough to draw blood but not enough to warrant stitches.

She's so silent, it's nearly unsettling.

Nearly, but not entirely.

My gaze is fixed on the tiny cut, watching as the blood seeps and pools, then slowly drips toward her thigh.

Raspberry...

Her blood is that perfect shade of raspberry.

Still straddling her left leg, I rise on my knees and spread them, nudging the inside of her right thigh to part our legs. I grab her hips, spread my palms wide, press my thumbs into the crease of her ass, and scoop up the perfect mounds of flesh. I'm careful not to cut her again, though my right palm still grips the open butterfly knife against her hip.

I squeeze her hard.

I lift her hips off the bed.

She yelps and twists her upper body, keeps her head turned back to watch me as I slip back just enough to bend over her backside.

I lift my eyes to look at her from beneath my lashes, holding her stare as my head lowers. I flatten my tongue against the bleeding mound, and with a long, languid lick, I sweep across the cut.

Tasting her blood feels indecent, transcendent...

And it seals our fate with the covenant of my obsession.

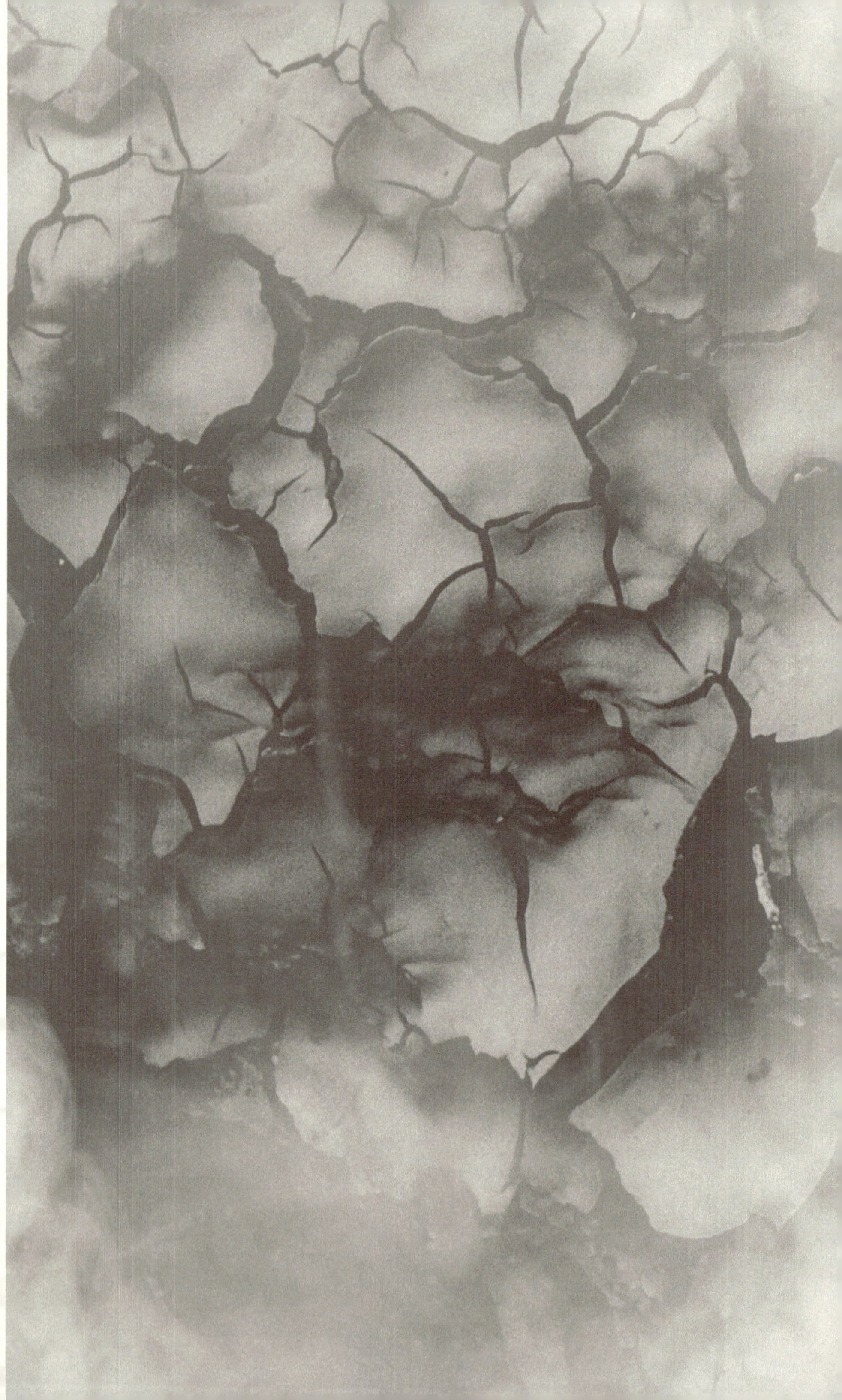

CHAPTER EIGHTEEN
He Bleeds

Gemma

I AWAKEN WITH a fright as I'm stung by something sharp. It delivers a searing pain near the bottom of my ass cheek.

My mind runs through a series of commands.

Fight.

Run.

Sleep...

I try to rise, but only my head lifts from the bed, and it quickly falls as a tidal wave of exhaustion crashes into my skull. The waves sweep me out into the sea of sleep but the pain prevents me from slipping under. It keeps my head above water in a weary floating state that's somewhere between sleeping and awake.

There's a weight on my leg, pinning it down, and I feel it shifting and pulsing against my calf.

Wake up, Gem...

Wake up, wake up...

I force my eyes to open, though they fight to stay closed.

Wake up!

With every ounce of strength I can muster, I manage to lift my head, twisting my neck to look over my shoulder. My eyes are wide as they search for whatever caused my pain, though I blink slowly, fighting each tug of my eyelids.

He's here...

My eyes snap up and they're easily captured by Ozlo Kincaid's passionate stare. Immediately, I recognize the desperate look of lust—the one that warns of danger—yet there's something more behind his eyes that I can't quite place.

The way he stares at me, the way his gaze latches onto mine feels as connecting as it does controlling. But I know I must be misunderstanding what I'm seeing. Men like Oz never want connection; they only want control.

"Just hold still for me, baby."

His eyes drop before a fresh pain sears my ass.

I suck in a breath, but I don't speak a word, stunned by the proximity of a knife to my back. I'm overwhelmed by the relatively minor pain of it—it drags me back in time to the night I was meant to die.

I'll never forget it.

I'll never forget the horror I felt.

I'll never forget the excruciating pain of each puncture as four men took an equal share of stabbing me in the back.

My mind slips, dragging me away from reality. Fear begs me to disconnect, to flee to the darkness and hide there until this is over.

I could let it happen...

I could slip away from the present.

But there's something in my soul demanding I stay.

The glow of the bathroom light behind Oz frames him with a halo of light, even though shadows move around him, shifting in the darkness. His stare is fixed. He watches me bleed. He seems fascinated by the blood trickling down the back of my thigh. He watches it drip with the intensity of a vulture tracking a dying man, waiting for his inevitable death with anticipatory glee.

Yet his stare holds something else, something like reverence, admiration… possession.

Wild possession.

All at once, he moves. His knee lodges against the inside of my thigh, and as he rises on his knees to kneel behind me, he spreads our legs apart together. He grabs my hips, his thumbs dig into my cheeks, and he jerks my bottom up off the mattress. My upper body turns, and though I feel too drugged by sleep to push myself up enough to swat at him, I keep my head turned to watch him behind me.

He drops his head, but he lifts his eyes.

They meet mine with a lightning strike that electrifies me, sending a jolt straight through to my core.

What the fuck was that?

His stare is intense, passionate, desperate… obsessive.

It's everything that terrifies me, yet it begs my curiosity.

Why does he look at me that way?

Why don't I hate it as much as I should?

He looks into my soul as he flattens his tongue against my cheek, then drags it over the cut to taste my flesh and blood.

My muscles tense as I suppress a shiver.

I see my blood coating his tongue as he lifts it from my skin. He drags it back inside his mouth and runs it over his teeth. His head remains low, and his eyes stay locked on mine. He flashes a feral grin to show me his bloody teeth.

Fucking hell.

I know I should be screaming and fighting, but I feel like I'm coming out of a damn coma. My head is throbbing, my heart is racing. I'm aching, anxious, tingling, and dizzy. If I try to fight him off right now, I'll fail. I need to bide my time until my body finds some equilibrium. And I need to shake off any feelings that aren't pure hatred for this man.

Then I can wrestle that knife out of his hand and cut *him.*

Blood for blood, you little bitch.

I keep my voice low and steady. "I didn't have you pegged as a kiss ass."

"Oh, you're just the whole damn package, aren't you? Sweet *and* funny."

"I'm not sweet. I'm gonna kill you… as soon as the room stops spinning."

"You're so fucking sweet, Gemma." I feel his finger trace the cut, collecting my blood before tracing diagonal lines down the back of my thigh.

I tense against each drag of his finger. I don't want to feel how gently he touches me or the strange way each swipe sends a tingle rushing up my thigh, shooting through my body, sending signals of shameful pleasure to my core.

"Just look at you, candy cane." He stares down at the back of my leg where I imagine he sees the bloody stripes he's painted with his finger, and he licks his lips. "You taste so much more delicious than I could have dreamed."

He slips back and bends deep, touching his lips to the back of my knee. There's enough space between us now that I could probably get out from under him…

He hums through his kiss, and the vibration of his lips against my skin ripples through me. It triggers an unexpectedly gratifying sensation, one that keeps me rooted to the spot. It's a feeling belonging to *him* that he shares through his touch—a pleasure found within a mixture of adoration and carnal indulgence.

He replaces his lips with his tongue, sparking something so hot that I have to stifle a gasp. A current of electricity flows from his tongue, and it surges all the way up, traveling the path he draws as he licks straight up the middle of the back of my thigh. He reaches the cut, licks the open wound again, and it sends the current rippling up my spine. I shudder at the shockwave that tears through me, shaking loose a whimpered moan that escapes me, unrestrained.

What the hell is happening to me?

I need to hate the way that felt… but I don't.

I think I kind of liked it.

Snap out of it, Gem.

He just cut you and made you bleed.

He wants to hurt you.

He took you from your opportunity to kill Seb.

Get mad at this motherfucker!

It's easy enough to dig up anger for a man when he makes me feel something good without my enthusiastic consent. And it did feel good… I can't deny it.

I should feel embarrassed at the way I moaned, that I felt something resembling pleasure that didn't make me feel disgusted with myself. That's how I always felt when Seb would force my body to respond against my will; he'd use toys with heavy vibration that would send my body through the motions of coming—the building tension, the spasming muscles, the release. But the release was devoid of pleasure, unsatisfactory, and provided no relief.

If anything, it was painful, both physically and emotionally. Compared to all the other ways he hurt me, the physical pain was slight and temporary. But the emotional damage he caused that fucked me up sexually—in some ways I'm probably not even aware of—will never fully heal.

The shame he made me feel, the anger I had for myself knowing my body would give him a false perception of pleasure, the disappointment in myself for having any kind of physical release—even one without pleasure or relief—are feelings that still exist within me to this day.

Seb made me hate myself.

I call on that self-hatred, throw it on the flames of anger building within me, and let it burn.

I snarl, grit my teeth, and say with a deep, insistent tone, "Get the fuck off me."

He shifts behind me, and for a moment, I almost think he's going to listen and move away. But of course, he doesn't. Instead, he brings both knees between mine, slips back as he grips my ass, and dips low behind me. He moves quicker than I can react, and without warning, his head is between my legs, face against my panties, and his nose gently brushes across my pussy.

I gasp, entirely shocked.

Get fucked, dickwad!

I finally lose it.

I turn violent, thrashing and bucking beneath his hold.

"Get off me! Stop!"

His palms curve around my hips and hold me down. His face barely brushes over my sex when I hear him groan—a deep, guttural, desperate sound that makes me tingle where his lips lightly rest against my panties.

I'm fucked.

This isn't like the shower where he rubbed me as though he was clueless just because he was pissed at the way I faked pleasure for him.

This isn't like that at all.

The way he lightly sweeps—his face barely whispering over my panties—is teasing, tantalizing, tempting.

It's purely physiological, Gem.

This doesn't feel good.

You don't like it.

You don't want more.

Except... it does feel good, I do like it, and I do want more.

Oz's grip on my hips is painful, and it's contradictory to the intentionally gentle way his face moves between my legs.

It's confusing.

Every molecule of my being bounces around inside me, chaotically colliding and rebounding, making it hard to know good from bad, right from wrong, up from down. I can't make sense of the way I feel, and I can only process that in one way... He's being deceptive.

He's trying to manipulate me.

His lips smack as he places a kiss on my panties, and I feel the pressure of it touch me at the center of my pussy.

"I wanna lick you, Gemma." His voice is soft, almost pleading. "Let me taste you right here... Tell me I can make you come, baby. Please."

Let me? Tell me? Please?

Why is he using words that empower me?

Those words allow me to give or revoke consent. They give me ownership; they give me control. He can't possibly mean them. He has to be manipulating me, grooming me, making me feel safe enough so he can lead me willingly toward unwilling abuse.

I can't let him do that.

"No," I reply.

He toes the line, keeps his face there against me so I can feel him, though he doesn't press in. But I can still feel him rubbing his nose, his mouth, his cheeks over my panties.

Fucking hell.

It almost feels good again.

"Gemma, *please*." I feel him shudder, hear the way his voice quakes with desperation. "Tell me I can taste it. Tell me it's mine. Let me fucking have it before I lose control and take it from you."

Ah, there it is.

The power play. The coercion. The manipulation.

He doesn't really care about my consent, because he's going to take what he wants from me whether I give it or not.

If he's going to be deceptive, then I'll deceive him right back.

"Ozzy baby," I say both words as if that's his name, "I'm gonna give you one chance, okay?" I wiggle my hips, deepen the bend in my knees to lift my ass higher. "This is your one chance to get the fuck off me before I clap your face with my ass and break your nose between my cheeks."

There's a pause, and then he chuckles through a deep groan.

"Goddamn, baby, ease up on the filth. My cock can't handle that kind of dirty talk coming from you."

I warned him.

In one smooth motion, I push up on my hands and knees, shift forward, then pitch my weight back hard, smacking him right in the face with my ass.

He grunts as I slam into him and his hands release my hips. I drop to my hip and twist sideways, looking back at him to assess for my next move. As his hands rise instinctively to his face, I see that he didn't drop the knife. He still holds that damn thing in his right hand.

What? Did he glue it to his palm? Fuck.

The knife points at an angle toward the ceiling, parallel to his face, as both hands come up to cover his nose. He blinks, clearly dazed from the impact of my ass striking him in the face.

I need him to drop that knife...

Laying sideways in front of him, I lift my leg and thrust it at him with all my might, slamming my bare foot into the skull tattoo on his hand still held in front of his nose.

Caught off guard, he grunts in pain, his body tilts, and he almost topples backward off the bed. Before he falls, he rights himself, leans then drops sideways onto the mattress to avoid landing on the floor.

"Shit," he groans, rolling on his hip.

And the knife is still in his fucking hand!

He rolls his head against the bed, aiming his nose at the ceiling. His hands fall away, revealing a bloody nose and a bloody forehead—there's a small cut above his left eyebrow where the knife must have nicked him when I struck.

I climb to my knees, move above him with my arm drawn back, fist cocked, ready to punch him in the nose and make sure it breaks. As I thrust down, his hand snaps up defensively, his palm closing around my fist, and he pushes back.

It's his right hand cradling my fist.

He dropped the knife...

I spot it on the mattress beside him, resting a few inches from his head.

There's a pause.

We look at each other.

Then, at the same time, we move.

I jerk my fist from his grip as he rolls sideways, nearly knocking me over. I lunge for the knife, but he grabs my waist and pulls me back. I fight him hard, thrashing and kicking my legs. I thrust myself higher along his body, using his thick thighs as a leverage point for my bare feet to push off from.

The shift of my weight has me slipping from his grip. The knife is within my reach. I stretch my arm, my fingers scrambling, clawing at the comforter, and with a grunt of determination, my palm wraps around the handle.

There isn't so much as a millisecond to celebrate. His arms instantly tighten around my waist, and he flips me onto my back. I tug on my arm, but it's met with resistance. I look at the knife, which hovers in the air between us.

His large palm encircles my hand that holds the knife.

"Let *go!*" I shout.

"You're gonna hurt yourself," he says with a feigned tone of concern. "Don't fight me on this."

"I'm not gonna hurt *myself*, you asshole. I'm gonna hurt *you!*"

He starts to smile, but it must pull a shockwave of pain through his face because he flinches, blinking hard. I pull down with all my strength but he's stronger, and he doesn't relent.

"You can hurt me all you want, pink... I might even like it. But it's not gonna get you what you want."

We fight for control over the knife, tugging back and forth. But he maintains power with brute strength, climbing to his knees and straddling my waist.

"Fuck. You." I grunt the words between tugs.

It may be hopeless to fight him, but I'm not going to stop.

"Is that an invitation? You should be careful with your words, baby. I'll give you everything you ask me for, and nothing that you want."

He rises higher on his knees, looming over me, making me feel smaller with each passing moment. His left hand is pressing down on my shoulder, and I feel myself succumbing to his strength.

And at some point, I realize there's been a switch…

We were both pulling on the knife before, each of us fighting to tear it from the other's grip.

Now, we're pushing, pressing, thrusting it toward one another.

What am I doing?

I *want* control of the knife.

When he pushes down, I relent, let my arm drop to the mattress at my side. He hesitates as I twist the knife in my palm, grip it tight, and when I raise it between us with the tip pointed at his throat, he sits back on his heels.

I let out a heavy breath of relief.

But then he grins.

He bends.

He lowers until the tip of the knife touches his throat.

"You wanna kill me, baby?"

I'm confused, surprised.

"Yeah," I reply. "I wanna kill you."

His eyes flash with something dark. "Do it. Push it in. End me right now."

We're both panting as we watch one another.

Do I really want to kill him?

Will he really let me end his life?

We might both be bluffing in this standoff of wills.

"I've killed before," I remind him between breaths. "Three men as big as you, all on my own. I can kill again… I can kill *you*."

Why am I still talking?

I should just stab him and get the hell out of here.

"I know you can." He drops lower, and the tip of the knife presses an indentation into his skin. "You can do anything you want, baby."

"You condescending motherfu—"

He slaps his palm over my mouth—the one with the skull tattoo—and presses down. "Quiet, pink, I'm not finished."

His hips are heavy on mine, his hard cock against my lower stomach. "There's a time and place for everything. Opportunities find us when the time is right, and if we don't take advantage of them, they scurry away… just like you, baby. I found you when I was meant to. You were an opportunity I took advantage of. I haven't wanted anyone the way I want you in a long fucking time."

He continues to drop his weight as he speaks. My gaze shifts between his face and the tip of the blade as the threat of him puncturing himself gradually strengthens.

"If I hadn't snatched you up, you would've scampered away from me forever. I knew when I saw you that I couldn't let that happen. Do you understand me, Gemma? Do you have a grasp on the value of acting without hesitation? If you really wanna kill me, this is your chance. *This* is your opportunity, and it's the only one you're gonna get. You should take advantage of it. I'd probably even be proud of you. But if you don't kill me now, then I'm taking that opportunity away from you for good. Try to kill me again after today?" He makes a sound of pure delight. "I'll make us both bleed, Gemma. I'll paint our bodies with blood from each of us, mix it together, see if the blend is as dark as our souls… And you know what?"

"What?" The word grinds through my clenched jaw.

"I think you'll like it. I think there's a darkness hiding inside you, and it's the same shade as mine. I think it turns you on to imagine your blood coating my fingers before I sink them inside you."

Violence.

He demands it, and I'll deliver.

With a quick slash, I drag the tip down across his chest. He hisses at the burn of the shallow scratch and instinctively pulls back. He only rises a couple of inches, but that creates the space I need between us to aim the tip at his heart and build enough momentum to pierce him.

I aim.

I breathe.

I thrust.

He bleeds.

CHAPTER NINETEEN
Like Twin Stars

Gemma

I FIND MY power with the thrust of a knife. It penetrates his flesh as an extension of my hand, triggers a release, and the flood of endorphins overwhelms me.

Fucking hell, that feels good.

Just before the blade plunged, my eyelids snapped shut, protecting my eyes from the spray of blood that would rain down from his wound. I didn't see the moment it sank inside him, but I had the satisfaction of hearing the surprised sound he made.

Did I puncture his heart?

Did I kill him?

I bat my lashes, blinking away heavy droplets of blood that splashed over my right eye. I still feel his weight. He's still on top of me, holding me down. Somehow, his dick is still hard; it's still heavy where it lays on my lower stomach.

My eyes open as he moves. He lifts away to lengthen his spine and sits back on his heels, adding more weight and pressure across my hips.

"Fuck," Oz groans.

The knife isn't in my hand.

When did I let it go?

Where is it?

My eyes flitter across his chest…

There's no wound over his heart.

His right hand—the one with the partial skull tattoo—rises between us and reaches across his chest. I spot the knife when his fingers wrap around the handle.

It's not where I meant it to be…

It's jammed into his left bicep.

"I missed…"

Shit.

I missed!

How the fuck did I miss?

He looks at the wound with some sick sort of fascination, watching blood ooze around the blade.

Then he looks at me, meets my eyes, and grins. "I'm proud of you. Damn, I'm so fucking *proud* of you. If I hadn't moved, that would've killed me." He looks at the wound again. "I know you pushed it in as hard as you could. I felt your strength, baby." He stretches his fingers away from the handle, then wraps them around again with a firm grip. "You did so fucking good."

His jaw visibly clenches as he braces himself, and with a grunt, he yanks the blade out of his bicep. He exhales with a heavy rush of air as fresh blood falls over me, oozing from the slit and gliding down his arm.

"Fuck, that hurt." He clutches his arm as his upper body twists, then he falls back on the pillows near the headboard.

His right leg straightens as he drops, and it lays heavily across my hips. If he flexed every thick muscle of his toned thigh, he could probably keep me pinned with that leg alone. But he's not flexing, not pressing down as though he means to trap me. The only tension he shows is in the strain of bracing against the pain. Another wave strikes him, and his expression tightens as he sucks air between his teeth.

Get out, Gem.

Go while the pain is still intense.

Now... this is your chance!

I kick my legs, dig my heels into the mattress to push myself backward. He doesn't try to hold me down with his leg, but it's still heavy. I manage to clear my knees, then sweep my feet out from under him. I roll sideways toward the foot of the bed, spin right off the end, and land on the carpet on my hands and knees.

"Where are you gonna go, Gemma?"

I rush to my feet, expecting to see him rise and come after me. Instead, I find he's still laying on the bed.

"Anywhere," I reply, slowly backing away. "Anywhere away from you."

I reach my hand out behind me as I step backward toward the door, searching for the doorknob without taking my eyes off him. My heel strikes something on the floor, and I nearly fall back, but I manage to catch my balance and stay on my feet. I have to look away from him to see what's blocking my escape— the twin mattress he laid sideways in front of the door.

Fuck.

"I told you before," he says, "even if it were possible for you to escape the Gates, you'll die out there on your own."

"I'll die in here with *you*." My fingers skim drywall until I find the light switch. I flip it on, flooding the bedroom with light. "I'd rather take my chances—"

"I was never gonna kill you."

His voice is soft, and I must be delusional because that almost sounded sincere. I know he's lying, trying to manipulate me... yet it makes me pause all the same.

"I just wanted to see the color of your blood," he admits.

I bend near the head of the twin mattress, grip the edges, and tug. I turn it and drag it away just enough to allow the minimum space needed to open the door.

"The cut on your ass is small. It's *nothing*."

I snap upright. My hair whips around me, flinging over my shoulder as I whirl to look at him. "Excuse the fuck out of me?"

He gazes at me down the length of his prone body, though his head remains on the pillow. "It was the only cut I was gonna make, and I would've cleaned it when I was done."

I take a bold step forward. "It was one cut too many. One *fucking* cut is too many! Do you have any idea what I've been through? What I've survived?" Another step. "I know the worst of men. My rage is the product of their vile intentions, and you—"

His head rises from the pillow. "You think my intentions are vile?"

I almost laugh as I cross my arms. "Do you seriously have to ask?"

"I do, actually." When I don't immediately respond, he drops his head on the pillow again. "Why are you still here? I thought you were leaving… Isn't there somewhere else you'd rather be than here with me?"

Good question…

Why the fuck am I still here?

"Yeah, you're right." I drop my arms and take a step back. "I have a revenge plot to finish."

"There's my girl," he chuckles. "There's that main character energy."

God, I hate him.

I lift both middle fingers as I take another step back. "Fuck you, Oz. I hope you fucking die."

"Well, fuck, princess…" He rolls onto his right side, his hand still clutching the wound on his left arm. I back up as he rises to sit, sweeping his legs around to drop off the side of the bed.

I take another step back and collide with the door. "If you had a dick, I bet it'd be fucking huge… Bigger than mine, no doubt."

"Oh, I wish." My eyes narrow as I push off the door and step forward. "I *wish* I had a huge fucking cock to sling around. I'd be the most powerful bitch you've ever met, and I'd tear you a new asshole for every girl you've ever raped with yours."

"Guess I'm stuck with the one asshole I already have, then."

I chuckle without humor, tilting my head as I look at him with disbelief. "You fucking liar."

I know I shouldn't engage, but I can't seem to stop. There's a constant push and pull between us, like twin stars in a binary system. He found me in the vastness and dragged me into his orbit.

I need to go… I want to leave.

Yet I already feel the drag that could keep us revolving.

Have we already been bound by each other's gravity?

Have we already begun circling in an infinite celestial dance?

If we have, this will only end catastrophically; we'll collide, we'll collapse, or we'll consume each other entirely. But one way or another, this will end—I'll make sure of it.

I'll eat him alive if that's what I have to do.

He turns his head sideways to look at me, and his expression is more serious than I expected. "I'm not a rapist. I'm a lot of things, but I'm not that."

I wanna scream.

I wanna cry.

I wanna choke the life out of him with my bare hands.

"I can't believe you just said that to me with a straight face."
I slowly shake my head as my eyes narrow to slits. "Have you
already forgotten what the fuck you did to me in the shower?"

"No, baby, of course not. How could I ever forget how hard I
came watching you fake it for me?"

I charge after him with nothing but violence raging through
my mind. My fist clenches beside my hip as I rush around the
side of the bed, and I only raise it the instant before I strike. I
throw a punch that lands hard against the side of his face.

"Motherfucker," I mutter, shaking my hand as a surprising pain
shoots through my knuckles.

I hit him hard, and it hurt my hand, but the impact only has him
twisting sideways for a moment.

He sits up straight, looks me dead in the eyes, and says, "Harder."

He doesn't need to ask me twice. With a flat palm, I slap him as
hard as I can across the cheek. I intend to hit him a third time,
but as I draw my hand back, he snatches my wrist.

"Gemma." He commands my attention with a simple yet
severe lift of his eyebrows, with the intensity of his needlessly
beautiful hazy blue eyes locked on mine. "I'll let you get back to
beating the shit out of me in a second, but I need you to answer
a question for me first."

"What?" The word is flung from my mouth with fury as I jerk
my arm from his grip.

"Did you say no?"

"Excuse me?"

"In the shower... Did you tell me to stop?"

"Of *course* I did!"

He cocks his head. "You sure about that?"

"Yes, I said..."

What did I say?

I'm sure I told him no.

I must have told him to stop.

But did I say the words out loud?

It shouldn't matter whether I verbalized it.

It doesn't matter, but...

Shit.

Did I ever tell him to stop?

I pause to search my mind. My gaze shifts, becoming unfocused, and I fixate on the pillow resting beside him. I find some mental images of what happened in the shower. A few of them are clear, though many are shrouded in fog. It's like the mist and steam from the shower had dissipated from reality and seeped into my mind to obscure the details.

It feels the same as my memories of the most horrifying moments from that summer with Seb and his friends. Those traumatic recollections existed for years as mental images obscured behind frosted glass. I could make out the abstract visual of the events that took place, but the details, the words spoken, and the emotions I'd felt were too blurred to recall.

They remained that way for years. My mind couldn't even begin to break the frosted glass until I found stretches of time where I felt safe. Even then, it happened slowly. I could only shatter one glass wall at a time for the suffering brought by each break of clarity.

So I have to wonder whether the details of what happened in the shower are hazy because Oz hurt me like Seb or because my mind is so broken that it no longer forms memories the way it should.

Either reality is unsettling.

And regardless of the reality, I'm stuck in a loop, quickly scanning the few clear mental images of what occurred in the shower.

Gently placing his hands, I feel Oz touch my hips, but I can't react. I'm still trapped in the search for what I said to him, what I didn't say to him, what I *wanted* to say to him but couldn't…

"I remember what you said, if you'd like me to refresh your memory."

The sound of his voice calls to me, bringing me to the present reality where his stellar gravity drags me into orbit. I blink, force my stare to focus, and search the blue of his eyes.

"You said, *Make me come.*"

I shake my head.

He lifts his hand, brushing a lock of hair from my cheek. "You said, '*Don't stop, Oz.*'" He tucks the strand behind my ear. "You said, '*Yes,*' and '*Oh, God,*' and '*Please.*'" His hand lowers to my hip again. "But what you didn't say was '*No*' or '*Stop.*'"

A breath rushes out of me, sinking my lungs, and my shoulders drop. "But I didn't need to say it…"

My head is spinning.

I feel flustered, mind-fucked.

He's playing mental games with me, and it's not fair.

"You're not fighting fair," I whisper.

He drags me closer, and my stupid body lets him.

"I know, baby." His hands rise just enough to lift the hem of my shirt so he can touch my skin, so he can curl his fingers around my waist. "I know." He leans forward and gently places a kiss over the fabric between my breasts. "It doesn't really matter what you did or didn't say, right?"

Does he mean that?

"What really matters," his hand moves beneath my shirt, glides smoothly over my skin, and stops just beneath my breast, "is what you did when I kissed you."

What did I do?

His thumb sweeps over my nipple, and I feel it everywhere.

I fill my lungs with a gasping breath when he does it again.

My back arches with the next brush.

"Take off your shirt. Let me look at you."

"What?" I'm swept up in an unanticipated haze of lust—a feeling I thought was lost forever. "No, tell me... What did I do?"

"When I kissed you?"

"Yes."

"You kissed me back—and there was nothing fake about it."

His hand glides up and down my side, dragging a little lower over my hip, then farther down my thigh on each sweep.

"I wanted to make you feel good; I wanted to make you come." His hand stops on my thigh, near the bottom hemline of my panties. "I still do." His thumb swoops in, rubbing the inside of my thigh in gentle circles.

I feel breathless, a little light-headed.

My body sways toward him. I put my hands on his shoulders to steady myself. "I can't."

His thumb moves higher. "Can't, what?"

I shake my head as my eyes drift shut.

I'm lost in the way he uses me, victim to the way he draws desire.

His hand turns, fingers slipping between my legs.

"Oz..."

"Just tell me you want it." He kisses my stomach. "Just say, '*Please.*'"

His fingers breeze over the fabric covering my pussy.

I clench.

I shudder.

I moan.

"I'll do it however you want me to," he promises.

His fingers graze my panties, lulling me into a quiet desire.

"I could stroke inside you with my fingers. I could lick your clit." His hand slowly slips, glides around my hip, flattens against my lower back, and pulls me against him. "You could use me if you want."

He lifts my shirt and lays gentle kisses on my stomach. The light touch of his lips fluttering over my skin sends a flurry of need through my core, and for a second, I forget to breathe.

"I'm already hard for you." His hand glides over the curve of my cheek and continues down the back of my thigh. He clutches behind my knee, lifts my leg, and I shrink back. "It's okay." He pulls my leg over his thigh, guiding my movement until my knee is settled on the mattress. "Now the other." He looks at me expectantly. "I can't lift your leg with this arm; you stabbed me so good, baby."

A dark, vast emptiness creeps into my consciousness.

It's like I'm floating into deep space, and the quiet is actually relieving. I don't feel entirely gone from my awareness; I'm not completely disconnected. I feel as though I've entered a peacefully thoughtless space that allows sensation to exist for what it is.

His touch feels inevitable in this strange moment. It's undeniable, like the chaotic harmony of the cosmos. Unexpectedly, my body responds with acceptance.

There's only sensation

There's only the need to follow desire.

And what I desire is to surrender to his inescapable gravity.

I lift my leg over his, straddling his lap.

His right hand strokes my hair, and it feels so good, I can't help but indulge. My eyes flutter shut, and I let my head fall heavy against his palm.

"Goddamn, you're beautiful. Why don't you just relax? Let me inside you… Sit on my lap, and I can hold you, kiss you, stroke your hair while you use me to come."

My body sinks, desperate for more sensation, fighting to keep my mind in the quiet darkness to remain in this physical state that just feels so fucking good.

His hand falls away from my hair, and I lift my head, opening my eyes. I watch the nebulous clouds dance across the blue of his eyes as he reaches between us. My lips part, and I gasp as his fingers sweep my panties to the side, tickling across my bare pussy as they tug the fabric.

"I need you wet, Gemma. You wanna be wet for this, don't you?" The tip of his cock grazes between my legs, sending tremors through my body. "Let me just play with you a little."

I think he grips his cock because the tip drags with precision, gathering my gradually pooling wetness so he can paint me with it. He barely dips the tip inside me, drags it away, and then swirls it over my clit. He draws out pleasure as he dips, drags, and swirls, repeating the pattern until I'm panting and rocking my hips.

"You can take it, baby. Just sit down and take it whenever you're ready."

Why do I want this?

Why do I need it?

I'm frenzied by desire, and I have to chase it…

I can't resist it.

With resolve, I lower my hips.

We moan as I lower steadily, impaling myself with the thickest, heaviest cock I've ever known. Inch by inch, breath by breath, I drop until I'm filled completely and there's not an inch of space between us.

Fucking hell, that feels good.

It feels so fucking good…

But then there's a flash of light in my mind that bursts through the peaceful darkness. It's like a distant star that explodes like a supernova, sending a brief flurry of thoughts bouncing wildly through my consciousness.

This is wrong.

He's gonna hurt you.

He coerced you into doing this…

How could you ever want him inside you?

He's toxic. He's dangerous.

You should be ashamed.

You don't like this.

You hate him.

You can't enjoy this...

Shame and the sense of wrongness begin to drag me from the empty peace... But the sensual, filthy way he whispers, *"Fuck,"* as he trembles triggers the same release, the same rush of endorphins I felt when I thrust the knife into his flesh. It scatters the bad thoughts, sends them away, and I drift back into the abyss of empty space and carnal recklessness.

"You're so warm, so fucking perfect." The hand of his wounded arm rests lightly against my hip, the other stroking my body, touching me everywhere he can reach. "Move for me. Rock your hips. Make yourself come."

I couldn't stay still if I wanted to—this need to use him for my own selfish gain is overwhelming.

I remain fully seated as my hips begin to move.

I lean forward and find a perfect angle where my clit pulses against his lower stomach with each forward grind of my rocking hips. I move steadily, slowly but heavily, as the drive for physical pleasure overpowers everything else.

My left hand moves from his shoulder, follows the curve of his neck toward his jaw, then slips around to cradle the back of his head in my palm. Panting, needy, my head lowers and our foreheads touch. My eyes are closed, but I can feel the way he watches me as I move for myself, for my *own* desire, seeking release for me and *only* me.

He sighs. "I'm so proud of you, baby. You took me so deep... You're doing *so* fucking good."

No, I don't want that...

I want him to hate this.

I don't want his praise; I want his spite.

With my forehead still pressed to his, I slowly shake my head while I firm up my grip on the back of his skull. I grind heavier, rock faster, pulsing my hips until my clit is throbbing with warning.

My lips part and remain that way as I pant and moan with quickened breaths. I open my eyes, turning my forehead against his to see the bloody stab wound in his bicep. My right hand slips from his shoulder, softly glides down the side of his arm to rest beside the wound.

I watch his blood ooze from the puncture.

I did that... I cut him.

I ripped his flesh, and I took control.

I tore his skin, and I took my power.

I fuck him harder.

I'm closing in on the relief I need... the relief I *deserve*.

And just as I feel it beginning, at the moment it rises to start its climb toward the peak, I lay my thumb over his wound and press.

Oz cries out in pain, and I breathe out a moan.

"Fuck, *stop!*" he groans, but that only spurs me on.

He tries to reach between us and across his chest to remove my hand, but I'm determined to hurt him while I peak. My strength amplifies as pleasure rises, as I take what I want and give him pain in return. I keep him firmly against me, my fingers splayed at the back of his head, and our foreheads press together so hard it causes an ache.

I bask in knowing he feels that ache, too, but the minor discomfort isn't enough—I want to hurt him deeper. I shift my thumb, press it harder, feel it creep into his wound…

And he howls in pain.

This is power.

This is what it feels like to conquer a man.

My hips thrust erratically as I near the peak, as the spectacular tingling in my pussy explodes, sends me flying over the crest with the most perfect pleasure I've ever felt. Shockwaves of prolonged bliss ripple through my body, and though my movements slow, I don't stop, lazily rocking my hips through the fall.

Relief.

Fucking hell.

I could cry tears of joy for the way this relieves me.

It wasn't just a release devoid of satisfaction.

It was enjoyable, gratifying.

It was everything an orgasm *should* be.

I let out a small laugh as I release him. I lean back, arching my spine, and let my head fall back on my shoulders. I take a moment to revel in my satisfaction.

But in a flash, the moment's gone.

Despite the pain he must feel in his injured arm, both his hands clamp around the sides of my waist with a warning squeeze. My head drops to level, and my wide eyes meet the depravity in his.

My hands snap to clutch his wrists. "Don't—"

In one motion, he lifts me off his lap, twists, and flips me onto the mattress, where I land heavily on my back. He moves over me, snapping something in my mind that floods light into the mental darkness. Every haphazard thought I'd suppressed while chasing desire rushes in, racing to fill all the empty space.

Just like that, control is taken, my power is seized, and pleasure fades to gray. He reaches across my body, and when he draws back to hover over me, I see what he was reaching for... He holds it in his hand—the knife. I'm so fucking stupid that I forgot all about it.

How could I forget?

How could I let this happen?

With haste, he reaches down, pressing the blade to my throat. Fearfully, I freeze, entirely overwhelmed by my senses and the flood of thoughts filling my mind.

Oz shifts between my legs. He grazes my pussy with his other hand, readjusting my panties where they bunched with the movement. He pushes the fabric toward my thigh, out of his way, then drives his cock deep inside me.

I gasp.

He groans.

He fucks me.

"Hold still for me." He thrusts. "I don't wanna slip and add another cut to your pretty little throat."

"Oz, please—"

"Yes." He bends over me, bracing his free hand on the mattress above my head, the knife still at my throat. "That's my girl, begging so sweetly."

"I'm not begging—"

"No, Gemma. I don't wanna hear any other words fall from your pretty lips if they aren't *Yes, Oz, Please,* or *Harder.*"

"I don't—"

He rears back, still thrusting as he lifts the knife from my throat, lays the blade flat to my chest, and slowly drags it between my breasts.

I hold my breath as tears fill my eyes.

"Does this scare you, baby? Do you feel how hard and deep I sink inside you and fear I'll do the same with this?" He lifts the knife, bringing the tip of the blade to rest at my sternum.

I'm terrified, seized with fear.

But I also feel my stomach clench with the way he moves inside me. Something deep within me is twisted, and I know it's wrong. It's the way that fear mingles with the desire to come again.

It's sick.

It's wrong.

It has to be some stupid kink developing from my trauma.

I feel him swell, grow, and throb inside me. It tugs on a thread from my core, one that pulls pleasure from that twisted feeling. I don't mean to make a sound, but involuntarily, I moan. The moan is meaningless, though—the tug of pleasure is fleeting, a quick jolt of something that feels good, and a moment later, it's gone.

I don't want him to fuck me like this.

I didn't ask for this.

But I can't tell him to stop under the threat of his knife.

Shame strikes as he thrusts hard.

Self-hatred settles as I endure his erratic movements, witness his loss of control, and feel the flood of warmth that spills inside me.

Fuck... He came inside me.

I drop off a cliff into an ocean of panic, and the knife no longer concerns me.

"Get off." I swat at his hand. "Get off me." I kick my legs. "Get *off!*" He removes the blade from my chest, and I jackknife, slap my palms to his chest and shove as he slips out of me. "Get away!"

I leap off the bed, jerk open the door, and dash down the hall.

"Gemma," he calls out. "Don't make me chase you."

His cum drips, seeping out from inside me, and tears fill my eyes. I've never been so confused and overwhelmed. I've never felt so hot and filled with so much hatred all at once. I've never wanted a man who terrifies me the way he does.

Oz will break me, but worse... I fear he'll change me.

I have to run. I have to leave.

I have to get away from Ozlo Kincaid.

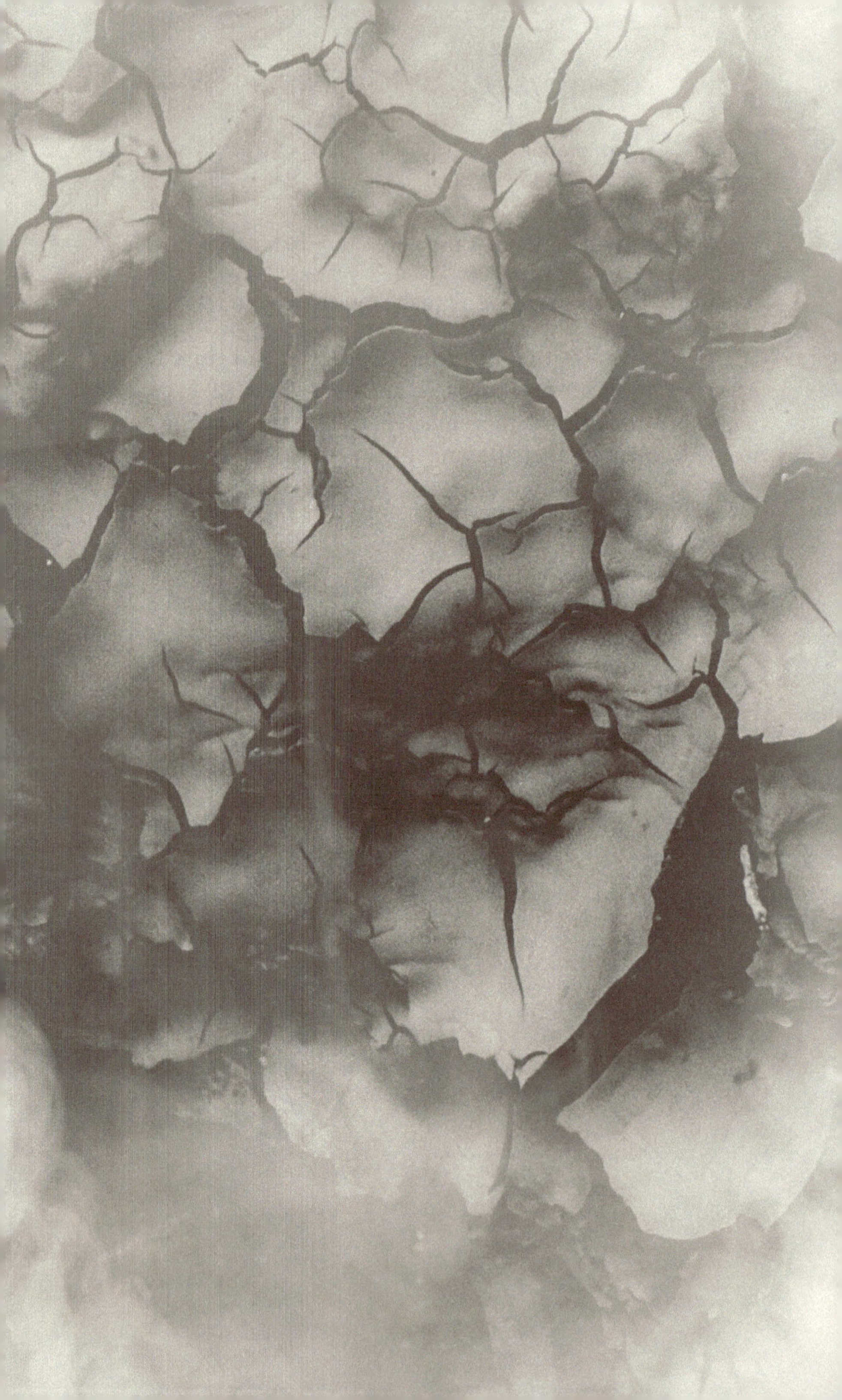

CHAPTER TWENTY
Let Her Run

Oz

I CRAFTED MY own coffin when I tasted Gemma's blood. I climbed inside it while she fucked me and closed the lid when she came on my cock. Beneath my knife, her fear was heavy, pounding through each heartbeat like a hammer driving nails to seal my casket. Then she dug a hole and buried me, sealed my fate within the pulsing embrace of her warm pussy as I spilled inside her.

Life as I know it is over.

I went too far.

Our privileged way of life exists within the Gates because we have rules, structure, order, and consequences. The land around our desert haven is occupied by men who live unrestricted, men without order, who do as they please. I lived that way for years before daring to dream of a better life.

I wanted a life that meant more than just fighting to survive the day, while at the same time, secretly wishing that day would be my last. The wandering lawless live without restraint and they suffer for it. Without community—without structure and shared resources—the odds of survival are low.

We have the means not only to survive but to thrive, and it's all because of this community—this privileged province I established from the ground up. The resources we've been granted to live as well as we do are solely because of our partnership with Prosperity—the city that sustains us—and that partnership lives and dies on our behavior. So good behavior is not just expected but obligatory; it's written into our contracts with the city and signed with our fucking blood.

The rules we have are necessary, and we enforce dire consequences when they're broken. But I bent the rules, twisted them nearly to the point of snapping...

I'm on the verge of fucking snapping.

And it's all because of Gemma—my stunning little desert rose.

I found her in the blinding sunlight, and she found the darkness I hide.

If I were in a rational state of mind, I'd calmly collect her things, go find her, and walk her over to the holding house where she'll be safe. I've already traumatized her, pushed beyond her limits, and broken the vaults inside her mind. I've used her, abused her, and made her fear me beyond reason.

Yet, despite all that, I can't bring myself to do the reasonable thing. I'm dangerously obsessed with her. I want her in a way that's breaking me. I want every little piece of her for myself.

I need her to be mine.

I pull on my boxer briefs and a pair of jeans before slipping out of the bedroom and walk barefoot down the hallway, knife still in hand. When I reach the top of the staircase, I pause, listening for movement to assess where she's gone.

A few seconds tick by before I hear a hurried whisper and the familiar sound of Angel's tail thumping against the wall.

Is she trying to take my fucking dog?

That spiteful, beautiful little bitch.

I wait at the top of the staircase with the knife held down by my side. The light from my bedroom casts a glow down the hall, shining just enough light down the steps to see her when she passes a few seconds later. The gray faded forms of Gemma and Angel appear in the faint frame of light as they creep past.

"Hey, pink," I call down to her.

She freezes, turns her head, and looks up at me.

"Where the fuck do you think you're going with my dog?"

She bolts.

I casually jog down the steps.

I'd turned off the lights in the kitchen and living room before I went up to bed—the first floor is dark aside from the dim glow of moonlight through the windows. There's just enough glow to see shapes and shadows moving in the dark.

As I step into the sunken living room, I hear a *click* when she unlocks one of the deadbolts securing the front door. I don't feel the need to rush because it's one of three deadbolt locks, and she'll still need to find and unlatch the other two.

I cross behind the couch to the sound of a second *click*. I step up from the living room into the foyer, then stop to watch Gemma's dark shadowed outline at my front door. She's frantic in her attempt to open it, but Angel merely stands beside her, shaking the entirety of her backend with wild excitement.

I can't even stay mad at Gemma for trying to take my Angel.

Look how fucking happy she is...

Angel doesn't know Gemma wants to take her away from me. She probably thinks she's going on a Daddy Oz-approved nighttime adventure walk with a new friend.

Another *click* makes three unlocked deadbolts.

It's impressive that she found them all in the dark.

But did she remember—

The door opens, barely parts the frame, then slams shut again.

Nope, she didn't remember.

"I think you forgot the chain lock."

Gemma makes a sound that's some combination of a scream, a yelp, and a grunt... It's fucking cute. "Shit!"

I stalk toward her as she struggles to find the chain and unlatch it in the dark.

I close in.

I reach out and grip her arm.

I drag her from the door, throw her back against the wall, and pin her body there with mine.

"I think you would've made it out if you hadn't stopped for Angel. I should be pissed at you for trying to take her, but fuck, just look at her." I glance over my shoulder at Angel. "She's as obsessed with you as I am, and that's the real problem here. I needed you to leave, baby. I needed you to escape. I needed you to get the fuck out of my house before I barricade us both inside and refuse to leave." I shift closer. "I needed you to be faster. I'm out of control with you here. In less than a day, you've upended my entire fucking world."

Her breaths are unsteady, quick, and heavy. "I can still go," she whispers. "I can still leave. Just step back, and I'll leave. I'll move faster. I'll get away, okay?"

I slowly shake my head. "I think it's too late."

"It's not... What do you mean?" Her voice shakes, lacking confidence and power.

I can't say I like the way it sounds. It makes me uneasy. It unsettles me, because I know I'm the one who brought her to this point. But maybe it's good that I feel a moment of unease... It means I haven't entirely devolved into a predator acting solely on the instinct to conquer.

Maybe the fear in her voice will stop me from grabbing hold of her before I drop over the edge. Maybe she can shine just enough light to keep me from falling into the darkness. Maybe she can still escape before I drag her down with me to the bottom of the black abyss.

"I need you to leave."

"I-I'm trying to... If you move, I can leave."

"I was supposed to protect you." My hand skims her waist as I drop my forehead to touch hers. "I brought you here to save you, but just look at what I did to you."

"You can make it right. Open the door for me."

She's nearly crying; I can hear it in her voice.

I hate it as much as I love it.

"Please, just let me go. Oz, *please...*"

Fuck.

She's finally begging, but it's not in the way I wanted.

Her hands slip between us, and she places them on my chest. "Ozzy, please." She sniffles. "Open the door and let me run."

Let her run?

Let her run...

Oh, I can let her run...

I don't trip over the edge and fall into the abyss... The darkness itself climbs out to greet me, rips me from the light, cloaks me in shadows, and drags me straight to the bottom.

I kiss her forehead, then dip my head to level our eyes. "You're right, I should let you run."

Her eyes dart wildly across my face, scanning every feature with skepticism. I step back beside the door and reach up to unlatch the chain lock—it *clinks*, then *clatters* against the wood. At the sound, Gemma pushes off the wall, rushes forward to stand in front of me with her chin raised high, and her eyes open wide.

I raise the knife, gently touching the tip beneath her chin as I bend. The tips of our noses nearly touch as I watch a silent tear slip from the corner of her eye.

"You're gonna run from me, baby. But I need you to run fast... Because if you don't run fast enough, I just might catch you. And you don't wanna know how dark this gets if I catch you."

It's a threat.

It's a promise.

It's the actualization of my greatest fear.

I've spiraled out of control, and I might destroy us both.

I step back, open the door, and fling it wide.

I twist my head, glance out through the doorway, and all I see is darkness—where she and I belong.

"Run, baby... *Run.*"

Gemma turns, runs, then vanishes into the dark.

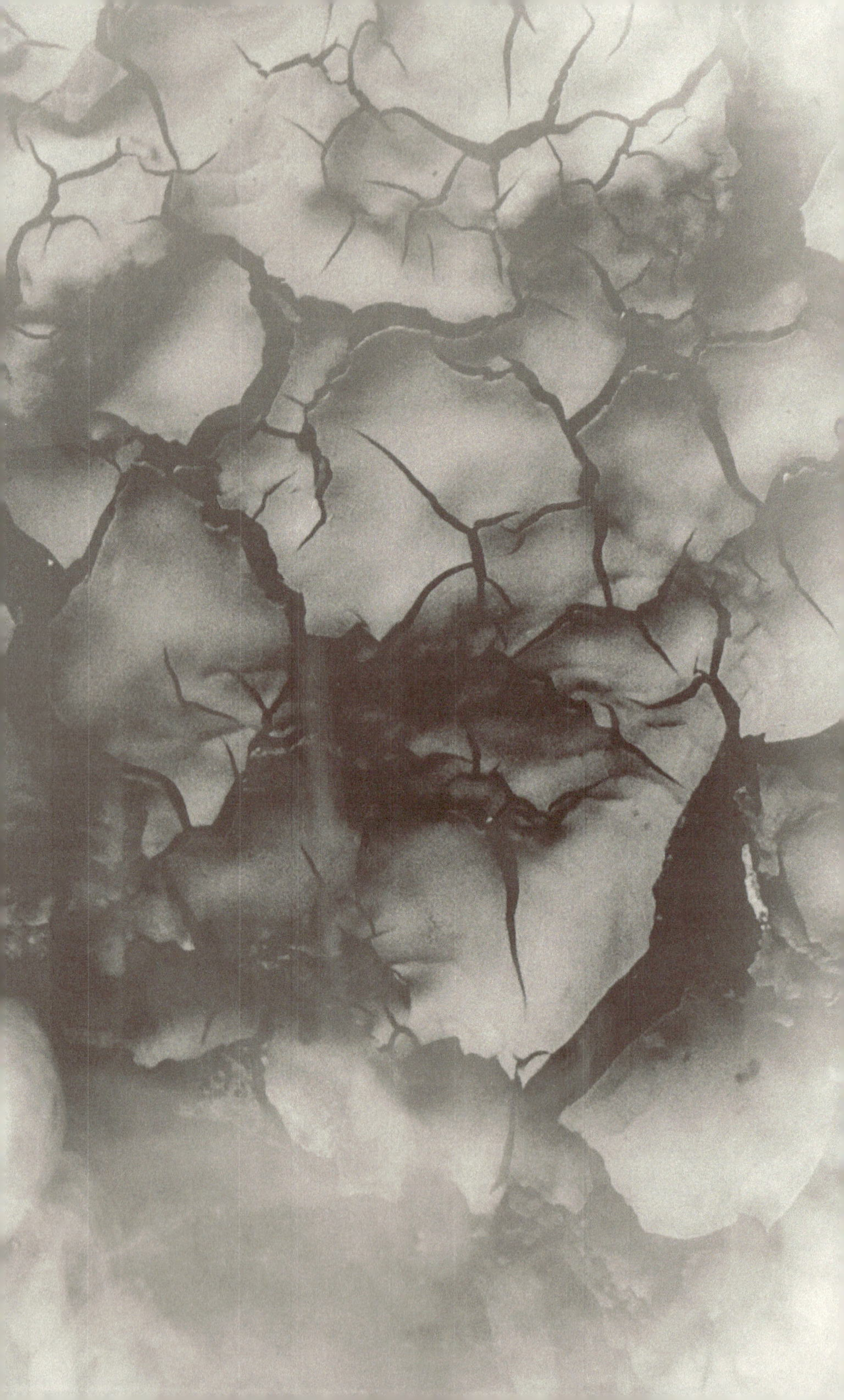

TO BE CONTINUED IN
Lawless, Book 2
COMING SOON!

SUBSCRIBE NOW

to Brynn Ford's author newsletter!
You'll get an exclusive FREE EBOOK
and email updates on Book 2!

GO TO

brynnford.com/connect

TO SUBSCRIBE

ACKNOWLEDGMENTS

It's been a long time since I've published a new book. When my last book released, I'd reached a point of burnout. I had to take a long break from creating anything, and it definitely put me out of the habit of writing. It would be a lie to say that getting back in the habit was easy—it most certainly wasn't. But Gemma and Oz wormed their way into my mind and insisted they had a story I needed to tell. I'm thankful they did, because it got me back in the habit!

I couldn't have done this on my own and there are a lot of people I need to thank. The first is my husband... Chris, you've sacrificed a lot for me to be able to do this work, and I couldn't be more grateful for you. I know it's not always easy being married to me, but you manage my chaos like a champ. He's one of the good ones, and ladies, I'm not sharing!

Danielle, it will never cease to amaze me the way you stick around, encourage, and support me despite my creative chaos. You're the most amazing friend a girl like me could ask for, and I don't know that I could get through the tough times without you. You're honestly amazing!!

Silvia, my incredible, wonderful, patient editor... What would I do without you? I'm so grateful to have you on my team. You always do the best work in polishing my words and your flexibility and patience with me is more appreciated than I could ever express!!

To my incredible beta readers, Annica, Echo, Mary, Brandy, and Danielle, thank you SO much for your time, thoughtfulness, and support! I can't thank you enough for sticking with it through this manuscript as I stopped and started several times. Your notes and feedback are so helpful to me, and I can't thank you enough! I also want to give a special shoutout to Annica and Echo for suggesting some character names early on—Gemma's killers were named with your help, and I sincerely appreciate the great suggestions!

The beautiful cover artwork was done by Black Widow Designs and the paperback interior was created by Qamber Designs—all absolutely amazing designers. Thank you so much for the amazing cover, Dee, and for the gorgeous interior, Nada!!

To my Street and ARC team and everyone who has taken the time to read, review, or post about this series...THANK YOU! Your support means the world to me, and I'm so incredibly grateful for you.

My final thank you goes directly to you, reader. You picked up this book, you read the words I wrote, and for that alone, I am grateful. If you connected with the characters or the story and enjoyed this read, just know that you and I have met through these words, and I'm forever thankful you took the journey with me.

BRYNN'S BOOKS

The Four Families Trilogy
Counts of Eight
Dance with Death
Pas de Trois

The Four Families Spin-Off
King of Masters

Ember Glen
Spark of Madness
Blaze of Misery
Embers of Mercy

Senseless
Unheard
Unseen

Lawless
The Darkness We Hide
...more coming soon!

Standalones
Jagged Line Paradise
Sugar Wood
The Alter

CONNECT WITH BRYNN

Website
brynnford.com

Subscribe to Brynn's Newsletter
brynnford.com/connect

Goodreads
goodreads.com/brynnfordauthor

BookBub
bookbub.com/profile/brynn-ford

Instagram
instagram.com/brynnfordauthor

TikTok
tiktok.com/@brynnfordauthor

Facebook
facebook.com/brynnfordauthor

Facebook Group
Brynn's Daring Darlings
bit.ly/brynnsdarlings

ABOUT THE AUTHOR

Brynn Ford is a USA Today Bestselling Author of dark romance for daring readers. She writes emotionally heavy love stories that will twist your soul and shatter your heart before pulling you back together with a hopeful happily-ever-after.

Brynn's books are dark, sometimes disturbing, and often overwhelming. But they're always brightened by an insistent, spicy romance that will live rent-free in your head long after you've turned the final page.

When Brynn isn't obsessively writing, you may find her binge-watching favorite shows while eating far too much junk food or fanatically reading, always seeking to lose herself in the emotional roller coaster of a damn good story. She's a firm believer that her characters continue to live outside the pages in the minds of her readers. Stories don't end just because there aren't any more pages to turn.